JONATH

THE TRUTH ABOUT ARCHIE AND PYE

A MATHEMATICAL MYSTERY

This edition published in 2018 by Farrago,
an imprint of Prelude Books Ltd
13 Carrington Road, Richmond, TW10 5AA, United Kingdom

www.farragobooks.com

ISBN: 978-1-78842-108-9

To Gail, as always

e

a mathematical constant discovered by Jacob Bernoulli
while studying compound interest; irrational and
transcendental; equal to 2.71828 (to six significant figures)

π

a mathematical constant known to the Egyptians and
Babylonians but first calculated by Archimedes;
irrational and transcendental; equal to 3.14159
(to six significant figures)

Chapter 1

As I put the phone back in my pocket, I already knew I'd done something that was at best reckless and at worst catastrophically stupid. But Christ, I felt better for it: revenge served, piping hot, on Wedgwood bone china with a silver service. There would be consequences, but they were for another day. Right now, I simply wanted to pump my fists while shouting 'IN YOUR FACE, YOU BASTARD!'

However, I didn't do this, because on this busy Tuesday evening I was standing on the westbound platform of Reading Station, waiting for the train back to Bristol.

The train was delayed by signalling problems further down the line and by the time it arrived, a significant percentage of the population of the Western Home Counties was already on board. I had to fight to defend my reserved seat from territorial incursion on two separate occasions, once when I got on and again ten minutes later when I'd succumbed to the inevitable desire for alcohol from the bar. Having successfully re-established my tenancy, I sat back, sipped at my can of warm Stella and stared into space, drifting off into a fuzzy crepuscular trance as the train crawled westwards.

A muffled phone went off overhead.

'Excuse me,' said the man in the window seat next to me, raising himself into an awkward half crouch. I leaned away from him as he grabbed at his jacket, which tumbled down towards me in an untidy cartwheel. He snatched it away at the last moment and fished the phone out of an inside pocket.

'Hello?' he bellowed. 'Splendid. I take it you... Good, good... So what did you—'

'Um—' I said, looking for support from the other passengers. The woman across the aisle from me glanced up from her Sudoku, shook her head, tutted and went back to it. 'It's—'

'Sorry?' he continued. 'Didn't catch that, someone's trying to interrupt me—' He turned away from me towards the window. 'You didn't think... Sorry? But... No, well obviously I wasn't suggesting... No, no, no, but as I explained when we first discussed this—'

'Excuse me,' I said, but he just burrowed further into his seat and continued his conversation.

'Sorry, I didn't... You think I'm... I... You... But I don't think it's offensive at all, I'm sure my readers will... No, but... But but but... No, please listen to me, listen to me... OK, OK, I can take that out, I can take that out, no problem at all, but if... Well, yes, that bit as well, that's all fine... But no, really I can't do that... I'll be left with nothing worth— Sorry, you're what? But you can't... Well, yes, I suppose you can, but... No, please, just let me, let me, let me, can I, I mean... Um... Can we talk this over in person? I can come over tom— OK, well next week perhaps? I can do Thurs— No no no please... PLEASE... I'm sure we can... But what's Hilary going to say when... She's going to be furious! Sorry? Well, FUCK YOU.' He ended the call and slumped back in his seat, letting out the keening moan of a mortally wounded animal.

'Um,' I said, pointing upwards at the sign. 'Quiet carriage?'

'Oh, sod off,' he said, turning towards me. 'What the hell do you know? It's people like you who—' He stabbed his hand in my face for emphasis, and in doing so knocked the can of lager out of my hand, causing it to spill into my lap. I lurched to my feet, intending to give the man a piece of my mind, but the effect of this was lessened when I hit my head on the rack. Someone in the seat behind me winced.

'What in God's name did you do that for?' I hissed, trying to maintain some semblance of dignity while leaning down towards him.

He looked up at me, then down at the stain that was spreading across my crotch and then up again. A look of horror pervaded his face.

'Oh my God,' he said. 'I am so sorry. What must you be thinking? Please let me buy you—'

'Jesus,' I said, shaking my head. I wanted nothing more to do with this idiot. I sat down again.

'I mean it,' he said. 'Please—'

I held up my hand and shook my head again. 'Really,' I said, 'it was an accident. It's done.'

'No, I insist,' he said. 'What was it?' He peered at the can. 'Stella?'

I shrugged in agreement. It wasn't as if I was going anywhere soon. The train had ground to a halt again.

The man hauled his body past me into the aisle and made off towards the bar, returning a short while afterwards with two quarter-bottles of Chilean Merlot.

'Bar's out of beer,' he said. We opened our screw caps in perfect synchronisation, and poured the contents into plastic glasses. He was in his mid-fifties, I supposed, shortish but overweight, with a straggly, grey beard and wire-rimmed glasses. He wore a maroon pullover with a stain near the collar – yogurt? toothpaste? something worse? – and a pair of ill-fitting navy blue corduroys. He took a long swig and grimaced.

'Worst day of my life,' he said, still with no concern for the 'Quiet Carriage' notice. 'If I ever see that little shit again, I will strangle him, swear to God I will.'

I couldn't help but raise an eyebrow. The Sudoku lady glanced across at us and tutted again.

'Sorry,' he said. 'Let's start again. Burgess. George Burgess.' He held out a hand. 'Don't bother looking me up on Wikipedia because the bastards removed my entry. Didn't meet their notability criteria, whatever that means. According to an editor who goes under the name gobblegobble23, anyway. Who are these people? Do you want another one?' He drained his glass and belched. A fine vinegary aerosol wafted over me.

'Well—'

'Splendid. How's it drying, by the way?'

'It's… on the way.' I was still damp.

'Good, good.' He started to get to his feet again.

'I'll come with you,' I said. Against my better judgement, I was intrigued enough to want to continue our conversation, but I was nervous about the looks we were getting from the other passengers.

Glasses refilled, we braced ourselves against the side of the carriage in the bar area as the train picked up speed and bounced its way westwards.

'I'm writing this book', he said. 'Or rather, I'm probably not writing it any more. Going to have to return my advance too, which I can't afford to. I'm really in the shit. All because of that twerp Vavasor.'

'Vavasor?' The name rang a bell.

Then I remembered. The Vavasor twins. Archimedes and Pythagoras. Famous mathematicians. There was a girl in the sixth form at school – what was her name? – who had been

10

obsessed with them. Kept reading bits out of the inquest report. One of them – Pythagoras? – had been found dead with a metal set square through his heart, and the other one found hanged in a wood a week later. Everyone assumed the second one – Archimedes? – had murdered his brother before killing himself in a fit of remorse. But no one had ever managed to work out why.

Dorothy Chan. That was her name. Wonder whatever happened to her.

'Yes, it's their ghastly little brother Isaac I have to deal with,' he said.

'So?'

'You see, the book's about the twins. Yes, I know, yet another one. But I've got a whole new angle. I've seen the Marginalia.'

I could tell the word had a capital letter. 'Sorry?' I said.

'The Marginalia. Hardly anyone gets to see them. Not since bloody Margot Evercreech.'

'Who?'

'But now that little shit says I can't use them,' he continued, ignoring me. 'I should never have shown him the draft. Said he thought the angle I was taking was unsavoury. Well, he should have seen it coming.'

'So… what was your angle, then?' I said.

'Psychosexual, of course.'

I choked on my wine.

'Sorry?'

'It's been obvious to me from the start,' he continued. 'And what I saw in the Marginalia confirms it.'

'Psychosexual?'

I was now well past the point of no return. I had to know the full story. The metaphorical car had crashed right across the road from where I was standing and the ambulance crew were pulling the twisted bodies out of the wreckage. I needed to see blood.

11

'Of course,' said Burgess. 'For one thing, the twins were lovers. Obvious. To be honest, I bet all twins are. Means, motive, opportunity. All present and correct from the cradle. Probably all bugger each other like bonobos.' There was an odd silence in the bar area.

'So, hold on,' I said. 'You suggested… in this thing you sent their younger brother… that the Vavasor twins had some kind of sexual relationship?'

'It's the gay thing, I suppose.'

'I would have thought it was the incest.'

'Really?' he said, with a sigh. 'Well, I suppose it is a bit of a taboo. But I'd always assumed they'd want the truth, however unsavoury. Wouldn't you?' He looked at me for a moment. 'Oh dear. I suppose you're right.'

The man's face was an exquisite portrait of a soul in torment. I didn't know what to say.

'Oh dear Lord. That's it, then, isn't it?' he continued. 'That's the final nail in the coffin. I'm going to have to tell my agent to return the advance. It's all gone, you know. Every last penny. I am well and truly shafted.'

'Maybe you could write a different book.'

'Dear boy, there are thousands of the buggers already. Vavaso-rology is a whole bloody industry. You need a new angle. Really thought I had one. Still do. Some of the things I saw in those papers would make your hair curl.'

'So why not just publish it yourself?' I said, emboldened by half a bottle of dodgy Merlot. 'That's what everyone's doing these days. What's the worst that can happen?'

'Well, they'll sue me and I'll end up bankrupt. But I'm damn close to bankrupt anyway.' He beamed at me. 'Great heavens. I do believe you're right. I shall go ahead as planned, with or without the little turd's permission. I shall publish and I shall be damned.' The train began to slow. 'Where are we?' he said, peering out of the window.

'Not sure,' I said. 'It's a while before my stop.'

'Ah!' he said. 'Swindon. The fragrant heart of Wiltshire. This is where I take my leave.' He shook my hand. 'Thank you so much for your advice, my good sir. You have no idea how helpful you've been.'

'My pleasure,' I said, relieved that our encounter was at an end. The train came to a halt, and he went on his way. It was only when I got back to my seat that I noticed he'd left his jacket there. In the overhead rack there was also a smart metal attaché case with a forbidding six-digit combination lock. I took them both with me when I got off, intending to somehow return them to him. However, this turned out to be not only the first but also the last time I ever saw George Burgess. Shortly after our meeting he was found dead, his jugular vein pierced by a mathematician's compass.

Chapter 2

By the time I got back to the flat, it was late and Lucy was already in bed. I stowed Burgess's case under my desk, undressed and crawled in beside her.

She was halfway through breakfast when I stirred the next day.

'Go well?' she said.

'Urgh,' I said.

'That good,' she said, raising an eyebrow.

I poured out a bowl of cereal and sat down opposite her.

'Working from home today?' she said, eyeing up my dressing gown.

'Urgh.'

'Can you sort out some food for tonight, then?'

'Urgh.'

'Was that a yes or a no?'

'Urgh.' The part of my brain that deals with language operates in some sort of standby mode until mid-morning and only switches on for emergencies. It's to do with conserving energy. Also, it puts off having to deal with anything awkward, like the fact that you have almost certainly pissed off a key client so comprehensively that you are very likely to lose your job as a result.

'I'll take that as a yes.'

'Urgh.'

'And call whatshisname about the leak in the bathroom. I've left the number by the phone.'

'Urgh.'

'Well, I can't sit here talking to you all day,' she said, standing up. 'I'm off.'

'Urgh.'

She turned at the door and looked at me. God, she looked good in a uniform. 'I… never mind,' she said, before leaving.

By the time I'd fetched my mobile, there were already three missed calls from Claudette at *m*KG.Q*, along with a text simply saying: 'Call. Now.' I turned it off. I didn't want to deal with this quite yet. I needed to consider my options.

I sat down at my computer and checked my e-mails. The first one was from a guy I'd once worked with at *m*KG.Q* who had moved on to a competitor with a less ridiculous name. I'd bumped into him on a training course recently and he'd mentioned something about a big project he was recruiting for. I was quite excited until I actually read his e-mail. Unfortunately, it turned out that owing to the present financial climate, his project had been placed into the chill cabinet in order to revisit potentialities for leveraging a soup-to-nuts flatpack reformulation of the entire paradigm. I was fairly certain this was bad news.

This was followed by a brief flurry of spam and a long missive from my mother, who had emigrated to Tasmania to rear pygmy alpacas – an extreme if understandable response to the breakdown of her relationship with my father. Finally, there was an urgent e-mail from Claudette, which I deleted without reading. Then I checked my bank account. As usual, this was a very bad idea.

I needed to earn more money. Given what happened yesterday, this was unlikely to happen at *m*KG.Q*; indeed, it was extremely likely that I'd be earning a lot less money very soon. So I needed to find something new. Provided I could persuade Claudette to give me a half-decent reference, I should be OK. I was good at what I did, even if I'd been a bit demotivated lately. All right, totally demotivated. But that happened to everyone from time to time, didn't it? I was sure it must. I had a good contact list. I just needed to start the process of finding a new job.

Then I caught sight of Burgess's case under my desk. What was I going to do with it? I really ought to give it back to him, if I could find him somehow. But what a strange encounter that had been, and how odd he should turn out to be writing about that thing Dorothy Chan had been so obsessed with.

God, Dorothy Chan. Wonder what she was doing now? And what was it about the Vavasors anyway? Wouldn't it be ironic if I was the one to sort it all out? Without thinking, I opened up Google and typed in 'Archimedes and Pythagoras Vavasor'.

At around half past six, I was deep inside a blog about how the Japanese Yakuza were seeking to dominate the world by seeding the clouds with some kind of mind control gas. I had no idea how I had got there and no idea how long I'd been there, although judging from the way my stomach and bladder felt, the journey had taken me the best part of the day. If it hadn't been for my subliminal reaction to the words 'Wake up, sheeple!' I would probably have still been surfing way into the night.

'Shit!' I said out loud and got up from my desk. I raced to the freezer and dug around for something to eat. When we'd first moved in together, I'd devised a brilliantly comprehensive system for maintaining control of its contents, involving a series of different-sized sticky labels, gold and silver stars and a ring-binder with colour-coordinated entries, but neither of us had ever bothered to follow this, with the result that every drawer appeared to be crammed full of small anonymous bags of vomit. I grabbed two at random and threw them in the microwave.

Then I went back to my desk and erased my browser history, just in time for Lucy to walk in the door.

'Did you phone the landlord?' said Lucy.

'What about?' I said.

'The leak. In the bathroom. I left the number by the phone.'

Shit.

'Sorry. Been busy.'

She gave a little sigh. I didn't like those sighs. 'So what are we having to eat?'

I glanced towards the microwave. 'Some sort of casserole. Microwave special.'

Lucy didn't comment.

We ate in silence.

(This is what I'd established. Archimedes and Pythagoras Vavasor were in their fifties at the time of their respective demises, which had occurred ten years previously. Nominally attached to Clare College, Cambridge, they lived a hermetic existence in a cottage in Little Wilbraham with their housekeeper, Mrs Standage, and their cat μ.)

'Two cats on a sloping roof,' I said, trying to lighten the atmosphere. 'Which one slides off first?'

'Sorry?' said Lucy.

'Two cats, sloping roof. Which one goes first?'

'I have no idea.'

'The one with the lowest μ.'

She stared at me. 'I don't understand.'

'μ. Coefficient of friction. It's a pun. Mew the sound that cats make and μ the letter in the Greek alphabet that sounds like mew.'

'Ah,' she said. 'It's not very funny, is it?' Lucy very rarely finds my jokes funny. 'Where on earth did you get that from?'

'Someone told me it yesterday.'

(Actually, I'd found it after Googling 'cats called μ'. It was number one in a list of the Best Mathematical Jokes of All Time. There was only one other joke in the list, and this involved a professor at a conference observing the line of people waiting for the toilets and remarking that pee implied queue and queue implied pee. I wondered if Dorothy Chan knew any other mathematical jokes. But I had to stop thinking about Dorothy Chan.)

' – Minsk,' Lucy was saying.

'Sorry?'

'Sandra's just got back from holiday in Minsk – '

(Who's Sandra? Oh, I remember. Short. Blonde. Married to one of the anaesthetists. Or was that Gina?)

' – apparently it's the new Irkutsk. They stayed in a real worker's flat, and they got taken to see an operational Uranium processing plant.'

(Why are we talking about holidays? We can't afford a holiday.)

'Are you listening to me, Tom?'

'Of course I am.'

(Pythagoras was born twenty-three minutes before Archimedes. In the days following his death, Mrs Standage came under considerable pressure to reveal the whereabouts of the missing Archimedes, but she consistently refused, asserting that she didn't believe that either of 'her boys' could have done anything wrong. She was the one who had discovered Pythagoras's body, and there was one entire strand of Vavasorology devoted to a theory that she had stolen some crucial papers from his desk. However, apart from Dinsdale Mazloumian's testimony – and there were many who dismissed him as a complete fantastist – no one had ever obtained

18

an interview with her. She was rumoured to be currently living alone with μ in a small cottage on the outskirts of Basingstoke.)

' – traditional *Znamenny* chant. They even went to a festival of puppetry.'

'Sounds wonderful.' Puppetry? Jesus.

(Dinsdale Mazloumian was typical of the denizens of the curious netherworld of Vavasorology. His thesis was that Pythagoras had solved the perpetual motion problem and had been put to death on the orders of the global military industrial complex. This claim was, he asserted, borne out by his conversations with Mrs Standage. However, in an interview for *Vavasorology.com*, he described Mrs Standage's cat as a grey, male British shorthair, casting considerable doubt on the veracity of the encounter, as it was well known that μ was a female of mixed heritage and black with white socks. His supporters, however, pointed out that it was entirely possible that either (a) Mrs Standage had acquired a new cat, also called μ, (b) the cat had spontaneously mutated or (c) the eternal spirit of μ was so powerful it had projected itself onto a feral intruder. Despite being barred from every Vavasor-related forum on the net, the influence of Dinsdale Mazloumian was still strong and his book *Perpetual Pye* continued to sell.)

' – don't you think?'

'Um… sorry?'

'A holiday. We need a holiday. Both of us do. You've said it yourself.'

'Yes, but – '

(I remembered now I'd ordered half a dozen books on Vavasorology today. Lucy didn't have any days off planned for the next week or so, so there was a decent chance they'd arrive when she was out.)

' – even just a week away would be good for us. Where do you fancy?'

'Not sure we can afford Belarus, although the puppets are obviously a major temptation.'

'I was thinking more of – '

(During the day I'd applied to join three forums: *Vavasorology.com*, which clearly regarded itself as the authoritative voice, *Vavasor: Truth and Consequences*, which was home to an eclectic selection of cranks, ranging from occultists through to breatharians, and the singularly unwelcoming – and oddly capitalised – *ePi Forum*. As far as I could tell, the ePis were the militant wing of Vavasorology – a bunch of hardcore mathematicians who were occasionally let out for the day but otherwise kept well away from the public. Dorothy Chan was almost certainly one of them, not that I cared either way.)

'You're staring into space again,' said Lucy. 'Are you OK?'

'I'm fine,' I said. 'Just a bit tired, that's all.'

(A scan of the public areas of *Vavasorology.com* – the other two forums were completely private – suggested there was still plenty of lively debate about the Vavasor twins, ten years on. The level of detail in the discussion was impressive. What was the significance, for example, of the fact that Archimedes had chosen to hang himself using a piece of rope exactly 3.14159 feet long? This thread went on for several pages until a weary moderator chipped in that this so-called fact was the result of a malicious Wikipedia alteration and would everyone please read the bloody FAQ before posting?)

'Well, I think that rather proves my point,' said Lucy.

'About what?'

'About a holiday, Tom.'

(Apart from the vociferous minority clustered around the likes of Dinsdale Mazloumian, most people seemed to accept that Pythagoras was indeed murdered by his twin brother. This view was also shared by the police and the local coroner, who returned verdicts of unlawful killing and suicide whilst the balance of his mind was disturbed, respectively. It was also generally agreed that the crime was committed in the heat of the moment, as the unusual and impractical choice of murder weapon pointed away from a pre-meditated attack. However, the absence of motive opened up the field for every kind of wild speculation.)

' – or would you rather go somewhere else? I'm doing all the work here, Tom.'

(Were we back in Belarus? I really didn't want to go to Belarus.)

'Tom!'

(As well as the question of motive, there was also the issue of what they were working on at the time. Neither twin had been seen in the vicinity of the Centre for Mathematical Sciences for years, but according to one rumour they were about to announce a proof of the Riemann hypothesis, one of the remaining unsolved Millennium problems, with a million dollar prize attached. This developed its own mythology in which the proof was so complex it could only be formulated by a pair of identical twins. There was a more extreme corollary to this, which was that this proof could only be *understood* by pairs of identical twins. This led to several candidates including the Russian Korsakov twins, the Austrian Dolmetsches and two of the Indian Kumar triplets being given privileged access to the Vavasor papers. The results were inconclusive, although the Dolmetsches claimed to have stumbled across a full proof of the twin prime conjecture. Unfortunately, one of them had spilt a mug of hot glühwein on the page in question shortly afterwards and their subsequent efforts to reconstruct the argument had so far come to nothing. I briefly looked up the Riemann hypothesis, but every synapse in my head began to scream in pain and I gave up after a couple of paragraphs. The twin prime conjecture seemed slightly more brain-friendly, but I didn't want to chance it straight away.)

' – so shall I phone the landlord myself tomorrow, then?'

'No, no, I'll do it. Don't worry. No problem.'

(But why would arguments over a mathematical proof have led to murder? In her testimony to the inquest, Mrs Standage insisted her boys never exchanged a cross word with anyone, let alone each other. It was easy to see how imaginations could run riot, even before the papers were withdrawn from the public domain by the Vavasor estate following the Margot Evercreech debacle. Which reminded me, I hadn't got round to Googling her yet.)

'Where are you off to now?' said Lucy as I got up from the table. 'It's T'ai Chi night.'

'Bit more work to do,' I said. 'Think I might have to skip T'ai Chi this week.'

She didn't look happy at this at all and didn't say another word before she went out.

But I didn't get very far with Margot Evercreech, because news had started to come out about a mysterious death in Swindon, and it didn't take long to work out who the victim was. Once I'd recovered from the shock, I spent the rest of the evening finding out as much as I could about George Burgess, every now and then glancing down at his locked case, which was still sitting under my desk and had begun to resemble a ticking bomb.

Chapter 3

I woke up at a quarter past three and lay awake for the rest of the night thinking about the Vavasors. The more I thought about it, the more I became convinced that with a little bit of work, I could solve the mystery once and for all. I would come to the problem with fresh eyes and – more importantly – the contents of Burgess's mysterious case. The fact that he had been killed suggested he was on the verge of cracking the thing wide open. That's the way it usually happened, right?

Obviously, I wouldn't be killed. I would be more careful. Burgess was clearly a careless idiot. After all, he'd told me his daft theories within a few minutes of meeting me. It's hardly surprising he got bumped off. For Christ's sake, the man deserved to die.

The obvious flaw in this plan was that I hadn't actually managed to open the sodding case yet. The lock had failed to yield to any of my guesses, and to work through all the combinations was going to take months. I'd tried forcing it, but it was made of solid steel and wouldn't bend a millimetre.

The other flaw in the plan was that I might be killed. I didn't want to be killed. Despite the best efforts of Claudette and the rest of the bunch at mKG.Q*, I had a good life and I fancied experiencing more of it. Lucy and I could get married and have babies and stuff. Twins, maybe.

Christ.

What was I thinking of?

And that's when I made my decision. I wasn't going to be sucked into this thing. I would go to Swindon, knock on Burgess's door and give the case to whoever answered. If there was no one there, I would wait until someone turned up. Someone was bound to, because there were things to be sorted out. I'd say sorry about your husband / father / weird Uncle George (delete as appropriate), hand the item over and then bugger off.

Once that was done, I'd forget everything about the stupid Vavasors. And Dorothy bloody Chan. I'd forget all about her too. I hadn't invited her back into my head and it was time for her to clear off again. Then I'd swallow my pride and go into the office and take whatever shit Claudette had to throw at me. I could blame overwork or the side-effects of medication or fears about terrorism or something. What kind of a PR man did I think I was? I should be able to do this in my sleep.

Which is why I got up at six o'clock to go to Swindon with Burgess's unopened case. The previous night's sleuthing had narrowed him down to a choice of three possible addresses.

'Where are you off to?' Lucy had said, appearing in the doorway to the kitchen.

'Work,' I said.

'Bit early, aren't we?'

'Yeah, well. Got a lot to catch up with.'

'What's that?' she said, nodding towards Burgess's case.

'Oh, some stuff from a client.'

'Oh.' She sat down at the table. 'See you, then.'

'Yeah.'

I was going to have to tell her about my mishap at work at some point, but not now. I had to sort this out first.

The first address took me to a boarded-up end of terrace in the middle of an estate. The roof looked likely to fall in at any minute and the place had clearly not been occupied for some time. George Burgess may have been an unusual character, but this wasn't his home.

I drove on towards the second possibility. This turned out to be a semi-detached Edwardian house in a quiet, middle-class, suburban avenue. This was more like it. There was a lot of activity around the house, some of it involving people in white overalls. Both sides of the road were already full, so I travelled on a bit further and parked a couple of streets away. It was a warm day, so I left my coat in the car, along with the case. I'd go back for it when I'd sorted out who to give it to.

There was a spotty young policeman standing outside the house, looking as if his mum had bought him a uniform several sizes too big so he'd have room to grow into it. I hadn't reckoned on a police presence, although it seemed obvious now that forensics would be scouring the place for clues. I wondered if I should go and offer the case to him. For the moment, however, he seemed to be involved in a heated conversation with another man. This one was tall, thin and weedy, wearing a paint-spattered hoodie that didn't quite meet the top of his jeans. He was bouncing up and down in an agitated manner. I hung back a little and listened in to their exchange.

'But I need to get in there—' There was a hint of an Eastern European accent.

'This is a crime scene, sir.'

'There are things—'

'Everything will be released to the family in due course.'

A white-overalled man emerged from the house carrying a computer.

'Hey!' said the hoodie guy, making a move towards it. 'You cannot take that!' The cop stepped in and barred his way, while the man in the white overalls continued walking with it towards a police van that was parked just up the road.

'Sorry, sir. Evidence. If you give me your name and contact details, I can let you know—'

'Yes, but… I need—'

'I'm sure you do, sir. But a crime has been committed and we need to gather all the available evidence.'

'No! Very important! You not understand—'

'Well, if you'd like to make a statement, sir—'

'No! Is no good. Is no good.'

The hoodie guy began to walk away, shaking his head. The cop seemed undecided as to whether he should be taking more of an interest in him.

'Wait a moment, sir,' he said, eventually, looking round to see if there was someone else who could take over his role guarding the front entrance. But the man in the white overalls had already disappeared back into the house and there wasn't anyone else around. This was an opportunity. I stepped up to the cop.

'It's OK,' I said. 'I'll go and get him for you.' He looked at me with a mixture of relief and uncertainty. He probably hadn't been doing this very long.

I set off after the hoodie guy. He obviously had something to do with Burgess. With any luck I could palm the case off on him.

'Excuse me?' I said. He glanced at me over his shoulder and continued walking. I followed after him. When he reached the end of the road, he started to run. 'Hey!' I shouted. 'I just want to—'. By now he was picking up speed. I wasn't dressed for jogging but I instinctively went after him. He hurtled off around another corner to the left, before dodging across the road to the right, without a glance in either direction. I was more cautious, but there was very little traffic and I managed to get across in time to see him disappearing around the next corner.

Pausing only to consider how unfit I'd become lately, I set off after him again. Fortunately, he was beginning to tire as well and I was now gaining on him. This gave me a new burst of speed and very soon I was within grabbing distance. But he could obviously hear me getting closer and the distance between us started to expand again. But up ahead some idiot had left a couple of wheelie bins lying around in the middle of the pavement and he had to check himself in order to avoid a collision. I launched myself forward again and grabbed hold of his top.

'What the fuck?' he said, trying to struggle free.

'I want to talk to you,' I said. 'About Burgess.'

'What about Burgess?' He'd lost his footing and was now grabbing at my jacket to stay vertical.

'Why did you—?'

He pulled away from me, spilling the contents of my jacket pocket on the pavement in the process. My mobile bounced once and then broke into two pieces. It then broke into several more under the weight of the hoodie guy's feet. My car keys didn't bounce at all. Instead, they just dropped straight down a grid in the road.

'You're with them, you bastard!' he screamed, backing away from me. 'Leave me alone, you murdering bastard!'

'What?'

'Leave me alone! I haven't done nothing.' He turned to run, back across the road. A large black Mercedes appeared from nowhere, screeching to a halt but not quickly enough to avoid hitting him. There was a horrible thud as he went down. Two men in sunglasses got out, picked him up and dragged him into the back of the car. I threw myself to the ground in the front garden of the nearest house. Then I peered over the wall at the Mercedes, which was still occupying the middle of the road. The driver had got out and was scanning the surrounding area. Then he shook his head, got back in and sped off.

'Can I help you?' said a warm, comforting voice behind me.

The room smelt of lavender and stale cabbage. A small army of china dogs surrounded me, fixing me with a uniform vacant stare.

'Biscuit?' said the woman, offering me a tin. She was short with grey hair and wearing a blue check housecoat.

'Er, no thanks,' I said. I didn't feel like eating.

'Have a drink, then, dear. You'll feel much better.'

I'd only managed a sip of the sweet tea she'd given me. I was shaking too much.

The car had hit him. He'd gone down like a sack of King Edwards.

'Go on, dear.'

They'd grabbed him. They'd bundled him into the back of the car.

'You'll feel so much better.'

They'd bundled him into the back of the fucking car.

'Really, you will.'

I took another sip of tea. I felt the warmth travel down my throat. I felt calmer. I drank some more.

'Thank you so much,' I said. 'You've been very kind, um… I'm sorry, I don't even know your name.'

'Daphne, dear.'

'Well, you've been very kind, Daphne.'

'It's no problem at all, dear. You looked as if you'd had an awful shock.' She peered at me with a look of concern. 'Are you sure you don't want a biscuit, dear?'

'No, honestly, I'm fine. In fact, I probably ought to be going.' I had to get home. Lie down. Wait for it all to blow over.

'Are you sure, dear? You're not going to drive, are you?'

'Well, yes, I… oh, sh—'

The keys. The fucking keys. How was I going to drive off without any fucking keys?

I'd have to break into the car and hot-wire it, wouldn't I? All I had to do was smash a window, open the driver's door and fiddle about a bit with the electrics. Right?

I had no idea how to do this.

I would have to get the train back home, pick up the spare set of keys and get another train back.

But I didn't have any money. My wallet was in my coat pocket. In the car. I'd locked my fucking wallet in the fucking car.

Shit.

I was going to have to text Lucy and ask her to come and bring the spare set of keys.

But I couldn't text her, could I?

Shit.

My mobile. My fucking mobile. My fucking mobile whose constituent parts were scattered over the pavement outside.

'I'm just going to get something,' I said, hauling myself out of the depths of her armchair. 'Back in a minute.'

In the short time I'd been inside having tea made for me, several kids had passed by the house and used bits of the phone for dribbling practice. I managed to gather some of them, but there was little chance they could be put back together in any form that would provide even the most minimal level of service. I went back into the house, after re-checking the grid to see if there was any sign of my keys. There wasn't.

'Um… can I use your phone?' I said, upon my return to Daphne's living room.

'Of course, dear.' I decided there and then that if Lucy and I ever did have a baby, it would be called Daphne. Even if it was a boy. And if we had twins, they would both be called Daphne.

Lucy would most likely have switched her mobile off by now, so I called the hospital and asked to be put through to her ward. After several rings, someone picked it up. I asked to speak to Lucy, explaining that it was a matter of life and death.

'What's wrong?' She sounded anxious. Maybe I'd overplayed the life and death thing.

'I was wondering… if you'd mind—'

'Where are you calling from? You sound a long way away.'

'I'm in some woman's house in Swindon.'

There was a long silence.

'Run that past me again, Tom.'

'I'm… oh, I see… no, don't worry, she's quite old… I mean, sorry, I didn't mean you were *old* old. Oh God – ' Daphne was looking at me strangely.

'Who are you talking to?'

'Her. The woman. Daphne. I'm in her house. She's not that old, that's not what I meant at all. I mean, she's—'

'Who?'

'She made me a cup of tea—'

'Why are you calling me, Tom? I don't have time for this.'

'OK.' Deep breath. 'Can you come over to Swindon and bring the spare set of car keys?'

'Why?'

'I've lost mine.'

'How can you lose the car keys? Why are you in Swindon?'

I had to admit these were two exceptionally good questions.

'I got into a fight.'

'You did what?'

'Well, I was chasing someone.'

'What? Who were you chasing and why? Why Swindon?'

Again, these were exceptionally well-chosen questions. Even if one was a repeat.

'I'll explain later. So can you come over?'

'Not now. I'm at work, you idiot.'

'Well, after work, then.'

'I've got Zumba.'

30

Sod Zumba, I'm stuck in Swindon. For Christ's sake, Lucy, this is serious. 'Can't you miss it just once?'

'No.' Long pause. 'I suppose I can come over afterwards.'

'Brilliant! What time?'

'I don't know. Depends on the traffic. I'll text you.'

'My mobile's broken. That's why—'

'Jesus, Tom. What have you been doing?'

'I said I'd explain later. Tell you what, let's say eleven p.m. Is that OK?'

'Suppose so. I'm not happy about this. I've got to get up early tomorrow morning.'

'I swear I'll make it up to you. Love you.'

'I know.'

I was about to put the phone down when I remembered. 'Hang on, I haven't told you where.' Having no precise recollection of where I'd parked the car, I gave her George Burgess's address, warning her there might be police outside.

'Oh, Tom,' was all she said before ending the call.

'Are you sure you don't want a biscuit, dear?' said Daphne.

'I think I will,' I said. 'I think I will.'

Chapter 4

I left Daphne's at eleven, spurning her offer of food and lodging for the rest of the day. She was lovely, but I'd already overstayed my welcome. More importantly, the china dogs were beginning to freak me out.

'You should be careful,' I said to her as I left, 'inviting strange men into your house like that.'

'Don't worry, dear,' she said with a twinkle in her eye. 'I've got a 9th degree black belt in Taekwon-Do. I could have taken you down whenever I liked.'

'Oh,' I said. Old people are amazing sometimes.

My first instinct was to go back to the cop outside Burgess's place and report what had happened to the hoodie guy. But after I'd played over the likely conversation in my head ('Did you make a note of the number plate, sir?' 'Er... no.' 'Why didn't you come back straight away?' 'Well, I ended up drinking tea in some woman's house.' 'May I enquire as to what you were doing here in the first place, sir?' 'Well, I thought I might be able to hand over something belonging to George Burgess.' 'What sort of thing might this be, sir?' 'Um... a case.' 'Where is this case now, sir?' 'Um...') I decided I'd already undergone enough humiliation for one day.

So I wandered around the town centre for a couple of hours or so dodging over-attentive sales assistants until it struck me that I could just go and sit in the public library for the rest of the day. I might even be able to use one of the computers to e-mail Claudette and establish how the land lay at mKG.Q*. However, it turned out you had to have a local library card and in any case you needed to book the computers in advance. This seemed grossly unfair. How was I to know I was going to break my phone today? I said as much to one of the librarians on duty, but she was having none of it.

'I'm very sorry to hear that, but those are the rules.'

'But I broke my phone. It wasn't my fault. I need to check my e-mails and stuff.'

'As I say—'

There was a cough behind me. I ignored it. 'It wasn't my fault. I got into a fight—'

She took a slight step backwards.

'I mean, I was running after this bloke, you see?'

She was staring at me now.

'I was just trying to talk to him but he ran away from me. No, that doesn't sound any better, does it?'

She pursed her lips and glanced meaningfully at somewhere over my right shoulder. 'I'm sorry, but I need to help these people with their books.'

'Right,' I said, turning round to see the small queue that had formed behind me. 'Right.'

It was almost as if she didn't believe me.

I found a seat in the study area and began to wonder what the hell I was going to do for the rest of the afternoon, then it struck me that I could read a book. It did at least seem possible to pick one off the shelves without having a signed consent form, but I couldn't make my mind up which one. Then I had an inspiration. I left my seat and went back to the librarian. I wasn't sure, but I thought I detected a slight roll of her eyes as I approached.

'Excuse me,' I said. 'Do you have any books by George Burgess? Local author, I think.'

This time there was a definite eye roll.

'Oh yes,' she said. 'We have several. Are you sure you want to look?'

'Why ever not?'

'You'll see.'

I suddenly felt sorry for the man. Here he was, scarcely cold, and this woman was badmouthing him.

'You know what's happened to him?' I said.

'Yes,' she said. 'And I'm not remotely surprised.' She gave me another odd look. I was getting tired of her odd looks. 'Are you a friend of his?' she said.

'Not exactly.'

This seemed to satisfy her. She jotted down a title and a Dewey Decimal code on a scrap of paper. 'This is the one people usually go for.'

'Thank you,' I said, taking the paper from her and looking at the name of the book she'd chosen for me: *Shroud of Ecstasy*. I recognised the title from my research the previous evening.

The central thesis of Burgess's breakthrough book was that the Turin Shroud was in fact the sheet from a bed in which Jesus Christ and Mary Magdalene had consummated their passion. According to the blurb, the image of a man's face had come to appear on the sheet via a mechanism which Burgess had christened 'orgasmic imprinting'.

I'd noticed that the online reception was polarised between reviewers who awarded the book an enthusiastic five stars, and some more doubtful readers whose one-star reviews noted the absurdity of the subject matter, the poor quality of the writing and the vast number of typographical errors. Several members of the latter group drew attention to the similarity in some of the phrasing used in *Shroud of Ecstasy* to that found in several of the five-star notices.

The book was dedicated to 'My Fellow Explorer, the Long-Suffering and Ever-Faithful Viv'. Based on my one brief encounter with Burgess, the first of these adjectives seemed entirely believable, and I felt a pang of sympathy for Viv, whoever he or she was. The book itself turned out to be an impressively heavyweight piece of work, both in physical terms and in the content. Although quite clearly the work of a madman, there was evidence of a herculean level of research. A casual flip through the references at the back threw up a whole cast of familiar fringe names such as Aleister Crowley, Wilhelm Reich and St John the Divine. Several popes were also mentioned, along with Adolf Hitler, the Medicis and the Illuminati.

I began to read the book itself, wondering how on earth Burgess could have parlayed this into getting commissioned to write a book on the Vavasors. I'd never heard of it before, so it couldn't have been a mainstream bestseller. Despite the salacious material, it was also a pretty stodgy read. Maybe it was because of this, or the warmth of the library, or the stresses and strains of the day catching up with me, but the next thing I knew was a voice telling me that the library was closing in five minutes and it was time to put my book away and go home.

I stumbled out into the street. It was colder than before and I felt the absence of my coat keenly. I was also starving and I wondered whether it was better to spend what little cash I had left on half a pint of bitter so as to rent a seat in a pub, or splash it all on a couple of Mars bars, in which case I'd have nowhere to go to keep warm. I was basically rattling about in the basement of Maslow's hierarchy of needs, where everything was focused on my raw physiological requirements. The lift up to the penthouse where I could begin to contemplate the cool stuff like esteem and self-actualisation was out of order until the engineer arrived to fix it. This wasn't a remotely pleasant place to be.

I began to consider the feasibility of pickpocketing. Surely it couldn't be that hard? I spent a couple of minutes observing the passers-by and wondering how I'd go about relieving them of their wallets. The first thing to do would presumably be to distract them somehow. Maybe some cheery banter or a magic trick. But I didn't know any tricks and right now I was all out of banter. And how did you slip your hand into their inside pocket without them noticing? What happened if you got caught? The more I thought about it, the trickier it seemed. I would have to choose between hunger and hypothermia after all. I decided to settle for hunger.

I headed for the nearest pub and managed to string half a pint out for an entire evening. I even succeeded in helping myself to a handful – or two or three – of nuts from the counter until the barman gave me a look and moved the saucer away. It's the little victories that count the most.

When I got back for my rendezvous with Lucy, Burgess's house was in total darkness. Curiosity got the better of me and I decided to have a peek through the letterbox. I sauntered up to the front door, squatted down awkwardly, nudged it open with my right hand and peered in.

'Tom,' said a familiar voice behind me, 'what the hell are you doing?'

I'd been so focused on the task in hand that I hadn't registered the sound of her car drawing up. I withdrew my hand quickly and with less care than I would otherwise have taken, stifling a yelp as the spring-loaded flap came down hard on the tips of my departing fingers.

'Jesus,' I said, staggering to my feet. 'Don't ever do that again.' I flapped my hand around in order to make the pain dissipate. It didn't.

Lucy observed my pantomime for a moment or two before holding out her own right hand, palm upward, with my keys dangling from her middle finger. I took them from her. She was still in her lycra, with her blonde hair tied back in a fierce ponytail.

'Seriously, Tom,' she said, 'what are you doing? Even by your standards, you're acting very strange.'

'Me? No, it's nothing. I'm just… visiting a client.'

Christ, that was really rubbish.

'You can do better than that, Tom. It's a quarter past eleven at night.'

She was right. But it had been a bad day.

'No, you're right,' I said. 'I'm… it's… well… look, I'm sorry. I'll try and explain—'

She shook her head. 'Not now. Not when we get home either. I have to get up early tomorrow.'

'I know. Me too.' Actually, I had no idea what I was going to do tomorrow. I guess it would involve going into mKG.Q* and doing whatever I could to jolt my flatlining career back into life. Lucy had turned and was walking away. 'How was Zumba?' I called after her.

She looked back at me, frowning. 'It was good,' she said. 'We had a new instructor. Quite sweet. He said I was making really good progress. It was nice to have someone take notice of me.' She paused, before adding, 'Hasn't happened for a while.' Then she got into her Micra and drove off.

Chapter 5

I found a spot in the car park and switched off the BMW's engine. *m*KG.Q*'s offices were located on the third floor of Ziggurat Mendip North, an out-of-town development built in the eighties using the then-popular technique of hanging pre-fabricated concrete slabs off the sides of a multistorey car park. It had won several awards in its time, including three for being the ugliest building in the greater Bristol area. Today it looked grimmer than ever.

Come on, Tom. Time to meet your destiny.

Once I reached the third floor, I was faced with the first hurdle. My pass didn't work. I waved it left to right, right to left, up and down and down and up, but none of these resulted in the usual satisfying click. So I ended up hanging around in the corridor trying to look nonchalant, waiting for someone else to arrive. Eventually, one of my colleagues emerged from the lift, smelling of cigarettes.

'Tom, hi,' he said.

'Hi Jezza.'

'The prodigal returns.'

'Yeah.'

'The prodigal returns.' He seemed to be playing with different ways of pronouncing the phrase, as if preparing to audition for a minor role in a school dramatic production.

'Yeah.'

Jezza tapped his nose. 'Claudette wants a word with you.'

'Yeah.'

'Well, good luck, mate.'

'Cheers,' I said. Jezza was a prick.

As soon as I'd snuck into mKG.Q*'s lobby in Jezza's wake, Claudette pounced. 'Morning, Tom,' she said, motioning towards her office. 'In here, please.'

I stepped into the room and closed the door behind me. I scrutinised Claudette's face for clues as to the agenda of our meeting, but she wasn't giving anything away. She was a tall, formidable woman. Raised in one of the toughest streets in St Paul's, Bristol, she'd worked her way up from flyposting for local reggae bands via the Arts Council to running mKG.Q*, which, whatever I currently thought about it, was reckoned to be one of the most dynamic PR companies in the South West. She wasn't someone to be trifled with. Unfortunately, trifle was all I had to bring to the table today.

As soon as I sat down, the door opened again and Melissa from HR scurried in, pink-faced, carrying a bunch of papers. I smiled at Melissa. She didn't smile back. This wasn't looking good.

'Well, then,' said Claudette when Melissa had sat down. 'The good news is that we have finally been given the contract for the Elk Balls promo—'

'Excellent—' I began. I'd worked hard for that. I'd come up with several really innovative ideas, too. Elk Balls would look great on my CV.

'However, the bad news is that ONE, in order to retain an understandably fractious customer, we have had to give him a discount, in fact such a heavy discount that we are almost GIVING AWAY THE FUCKING THING. And TWO, he does not want you, Tom, within an exclusion zone of TWENTY MILES OF HIS PREMISES.'

I hadn't seen Claudette this angry. Neither, it seemed, had Melissa from HR. The poor woman's eyes, normally a couple of tiny pinpricks, were currently the size of twelve-inch dinner plates.

'But I—'

Claudette held up her hand. She hadn't finished yet. She leant forward on her desk and steepled her fingers, peering over the rims of her glasses. 'Tom, what the HOLY GODDAMNED FUCK were you thinking?'

'I… don't know. I guess I lost my temper. I'd been up until three the previous night and—'

'"I guess I lost my temper",' she repeated. 'Tom, if that was all you'd done, it's possible that it could have been managed, even if Benny did walk in while you were describing him to one of his junior staff as a "devious little cunt who – "' She consulted the tablet in front of her '" – wouldn't know a set of principles if it bit him in the bollocks".' She looked up at me and took her glasses off. 'Did you really say "cunt"?'

Melissa winced.

'I… may have done,' I said. I was having a bad day.

Claudette leaned back in her chair and swivelled from side to side, apparently deep in thought. 'Thing is, we could – just about – have handled that. Even the "cunt". Although, strictly speaking – ' She looked across at Melissa ' – what exactly is our policy on "cunt", Melissa?'

Melissa's face was hard to read. There were several conflicting emotions fighting for space, although the main one seemed to be an overriding desire for Claudette to stop saying the word 'cunt'. 'Use of an obscenity in relation to a client would normally constitute grounds for instant dismissal,' she said, finally.

'Hmmm. Thank you, Melissa. Is this a clause we have invoked very often?'

'Not to my knowledge, no.'

'However,' Claudette continued, 'as you will no doubt be aware, that is by no means the end of the story. Is it, Tom?'

I stared at her. Shit. She knows.

'Benisons gave you the login details for their Twitter account, did they not?'

'Ye – es.'

'Yes, they did, Tom. Benny himself told me. And at ten to six on Tuesday evening, following your eviction from Benisons' premises, a series of unusual tweets appeared on their feed, seemingly referring to the very issue with their Supersonic Reindeer Burgers that you had gone in to resolve.'

'Really?' I said.

'Yes, really, Tom. Let's take a look at them, shall we?' She consulted the tablet in front of her. '"Benisons – from deer whose antlers glow in the dark, hashtag geigerburgers." "No need for an oven, Benisons are hot straight from the pack, hashtag geigerburgers!" Need I go on?'

'No, no – ' I shook my head. This wasn't going as well as I'd hoped.

'"Benisons made my nose glow red, says Rudolf, hashtag…" I mean, it's actually quite a snappy hashtag, Tom. In other circumstances – although I have trouble beginning to imagine what those circumstances might be – it is possible that I might even be applauding your coruscating wit.' She shook her head with a sad, almost sympathetic smile.

'Um – ' Say nothing, Tom. You might still get away with this.

'Those tweets were posted from a mobile phone somewhere in the region of Reading Railway Station,' continued Claudette.

'Could have been anyone, surely?' I said. Good riposte, Tom. Reading Railway Station must be absolutely heaving with trolls on a Tuesday night.

'In theory, yes,' said Claudette. 'However, there was also an amendment made to Benisons' Wikipedia page at roughly the same time. Do you remember that, Tom?'

I said nothing.

'"Benison International is a fast-growing supplier of down-market venison-based foodstuffs. Their most famous product is the Supersonic Geigerburger, so called because the meat content is primarily sourced from a supplier downstream from the *Łuszcząca się jak Skurwysyn* nuclear reprocessing facility in north-east Poland, which suffered a substantial leak in 2017. Benisons' owner, the larger-than-life Benny Olafson is a devious – "' Melissa squirmed in anticipation. Claudette looked up at me. 'I think we know what's coming next, don't we?' she said. 'Bit careless to use the exact same phrase, Tom.'

Too bloody right. 'That doesn't necessarily—' I began.

'Indeed,' said Claudette. 'However, call me a geek, but I noticed that the IP address associated with the Wikipedia amendment was an exact match for the source of an e-mail you sent me round about the same time to say you'd had a few differences of opinion with Mr Olafson regarding how to pro-ceed with respect to his radioactivity problem and you would be coming in the following day to discuss the situation. Again, it's not a hundred per cent conclusive, but...' Her voice trailed off, and she raised her eyebrows at me. 'Tom?'

'I got stuck,' I said. 'In Swindon.'

'Sorry?'

'That's why I didn't come in.'

'I'm not asking why you didn't come in, Tom.' She paused and a silence enveloped the room, like the silence before the guillotine dropped.

There was no way out. I shrugged and pulled a face. I shrugged again and pulled a different face. I shrugged for a third time and tried to speak. But no words presented themselves and I ended up doing a passable impression of a slow-witted goldfish. There wasn't anything remotely sensible to say.

Claudette sat up in her chair and sighed. 'OK, let's get this over with,' she said, nodding towards Melissa. Melissa shuffled through the papers in her lap and removed a single, handwritten sheet, which she wafted across the desk in my direction without meeting my eyes.

I scanned the scrap of paper. It stated that I would be resigning my position with immediate effect and that I was happy to forego my notice period in return for a pay off amounting to a week's salary. 'What's this?' I said.

Claudette sighed again. 'There are two ways of doing this: the quiet way or the noisy way. The noisy way is, I agree, more contractually correct, but it would also be very messy for all of us and if we go down that particular road I will make it my business to ensure that you never work in this business again. However, if we go the quiet way, you have my word that I will provide you with a reference that will glow so brightly you'll need to wear two pairs of sunglasses to avoid being blinded by the glare.'

'But it's unethical,' I said. 'Isn't it?' I wasn't sure. It certainly seemed unethical. I looked at Melissa. Melissa didn't say anything.

'You're not in a position to debate ethics, Tom,' said Claudette.

'For heaven's sake, I've already said I was tired. I'd been working all weekend on the action plan and then Benny comes along and tells me to stuff the whole thing. The man's a dickhead.'

'We know he's a dickhead, Tom. But it was your job to manage him and steer him towards an appropriate strategy for getting him out of the unfortunate situation he had landed his company in. Not hurl abuse at him and then walk out. Then compound it all by libelling him while you were waiting for the train home.'

'But it was just a joke—' I began. Shit.

Claudette gave me a significant look. In that instant, we both realised what I had just admitted, and I began to sweat. 'Those tweets didn't get deleted for three hours, Tom,' she said. 'Three hours, two of which had geigerburgers as a trending topic.'

'What? I mean, why?'

'No one could find the password.'

'You're kidding.'

'I assure you it's true.'

'Told you he was a dickhead.'

'But also *our* dickhead, Tom,' said Claudette. 'I had to fix Wikipedia myself.'

Which, of course, was how she'd spotted the IP address. I sighed. I'd had enough now. 'Glowing reference?' I said.

'Scintillating, Tom.'

I scribbled a signature and handed the agreement back to Claudette, who passed it on to Melissa. Then she reached down beside her and brought out a cardboard box, which she placed with great ceremony on the desk in front of her. 'Your – uh – stuff,' she said.

'Great,' I said, reaching for the box.

'One moment,' said Claudette, glancing at Melissa.

'Ah, yes,' said Melissa, holding her hand out. 'Keys.'

'What?'

'The keys to your car.'

I fished in my pocket and handed them over.

'We'll need the other set as well.'

Bugger. 'Ah. That may be a problem.'

'Why's that?'

'They... got lost.'

'We'll deduct the cost, then.'

'But that'll cost a bloody fortune,' I said.

Melissa gave a 'not my problem' shrug, scribbled something in a notebook and then started to gather her papers together.

Claudette looked up at me, put her head on one side and seemed to be about to say something. Then she shook her head and turned back to her tablet. I waited for a few seconds. 'You can go now,' she said, waving me away.

I wasn't sure what I was supposed to do. Should I shake her hand? That didn't seem right. But whatever anger there had been had dissipated, so storming out and slamming the door would have been ridiculous. I picked up my box and walked out of *m*KG.Q* forever. Outside, it had begun to drizzle.

I was still without a mobile and there were no public telephone boxes nearby. In any case, after the previous day's debacle, I felt it was not a good idea to pester Lucy for a lift. We'd exchanged fewer than a dozen words since we'd driven back from Swindon in separate cars. It was best to make sure she was in a receptive mood before announcing that I had just lost my job and might have a few problems in the not-too-distant future paying my share of the bills.

It took a couple of hours to walk back to the flat, by which time both I and my cardboard box were wet through. I dumped the box on the kitchen table, took off my jacket and grabbed a towel to dry myself. It was lunchtime, so I made a sandwich and helped myself to a much-needed beer from the fridge.

As I ate, I sifted through the boxful of detritus that consti-tuted the physical remains of my career at *m*KG.Q*. The first thing I pulled out was a selection of Lego bricks glued to a varnished wooden base. Peeling away from this was a Dymo label that read 'Empire Builder of the Year'. God. I was an ambitious little sod once. The next thing I found was a mouse-mat featuring the logo of Northern Soul Pies, one of my early triumphs. A four-year-old 'World of Lard' calendar. A desk tidy from Patsy's Pasties containing two blunt pencils, some rusty paperclips and a dried-out felt-tip pen. A novelty pig ornament from Pork On A Stick. And finally a mug with two handles (one slightly chipped) in the shape of a pair of antlers. From Benisons.

I opened another beer.

I wanted to be a music journalist once. I wanted to hang out with bands, travel the world and do cool things. Never managed to break into it, so I thought I'd try my hand at music PR, which would have been even better, because then I'd get to hang out with bands and they'd pay me for doing it. The best I could say is that I'd achieved fifty per cent of my ideal career. Trouble was, it was the wrong fifty per cent.

I opened another beer.

It was time to consider my position.

On the negative side, I had just lost my livelihood. Worse, I had lost it through my own stupidity. There were no two ways about it: I was an idiot. On the positive side, I now had more time to devote to finding out what really happened to the Vavasor twins.

Was that really a positive?

Maybe I should try to find a new job first, and then go and play detectives. But maybe the loss of my job was a sign.

Or maybe it was just a sign that I should get off my arse and go and look for another job.

But this was my big opportunity to find my true path in life.

Then again, if it looked like the Vavasors were my true path, perhaps I needed to find myself a better SatNav.

There were no more beers in the fridge. There was, however, a bottle of scotch in the kitchen cupboard, a present from The

Mechanically Reclaimed Mutton Company. This seemed an appropriate time to open it.

How much worse could things get? If I failed to get another job, a lot worse. I didn't want to face up to this, so I went into the lounge, turned the TV on and slumped in front of it, pressing buttons at random on the remote and feeling more miserable with every hour that passed.

At about six o'clock, I decided it was about time I pulled myself together, so I turned off the television and switched on the computer. The first e-mail I received was the acceptance of my application to join the *Vavasorology.com* forum. Now that definitely was a sign. I logged in and posted a quick message in the newbie area about how I'd come to be interested in the subject.

I then scanned the various threads on the closed area of the forum, marvelling at how madly inventive some of the folk there were and wondering how they'd spent their time before the days of the internet. The first thread that caught my eye was one discussing the possibility of both twins being assassinated by the Belarusian mafia, although there was little evidence or indeed motive advanced to support the theory. This didn't prevent several other users joining in to help to plug these significant gaps.

I gave up after a while and focused what attention I still had on a more coherent thread started by user *UltimateTruth* and headed 'Did GB have the crown jewels?': *Hey Guyz, Anyone heard anything bout wot happened to the crown jewels after GB got plugged? Turned up anywheres?*

The remainder of the thread consisted mainly of feverish speculation between *UltimateTruth* and another user called *AbsoluteTruth* as to whether someone like 'GB' really would have been given access to the 'crown jewels'. This exchange was punctuated at intervals by posts from the considerably less literate user *WhereTheBodiesAreBuried*, hinting opaquely at the identity of GB's killer, much to the annoyance of both the other posters.

Even with several measures of TMRMC's Famous Grouse inside me, I realised that 'GB' was George Burgess, and the 'crown jewels', whatever they were, were almost certainly in the case that Burgess had left on the train the day we met.

The case that was, I now remembered, in my car.

The car whose keys I'd handed back to Melissa from HR earlier on that day.

Chapter 6

'You did what?' said Lucy, withdrawing from me slightly.

'Said something bad about Benny Whatsit. Called him a – '
I decided not to say the word. It wasn't going to help.

'A what?'

'Bad word.'

'To his face?'

'Noooo. To someone in his office. And on Wikipedia.'

'Oh God.'

'Might have tweeted a bit as well. From their account.'

She shook her head. 'I despair of you.' She sniffed the air around me. 'Have you been drinking?'

'Ordered food. Jalfrezi and Dhansak.'

'I wanted Chinese. Tom, have you been drinking?'

'Bit. Going to sit down now. Not happy.'

'You're not happy – how do you think I feel?' She started bustling about the kitchen.

'What you doing?'

'There's rubbish in the sink. God, look at the state of this place.'

'Didn't get round to it. Sort it out later.'

'No you won't. You'll probably break something.'

'Not fair.'

'Completely fair, Tom. You're clumsy at the best of times.' She squirted some washing-up liquid into the bowl, filled it with hot water and put the breakfast dishes in to soak. Then she sat down opposite me.

'Still don't think you're being fair,' I said, belching.

'Tom, try not to do that when you're looking at me. You smell like a brewery.'

'Only had…' No. I couldn't remember how much I'd had.

'Tom, why didn't you tell me this before? You must have known what was going to happen.'

'Um. Don't know. Felt bit stupid.'

'What are you going to do?'

'Don't know.'

'And what were you doing in Swindon, then?' Lucy narrowed her eyes. I hated it when she did that.

'Long story.'

Lucy looked at her watch. 'I've got plenty of time.'

I paused, wondering where to start. Fortunately, at this moment, the doorbell rang. I answered it and was met by a figure with an impressive beard protruding from the bottom of a motorcycle helmet. He was holding a carrier bag. 'Your food,' said the figure, opening the visor. 'Two random chicken dishes, two pilau rice, couple of popadums and a bit of that manky salad my dad always chucks in for no good reason.' I recognised the voice.

'Mo! You're back! Hey, Lucy, it's Mo! Come on in, have a drink,' I said, taking the bag from him and waving him into the flat. Mo's dad ran Admiral Akhbar's Tandoori Cantina, Bristol's only Star Wars-themed Indian Restaurant. I'd given him some free PR advice in return for a couple of months' worth of Korma, which is how I'd come to know Mo.

Mo shook his head. 'Sorry, mate. No drink allowed.'

'Ah, of course. You're on your motor thingy.'

'Well, it's not just that, mate. I'm—'

'Never mind, never mind. Understand. Understand. So where've you been?'

'Been to uni, innit.'

'Really? Where?'

'Imperial, innit. Maths.'

'Whoa. You must be really clever. I'm rubbish at maths, I am.' Then a thought struck me. 'Ooh, hold on a mo, Mo. Sorry. Ha ha. Mo mo. Sorry. You must know all about those whatsit twins.' Mo frowned at me. I couldn't remember their stupid name. 'Begins with V, that's it. Va – Va – Vava – Vavavoom. No, not that. Va – va – .' It was on the tip of my tongue. Wherever that was.

'Oh, them,' said Mo. 'The bleeding Vavasors. Archie and Pye, innit. Nah, listen mate. Steer clear of that stuff. Leave it to the mentals on the internet.'

'But I met this bloke. Gave me his case.'

'Seriously, mate, don't go there.'

'I lost it though.'

'Good thing too, mate. If you want my advice, stay well clear of that rabbit hole.'

'Lost my job too.'

'Sorry to hear that, mate. Listen, next time you drop into the restaurant, give me a nudge. Got something to show you.'

I paid for the food and Mo left.

How was I going to get that case back?

'What was that all about?' said Lucy as I took the containers of food out of the bag and put them down on the kitchen table.

'I lost the case.'

'What?'

'Doesn't matter.' I got a couple of plates and some knives and forks.

'Tom,' she said, clicking her fingers under my nose. 'No, Tom, look at me, look at me. Look at my eyes, Tom. What are you up to, Tom? There's a load of stuff you're not telling me.'

'Bit confused about things.'

'That makes two of us. It's like you've been somewhere else all week. Occasionally your body drops in but your brain hasn't turned up for several days. I think you've given me the Dhansak, by the way.'

'Sorry. Can't get anything right.'

'Right now, no.'

'Met this bloke on a train. Then he got killed. But that was later. Left his case behind. Full of stuff. Can't open it. Took it to Swindon. Brought it back. Left it in the car. There's these mathem… mathemagician… oh, I dunno. These blokes. Twins. They're dead, too—'

'Tom, this isn't making any sense at all. And it's also slightly scary. Maybe we should leave it until you're sober.'

'Maybe we should. You sure this is Dhansak?'

'This is definitely not Jalfrezi.'

We came to a mutual decision that the best way to spend the evening was to watch a film, mainly because this would remove the need to say anything to each other. I can't remember what we watched, because I fell asleep half an hour in, not waking up until the Icelandic copyright notice. I wiped the drool off my cheek, switched the television off and got ready to turn in.

Lucy was already in bed and as I lifted up the covers, I caught a glimpse of her lovely back and I was suddenly overcome by a sense that everything was going to be wonderful and all right with the world after all. I didn't have a job, it was true, but I was still young, carefree and virile.

'Tom,' said Lucy, sleepily. 'What's that?'

'Nothing,' I said.

'You're poking me with it. Put it away.'

'Happy. Love you.'

'It's damp.'

'Sorry. Been for a wee. Love you.'

'Seriously, Tom—'

'Want babies. Twins.'

'Tom,' said Lucy, turning to face me. 'What's got into you now? Hasn't it occurred to you that the day you've lost your job might not perhaps be the best time to consider starting a family?'

'Dunno. OK, maybe not babies. No babies for now. Just, you know...' I put my hand on her buttock. She removed it.

'Sorry, Tom. I don't think it would be a very good idea now. Not even out of sympathy.'

'No. 'Spose not.' She turned away from me and I turned away from her. 'Love you,' I said.

'Yeah, I know.'

The one good thing about Saturday morning's stupendous hangover was that it gave me another excuse not to enter into conversation with Lucy. I guess I would have to tell her everything eventually, but I hadn't quite worked out the best way to do so without looking like a complete idiot. The fact that she was already predisposed to think of me in those terms didn't help, either. Maybe I shouldn't have told her about losing my job.

We spent the afternoon looking for a new sofa. I didn't remember agreeing to this, but apparently it had been weeks in the planning. It was hard, but I think I managed to maintain a reasonable level of enthusiasm despite my frail state. We even managed to agree at one point on a nice two-seater leather model, but this all fell apart when it turned out to be considerably more expensive than I'd been expecting. Even worse, the zero per cent finance deal they were offering was only available to customers who were in regular, full-time employment. Without thinking, I glanced at Lucy. This was a dreadful mistake.

'Oh,' she said. 'Well, yes, I wasn't expecting to, but I suppose there's no reason why I couldn't pay for it myself.'

'No, no, no,' I said, pleading. 'I didn't mean you to think that at all. We'll come back when—'

But Lucy had already left the shop in a huff. I followed after her, a short distance behind.

'Look, I'm sorry,' I said as we got into her car. I was still struggling to come to terms with my new credit status.

'It's all right,' she said, although it clearly wasn't.

'I'll get a new job.'

'But how long's that going to take?'

'I don't know. Claudette said she'd give me a good reference.'

'Do you believe her?'

I hadn't thought of that. 'I think so,' I said.

'Are there many jobs available?'

'I don't know.'

'You mean you haven't looked yet?'

'It only happened yesterday.'

'But you must have had some idea.'

'Well, yes. But I still haven't had time to look into it.'

'I really liked that sofa.' Lucy started the engine and we drove home in silence. I was beginning to realise that every new thing that went wrong was making it harder for me to tell her the whole truth about what I was up to.

For the rest of the weekend we did our best to avoid each other, which wasn't easy in a small flat. Every so often I worked out in my head what I wanted to say and opened my mouth to say it, before seeing the expression on her face and then shutting up again. At around eleven o'clock on Sunday morning she disappeared into the bedroom and re-emerged wearing her tracksuit. Then she went out, mentioning in passing that she was going for a jog around the block.

She didn't come back until a couple of hours later.

'Where did you go?' I said, looking up from the crossword.

'Bumped into Arkady,' she said.

'Who's Arkady?'

'Teaches Zumba.'

'Ah.'

'He's from Minsk.'

'Right.' I was vaguely aware we'd had a conversation involving Minsk some time in the previous week, but I couldn't remember the context. I hoped it wasn't important.

'I'm going to have a shower now.'

I briefly toyed with the idea of responding with 'Cool, I'll join you' or 'Mind if I watch?' but discarded both options after a moment's reflection. 'OK,' I said instead. I went back to the crossword but gave up after a couple of minutes of fruitless anagramming. My brain was elsewhere.

I went out for a walk to clear my head. I needed to make a plan. Identify goals and priorities. Strengths, weaknesses, opportunities and threats. Strategy and tactics. Get things back on track. Eyes on the prize.

But what was the prize?

A new job, obviously. I needed to pay my share of the rent and sofas and stuff. So the number one priority was to find a new job. Lucy was right. I should have got going on this earlier.

Then again, if I wanted to retrieve Burgess's case, I'd have to move on that pretty smartish too. God knows where it might get dumped when the car got handed on to its next owner.

So the number one priority was actually Burgess's case. I'd get onto that first thing Monday. And I'd start job hunting on

Tuesday. Or Wednesday at the latest, allowing for any overruns in the Burgess case hunt.

Sorted.

I sat down on a bench overlooking the docks and watched as a coxless four headed off towards the Avon Gorge, battling against the swell and a small posse of angry ducks who had taken exception to the alien presence in the water. My mind drifted back towards the Vavasors.

These were the facts as I knew them.

One, Archie and Pye Vavasor were – indisputably – both dead. No one knew for certain why this had happened or who was responsible, although the finger of blame pointed in the direction of Archie.

Two, George Burgess was also dead. The nature of his death (compass point through jugular vein) and Pye's (set square through heart) suggested a connection between the two events: one that would potentially absolve Archie from any blame, while at the same time reactivating up a whole range of alternative ideas previously dismissed as the preserve of conspiracy theorists. Then again, the fact that they were ten years separated in time was problematic. Perhaps we would have to wait for the next murder before a definite pattern could be established.

Three, at the time of his death, Burgess had been commissioned by the Vavasor estate to write a book on the affair, only for the permission to use some significant papers to be removed at the last minute. This was the weirdest aspect of the whole thing. Why, of all the available writers out there, did they pick Burgess? Why now? And why did they change their minds? And did this have anything to do with his murder?

Then there was the bloke I'd run into outside Burgess's house. Who was he and what was his connection to Burgess? Why did he run away from me? And who were the thugs who ran him down and bundled him into their car?

In the meantime, George Burgess's case was still out there somewhere, maybe in my old car, maybe somewhere else altogether, waiting to reveal its secrets to whoever could crack open its combination. I was determined that person would be me.

When I got back to the flat, I found a note from Lucy on the table saying that she had gone out with Samantha to discuss man problems. Samantha's boyfriend was an arse, so I wasn't a bit surprised by this. She wasn't back by the time I turned in for the night, so I added a note of my own to hers asking if it was OK to borrow the Micra tomorrow. I didn't like the idea of traipsing all the way to Ziggurat Mendip North and back on foot. On further reflection, the request to borrow Lucy's most valuable asset looked a little bald on its own, so I appended 'I'll try not to break it', followed by a smiley face and three x's.

Next morning I found the keys on top of the note, without any further comment from Lucy.

Chapter 7

I didn't fancy rolling up to my old company's offices in a borrowed Nissan Micra, so I parked a discreet distance away. Unfortunately, I succeeded in scheduling this manoeuvre for the exact moment my ex-colleague, Jezza, passed by on his way to the corner shop.

'Nice wheels, mate,' he remarked, raising his index finger in mock salute.

'Piss off, Jezza.'

Jezza grinned back at me and then grabbed his crotch in an alarming manner. 'Guess what I've got,' he said.

'I have no idea, Jezza.'

'Elk Balls. Get it?'

I sighed and headed off in the opposite direction, towards mKG.Q*. Jezza was still a prick.

There was no sign of my old car in the car park. I went into the building and was about to walk past the front desk when the receptionist called out to me.

'Can I help you?'

'Need to go up to mKG.Q*.'

'Sign in, please.'

'But I… Look, you know me. I always go straight up.'

'I'm afraid that's no longer possible.'

'What?'

'No longer possible.'

There seemed to be no basis for negotiation, so I signed in.

'Who is it you wish to see?' she said.

'Um… whoever deals with cars, I suppose.'

She waved a hand in the direction of a row of chairs and made a call. 'Someone will be down soon,' she said.

I sat down and waited. Every now and then someone I used to work with wandered past and I pretended not to notice. Eventually, Sunil from Accounts bounced down the stairs and came over to me, holding out a hand. I shook it.

'So is this about paying for the spare key?' he said. 'You could have just done a transfer, you know, and there may be other charges, depending on what they say about the condition of the vehicle.'

'Sorry, what?' I said, confused. What other charges? 'No, it's about something I left in the car. A case.'

'Ah, I wouldn't know about that. You'd need to speak to the leasing company.'

'You mean you haven't got my case? But—'

Sunil looked around himself and then spread his hands. ''Fraid not, Tom. We just arranged for the leasing people to come and pick the vehicle up.'

'What? You didn't check it over first?'

'Why should we?' Sunil seemed baffled by the idea.

'Well, in case I'd left something in there, of course. Jesus.' It seemed obvious to me. Why wasn't the man getting it?

'Hey, calm down, Tom,' he said, holding his hands up. 'Look, I'm sorry. I really can't help you. Here's the guy you need to speak to.' He gave me a card. 'Talk to Damien,' he said, tapping the card. 'He'll sort you out.'

'So you definitely don't have the case?' I said. 'It was in the back, behind the driver's seat. It's about yea big, combination lock…' I mimed its dimensions in the style of the big fish, little fish, cardboard box dance.

'No, Tom,' said Sunil. 'We definitely don't have your case.'

'You're absolutely sure?'

'Yes.'

'Maybe someone went down with the key…'

'I handed it over to them myself.'

'So no one else could have cleared the car out first?'

'Tom, give Damien a call.'

I shook my head. This was awful. That case was my lifeline. 'I'm not happy about this,' I said. Sunil shrugged and went back upstairs. I went back to the Nissan and drove straight to the garage where Six Star Leasing was based.

There was no sign of the BMW at the garage either. I went in and found the service counter. Somewhere a radio was playing 'Africa' by Toto.

'Hello?' I called out. No one responded. 'Hellooo?'

There was a bell push on the counter. I pressed it. Somewhere a long way off there was a buzzing sound. I waited several more minutes.

Eventually, an oldish chap with thinning, grey hair emerged, wiping his hands slowly on an oily rag. He was wearing a filthy blue boiler suit. 'Can I help you, mate?' he said, eyeing me up suspiciously.

'Yes,' I said. 'You've got my BMW. Well, it isn't my BMW any more, but anyway, I left something in it and I was wondering if you had it anywhere.' Then I remembered the card. 'I was told to ask for Damien.'

At the mention of Damien's name, the man's face clouded over. 'Damien, eh?' he said.

'Yes, Damien.'

'It's a lease vehicle we're talking about, then.' This was clearly a very disappointing turn of events.

'Yes. You see, I—'

'Who'd ever lend a vehicle to a stranger, eh?' he said with a sad shake of the head. 'You should see these cars when they first arrive. Things of beauty, they are. And the smell! Oh, there's nothing like the smell of a new car, is there? And then there's the sensual growl of a new virgin engine, like a stallion in its prime waiting to gallop...'

'Um...'

'And then it gets hired out to some tit in a suit. Who does marketing. Or sales management. Or – God help me – PR.' I quailed slightly. He was spitting the words at me in an alarming manner.

'Sure, but—'

'The thing is, my friend, every single pressed steel and re-inforced glass masterpiece that rolls out of Bayerische Motoren Werke AG is worthy of the same care, respect and attention as a newborn baby. Even' – he looked me up and down – 'the 3 Series compact executive models.'

'Well, yes, but—'

'You should see them when they come back to us. Scratched bodywork, torn seat leather, chipped windscreen, overflowing ashtray, and the engine crawling in on its knees begging for just one scintilla of love or understanding.' He looked me directly in the eye. 'Do these men treat their women like this?'

'I don't know,' I said, wondering where all this was going. 'Look, can we talk about my case?'

'It makes me weep sometimes. There was one came in this morning—'

Ah, so that was where it was going. 'Look, if it's about that little nick underneath the petrol cap,' I said, 'I really meant to get it fixed. It's just the bastards took the car away from me before I had time to.' I was blushing. Why was I blushing?

He shook his head sadly. 'If I had a pound for every time I've heard that.'

This was getting me nowhere fast. 'So have you got my case or haven't you?' I said.

'Mikey's got it.'

'Mikey?'

'Yeah. Didn't want to leave it lying around here in case it got nicked.'

'So where's Mikey?'

The man turned round and bellowed, 'Mikey!'

Another man appeared. 'He's gone home, Terry.'

'What?' said Terry.

'Gone home. Wife just gone into labour.'

'Well, there's your answer,' said Terry, turning back to me. 'Last one took seventeen hours, so I wouldn't hold your breath.'

'So what about my case, then?'

Terry sighed. 'Mate, I think your case is going to be a little way down Mikey's priorities right now. Have a little patience and come back this time next week, OK?'

I started to say something but gave up. Terry was right. I headed for home.

On the way back, I passed a phone shop and decided it was about time I got connected again. My contract still had several months to run, so I would have to look at buying a replacement outright.

I had forgotten how much mobile phones really cost. There was no way I could begin to think about buying the same model again, even if it was a year and a half since it originally came out.

'Do you have anything, y'know, a bit less expensive?' I said.

The assistant sighed and began scrolling down the screen in front of her.

'How about this one?' she said, turning the screen around to show me.

'Maybe a bit less?'

She turned the screen back and continued scrolling downwards.

'This one?'

'What about that one underneath it?' I pointed to a boxy contraption that looked like the remote control for the television in a care home. From a brief glance at the specification, its level of technological sophistication didn't go much further than that either. However, it was astoundingly cheap. I hadn't heard of the make before, but for the sake of conserving my dwindling finances, I was willing to take a punt on the Happy Wednesday Corporation of Chongqing.

'That thing?' she said.

'Yes. Why not?'

She tutted and shook her head, before turning the screen back. She tapped away a bit longer, then disappeared into the back of the shop. After a while she returned with a box containing my new Happy Wednesday Gold Star 3000. She completed the process of setting the phone up without looking at me once.

I left the shop with a spring in my step. At least one thing had gone right today: I was in contact with the rest of the world once again.

When I got back, there was an e-mail waiting for me from someone called Rufus Fairbanks, requesting a meeting the very next day. I googled the name of the venue, which turned out to be an exclusive members' club in the City of London. I also googled Fairbanks himself. He turned out to have his fingers in a lot of expensive pies, although it was hard to tell precisely what ingredients he was actually contributing. I replied, thanking him for his kind invitation, protesting that it was a little short notice, especially when I didn't even know the reason for our meeting.

Fairbanks replied almost immediately. *I'll make it worth your while*, he said. *And you're not exactly busy right now, are you?*

The hairs prickled on the back of my neck. *What do you mean?* I wrote.

What I said, replied Fairbanks. *I'm guessing right now you're spending most of your time slouched in your pyjamas flipping between PornHub and Russian Dash Cam videos. Am I right?*

Bloody cheek. *Is this about work?* I wrote.

I think you know what it's about, replied Fairbanks.

The ticket will cost a fortune, I thought.

At that precise moment the doorbell rang. I opened it to find a courier standing there in full motorcycle gear.

'Package for Mr Winscombe,' said the muffled voice behind the helmet. The figure thrust an envelope at me.

'Sorry?' I wasn't expecting anything.

'Sign here.'

I signed the screen of his handheld device. 'How come you popped up at that precise moment?' I said. The figure shrugged and left.

I opened the envelope to find a first class return ticket to London, dated Tuesday. Another e-mail pinged into my inbox.

Deal? wrote Fairbanks.

Deal, I replied. I didn't really feel in any position to argue.

Chapter 8

The steak was so tender that all I had to do was wave my knife at it and it deconstructed itself into a perfectly regular array of quivering, bloody slices.

'Exquisite, isn't it?' said Fairbanks. He was balding, in his fifties and had clearly not stinted on the finer things in life. Judging by the quality of his suit, his tailor probably earned more in a day than I'd ever managed in a month.

'It's extraordinary,' I said.

'Apparently they have a team of masseuses working on the animal twenty-four hours a day for its entire life.'

'Good grief,' I said. I couldn't begin to imagine how much it must have cost. 'Do the cows enjoy it?'

'I don't know,' he said, with an amused expression. 'Hadn't really crossed my mind.'

I took another bite. Regardless of the feelings of the animal, it was a remarkable experience for the diner.

'So, then,' said Fairbanks, after we had finished our main courses. 'The mysterious Vavasor twins.'

'Indeed.' Fairbanks had already established that this was the agenda for the day's discussions. Any hopes that he might have been head-hunting a PR guru had been very quickly dashed over the carpaccio and avocado foam.

'Look, I'm going to lay my cards on the table. Kimono open and all that stuff. I'm a pretty straightforward chap.' He leaned back and began to fiddle with his napkin. 'The thing is, you and I both know we're in a minority here. Am I right?'

'I'm not sure—'

'I mean, now that poor old Burgess is no longer with us – and frankly he had his moments – there are very few of us left working on this who still have a full suite of upstairs furniture.'

'What about the police?'

He gave a dismissive wave. 'What about them?'

'Well, Burgess for one thing. Won't that have opened up the whole case again?'

'Why?'

'Because of how he died.'

'Hmm. I see what you mean. Well, yes, maybe they will come up with something. Maybe they won't. Either way, you and I are a little way ahead of the game, are we not?'

Fairbanks hesitated before continuing. 'I think,' he said finally, 'that from this point on, we had better take this conversation completely off the record. So can you please place your phone on the table where I can see it?'

I took my Happy Wednesday Gold Star 3000 out of my pocket and laid it out in front of me. Fairbanks picked it up and looked at it.

'Are you sure this is a phone?' he said.

'Yes,' I said.

'Oh.'

'Long story,' I said.

'Hmmm. Well, if I find out that you have any other recording device on your person, be assured that I will take said device and thrust it several feet up where the sun does not shine.' He mimed an appropriate action with his right hand. 'Understood?'

I gulped. 'Understood.'

'So then. You saw Burgess just before he died, didn't you?'

'I—' I really did need to learn how to stop blushing.

'The post was deleted shortly afterwards, but someone with the username "arsebiscuits89" went on the – ah – Vavasorology forum to claim that they had met George Burgess on a train the day he died.'

Bugger. That was careless.

'Poster "arsebiscuits89" was otherwise inactive on the forum – presumably because he now realised the stupidity of posting anything there remotely on-topic – but a simple search led me to an account with the same absurd name on a music forum where, seven years ago, "arsebiscuits89" had conveniently linked to a rather tiresome and jejune blog post reviewing a concert by a Mexican, death-metal, mariachi band.'

Bloody hell. Las Palomas de Fuego del Infierno. I'd forgotten about them. Unusual cover of 'No Woman, No Cry', but otherwise pretty dreadful.

'I made a note of the name at the end of the review and a cursory search established that there was only one person with that name living close to a station on the route that "arsebiscuits89" had so helpfully described. In all, it took me less than five minutes from seeing your *Vavasorology.com* post to getting both your home address and your e-mail. Now, tell me what Burgess said to you, please.'

The steak had developed an unpleasant aftertaste.

'Come on, Tom,' he said. 'There's no such thing as a free lunch. Especially around here. Don't worry, you won't go away empty-handed. I have information for you too. But you can go first.'

'He said he'd seen the Marginalia.'

Fairbanks raised both eyebrows.

'Did he have the documents with him?'

I shook my head. 'No,' I said. I wasn't going to open my kimono quite yet. Not until I'd had a good look inside his, anyway.

'Pity.' He looked at me long and hard. 'What did he say about the Marginalia?'

'Oh, he had some crackpot theory that it was all about them having sex with each other.'

Fairbanks burst out laughing. 'Really? That was it?'

'Apparently so.'

'But he never showed you anything?'

'How could he?' I wasn't going to be caught out. 'He didn't seem to have any papers with him.'

'As you say,' he said. 'As you say.' Fairbanks stroked his chin. 'Did Burgess say anything about the main body of the papers?'

'What sort of thing?'

'The mathematics, Tom. That's what this is all about, isn't it?'

'I suppose it is. But no, he didn't. Didn't strike me as the sort of person who'd be interested in that.'

'No,' said Fairbanks. 'Odd, isn't it?'

'Are you interested in the mathematics?' I said. What was Fairbanks's angle?

'Everyone in the City of London should take an interest in mathematics, Tom.'

'Really?' I had no idea.

'How much do you know about the City?'

'Very little.'

'I thought not. The City of London, Tom, is a place where the strong and the smart make money out of the weak and the dim. How do we do this? Well, one of the ways is to construct ever more complicated things for people to invest in. Or, as you might put it, to bet on. For example, we might separate the interest from the principal in a mortgage and make them two entirely separate instruments. Then we might take some of these halves and throw in an option to swap a basket of them for a portfolio of Moldovan municipal bonds in five years time. Then we might take that option and re-value it in Vietnamese Dong.'

'You're losing me.'

'My point exactly. And the smart folk are the ones who have this all set up and ready to go knowing its true value. So when everyone else wants a slice of the action – because we'll sell it as, I don't know, perhaps a sure-fire way to hedge against downward movements in the Costa Rican overnight coffee price – we're the only ones who have a chance of making any money. Eventually, the rest of the market catches up, but by then we've moved on to something else. Financial engineering, they call it.'

'That's a bit sad, isn't it?'

'Why?'

'You're using mathematics to help invent worthless stuff to fool gullible investors.'

'Tough titties. If someone wants to buy something, who's to say the City can't sell it to them?'

'But it's still a bit... you know—'

'Let me tell you a story. Did you ever hear about the Grannies?'

'Sorry?'

Fairbanks leaned back in his chair.

'Couple of years back, chap in our financial engineering team came up with an idea for a new financial instrument. Called it the Granny. Thought it was the most exciting thing to hit the City since the eighties. The way he saw it, the combination of a squeezed, middle class and an ageing population had led to something close to a perfect financial storm. Our world was full of people with a non-productive Granny on their hands – a Granny who was costing them a small fortune to maintain, to boot. Nursing home fees, gin allowance, you name it.

Ultimately, of course, they stood to gain a nice wedge from Granny's will, but right at that moment, mainly as a result of the fun and games of the last few years, they were stonybroke. Wouldn't it be nice to get their hands on the dosh now?'

Fairbanks spread his hands and gave me an encouraging nod. I gave a cautious nod back.

'OK, then. Let's do a deal. We'll find someone who can give you a good price for the Granny now, as well as taking over the maintenance responsibilities, in return for eventually getting your share of the will. We'll take a commission for introducing the old girl to the market and arranging the deal, so,' – here, he counted off on his fingers – 'one, easy money for us, two, instant cash for the family and three, an entertaining punt for the counterparty.'

My mouth was hanging open. I shut it. 'But this didn't actually happen, did it?'

Fairbanks ignored me.

'The focus groups were exceptionally positive,' he said. 'Mumsnet – whoever they are – I'm told they're terribly influential – thought it was wonderful. And in the meantime, our modelling teams were coming up with some fascinating stuff about the potential secondary market.'

'Secondary market?'

'Yes. Once the Granny had been established as a tradable instrument, the secondary market would kick in. Institutions would start buying and selling them. Any properly balanced portfolio would be required to take a position in Grannies. Which gave us two problems: storage and real-time valuation. Storage we reckoned we could solve by turning one of the disused dealing rooms into a hall for bingo or whatever it is old women do these days. But valuation was trickier.'

'And that's where the maths comes in, right?' I said, struggling to keep up.

'Good Lord, no. This wasn't a job for mathematicians. This was a job for the medics. Of course, when we explained the concept to a few Harley Street types, they were on board immediately. Think about it: a good terminal diagnosis could send a Granny's price sky high.'

'Hold on—'

'I can see what you're thinking. Granny nobbling. Yes, we modelled that, too. It was a risk, in an unregulated market, but we felt it was a risk worth taking. And then, we wondered, could we come up with some derivatives?'

'Derivatives?'

'We started off with swaps. Exchange your wealthy but cranky Granny with another one who's skint but wonderful with knitting and a great babysitter. But that was tame. Cross-border swaps were far more interesting, because not only was there the lifetime forward foreign exchange calculation to consider but also the difference in death duty rates between the two territories. Much messier.'

'Good grief.'

'And then, what about options? In the end, we reckoned these might not work so well. Thing is, by the time you get round to exercising your option, there's a distinct possibility that the underlying Granny might already be dead, rendering the instrument completely worthless.'

'But this never happened, did it?' Please tell me it didn't.

Fairbanks shrugged. 'No. So they say. Or perhaps it's just gone underground. Put it this way, if you wanted to sell, I could probably find you a buyer. That's all I'm saying.'

Jesus. I thought about this for a long time.

'So did you know Pythagoras, then?' I said, eventually. I wanted to get the conversation back to relatively solid ground.

'Ha. I see where you're going, Tom. But no. I never knew either of the Vavasors. And I should perhaps point out that on the day Pythagoras died I was actually in New York, speaking at a conference.'

'I saw something on the internet about him being killed by the Belarusian mafia. He was working for them or something.' I'd been pondering this and getting increasingly worried by the implications, however absurd it seemed.

Fairbanks stared at me and then burst out laughing. 'What an extraordinary idea!' he exclaimed.

I joined in the laughter, feeling somewhat relieved. 'Actually,' I said, 'if you say it out loud, it does seem rather absurd. I didn't even know they had a mafia in Belarus.'

'To be fair, Tom, every country has a mafia.'

'Even the UK?'

Fairbanks spread his arms wide. 'What do you think the City of London is? I suppose there are a few straight dealers around, but most of what goes on here would come under the heading of organised crime in any other field of human endeavour.'

I was beginning to see his point.

'The thing is, in the absence of any more information, we just don't know what old Pye was up to. The family certainly aren't saying anything. Until they let Burgess in, everything was pure speculation.' He paused. 'And now the poor chap's dead. If only we had access to the Marginalia.'

'If only,' I said. 'If only.'

'You're sure—?'

'I'm sure.' I'd made my mind up. If I ever did get my hands on Burgess's case again, I wanted to have first dibs at the contents, especially now the stakes seemed to be getting higher with every day that passed.

'Pity,' said Fairbanks, signalling for the bill. 'Pity.'

As we both got up to leave, I was feeling more confused than ever. The whole affair seemed to be getting more and more impenetrable. I needed someone to throw me a bone.

'One thing,' I said. 'Why did the Vavasors call in Burgess?'

For the first time that day, Fairbanks looked genuinely perplexed. 'I have no idea,' he said. 'No idea at all.'

Well, it was worth a try. As we emerged onto the street and made our farewells, I noticed a guy in a black T-shirt and sunglasses loitering across the road. He immediately took out his mobile and made a call. I decided to take a detour round the block before going down into the underground. When I came back to my starting point, he had gone.

Chapter 9

By the time I got back to Bristol, it was getting dark. My enjoyment of the privileges of the first class carriage had been tarnished by a nagging feeling that I was being watched. The Paddington concourse had been populated exclusively with suspicious-looking men speaking into mobile phones, each one of whom stopped talking whenever I caught sight of them. At least two of them got on my train and I was convinced I was likely to be jumped at any minute.

When I arrived, I took a careful look at the rest of the disembarking passengers, but thankfully they all looked pretty normal. However, as the train pulled out, I glanced at one of the carriages as it went past me and I was convinced I saw someone holding a phone up to take a picture.

No, this was absurd. It was paranoia brought on by a heavy lunch, pure and simple.

I got back to the flat to find a note from Lucy saying she was out again, this time with Jeanette. I had no idea who Jeanette was, but at least it meant that I could put off the interrogation about what had happened in London. To be honest, I still wasn't sure what to make of it all myself. I'd replayed the meeting over in my head several times on the way back, and it made less and less sense with every iteration. Not only that, but I had this horrible feeling that the transfer of information had been in one direction only, from me to Fairbanks.

Also, despite Fairbanks's dismissive comments, I still couldn't get the Belarusian mafia out of my head. Were the people in the black Mercedes in Swindon Belarusian? How about the bloke they'd knocked over? He certainly seemed to have an East European accent. I did a quick search on the *Vavasorology.com* forum but the thread I'd been looking at the previous day had disappeared and hardly anything else turned up, apart from a brief report of an encounter between forum member *PyeNChips* and an unnamed gentleman from Grodno who was trying to promote a theory that Pye had been murdered by a team of highly trained cats led by μ. Even by the liberal standards of *Vavasorology.com*, this was an impressively unusual position to take, and there had been very little follow up.

The problem was, I couldn't make any public enquiries of my own about all this, because Fairbanks was very likely to see whatever I posted. Even if I deactivated my account and rejoined under a new username, chances are he'd be onto me as soon as I posted the question. A newbie asking about a possible Belarusian connection would stick out like a delegation of sore thumbs at a metacarpal health convention. If I knew what his handle was, I could perhaps have blocked him, but I didn't have a hope in hell of working that out. For all I knew, he was nothing more than a lurker in the shadows.

I realised now that any idea I may have entertained in the last few days of using the forum to find out anything about my investigation was completely doomed. I had no reason to suspect Fairbanks of anything underhand, but the man scared me. I had a strong feeling that I needed to keep him at arm's length, where the arm was holding an outsize bargepole.

That reminded me, I also needed to remove the blog post linking *arsebiscuits89* to my real name. If Fairbanks could put two and two together, so could a whole load of other folk. I spent a few happy minutes revisiting old posts, before deciding that the entire blog could go. It belonged to another, less complicated, more innocent era.

If I couldn't use *Vavasorology.com*, what else could I do? I'd get Burgess's case back at the beginning of next week, but there were still several days to fill in the meantime.

I drew up a list of names of people worth talking to.

In his phone call on the train, Burgess had referred to someone called Hilary who would be furious about the Vavasor estate withdrawing permission to use the Marginalia. I assumed she must be his editor. I had no surname, or indeed any idea of the name of the publisher, so short of contacting every single Hilary in the publishing industry, that didn't seem to be a goer.

What about Burgess's agent? I googled 'George Burgess agent' and found him listed as a client of Cheeseman, Hollyfoot and Finch, a long-established agency with an impressive list of high-profile clients. It didn't sound like the sort of place that would give house room to someone like Burgess, but his mugshot on their website convinced me otherwise. The hapless photographer had done their best with the given material, but the man was still instantly recognisable.

I added all the other names I'd gathered along the way to my list:

Isaac Vavasor, Archie and Pye's younger brother
Mrs Standage (and μ, the cat, if still alive)
Margot Evercreech
Dinsdale Mazloumian
'The Long-Suffering and Ever-Faithful Viv,' the dedicatee of *Shroud of Ecstasy*.

I didn't hold out much hope of getting access to Vavasor himself. He was notoriously reclusive and the whole business with Burgess would have only heightened his desire to keep out of the public eye. Mrs Standage, on the other hand, had disappeared off the face of the earth. Apart from the disputed claims of Dinsdale Mazloumian, there had been no sightings of her since the inquest on the twin brothers' deaths ten years ago.

Margot Evercreech did at least have a splendidly mad website, full of random font changes, sparkly spinning GIFs and a style of writing that gave all the appearance of an explosion in a punctuation factory. It had clearly been designed by a hyperactive ten-year-old in recovery after a Haribo overdose. However, while the existence of the contact form on the site offered a way of getting hold of her, the content made me even more inclined to save that option for when all other avenues had been exhausted.

If Dinsdale Mazloumian really had succeeded in tracking down Mrs Standage, he might be worth talking to, even if his own theories were as bonkers as everyone else's. He had less of an online presence, but I could probably get to him through his publisher.

And that left the mysterious, surname-less Viv, and I had no idea where to start with her. Or indeed him.

On balance I felt that Cheeseman, Hollyfoot and Finch would be the best starting point and I decided to get in touch with them the next day.

Next morning over breakfast, Lucy was less interested in my trip to London than I'd anticipated.

'So who did you see?' she said.

'Oh, a bloke. Someone in the City.'

'Did he have anything to offer you?'

'Sorry? Oh, I see. Possibly.' I knew what she really meant, but it was a plausible answer either way, so I wasn't technically lying.

'Would you have to move?'

It struck me later that she didn't say 'we'. 'Um... don't know,' I said.

'Oh well.'

And that was it.

I decided not to bother e-mailing Cheeseman, Hollyfoot and Finch because there was very little chance they'd take the trouble to respond. When I called them at ten o'clock, however, everyone seemed to be in a meeting apart from an intern called Bella, who had been left in charge of the switchboard. I tried again at hourly intervals throughout the morning, all to no avail. Life at Cheeseman, Hollyfoot and Finch was clearly one long series of meetings.

At one o'clock, I changed tack. I withheld my number and adopted a mild Scottish burr.

'Cheeseman, Hollyfoot and Finch, Bella speaking,' said the intern.

'Well, hellooo. I wonder if I could speak to... eh... Diana Cheeseman,' I said, picking an agent at random. God, that was a rubbish accent. My only hope was that Bella had never actually met anyone from north of the border. Fortunately, it turned out she hadn't.

'I'm awfully sorry, but she's in a meeting.'

'Oh, that is moooost disappointing. Most disappointing indeed. You see, I need to speak to her about George Burgess.' In the pause that followed, I could have sworn I heard her ears prick up. 'It's just that Hilary has asked me to speak to Diana about his estate and—'

'Ooh. One moment, please,' said Bella, with an urgent tone to her voice. 'She's out of the office right now, but you can reach her on – ' She gave me a mobile number. Bingo. I was in. Now to see if I could hold Diana Cheeseman's attention for long enough to extract some useful information.

I withheld my number again, dialled the number I'd been given and after a couple of rings, a female voice answered.

'Cheeseman,' she said. I heard the clink of glasses in the background, and her muffled voice saying 'One more bottle of the Sauvie Blanc, please, darling.'

'Ah, hellooo,' I said. The accent was improving with practice, I felt. 'I need to speak to you about… eh… George Burgess. I work with… eh… Hilary and she… eh—'

'Look, I don't know who you are,' came the reply, 'but first of all, you're not from anywhere remotely near Scotland.' Bugger. I'd been doing so well. 'And secondly, I know every single person who has or has ever had the misfortune to work for Hilary van Beek and you, sir, are most definitely not one of them.'

Shit.

'So, who are you?' she continued. 'Are you from the press? You don't sound like it, because you'd have butted in several times by now to protest. I wouldn't be getting a word in edgeways.' She paused. 'Well?' she added, and then, *sotto voce*, 'Awfully sorry about this, darling. I'll get rid of him as soon as I can.'

'I'm—'

'God, you're not an author, are you? Because if you are, please do bugger off right now and read the submission guidelines on our website.'

'I'm a friend of Burgess's,' I said.

'Good God. Surely not. I didn't know he had any. No offence, but he was a loathsome little man.'

'Um – '

'No, you're not a friend of his at all. Don't believe that for one moment. But you've got something of his, haven't you?'

79

For the second time today I could clearly hear the change in someone's facial expression. This time, it was the narrowing of Diana Cheeseman's eyes.

'No,' I said. I wasn't going to reveal my hand quite yet. 'I just wanted to know a few things.'

'You are a journalist, then. OK, I think this discussion is over.'

'No, wait. I'm not a journalist. I'm not even a friend of Burgess's, although I did meet him once. I'm just an interested party. I was wondering if you could give me some information.'

I heard her say 'One moment, darling,' to her companion, and then a succession of bumps and clatters before the acoustic at her end changed to the street outside. 'OK, What kind of information?' she said. 'I'd need a pretty good *quid pro quo*.'

'What do you mean?'

'Maybe you could help me out in return. Thing is, we're a bit stuffed as far as this sodding book of his is concerned. He was supposed to deliver the final manuscript this week after little Isaac had given it the once over and no one knows where the bloody thing is. Silly arse used to write it all out in longhand, so it's not even as if we could get it off his computer once we get it back from HM Constabulary.'

'Go on,' I said. An idea was forming in my mind.

'You see, given recent events, interest in the story is at an all-time high, so we want to get the damn book published as soon as we possibly can. From the point of view of sales, getting murdered was the best thing that Georgie B could possibly have done, and Hilary is expecting to make an absolute killing.'

'No pun intended,' I said, trying to lighten the tone.

'I'm sorry?'

'Never mind.'

'What I'm saying,' she said. 'Is that if you could lay your hands on Burgess's manuscript – and I have this odd little feeling you can – I might be willing to help you.'

This was getting more interesting by the minute. My original intention in contacting Diana Cheeseman had been merely to get her talking and harvest whatever random facts I could. But I now realised I might actually have something of value to her, because Burgess's handwritten manuscript was almost certainly in his case. What's more, it was also becoming abundantly clear that neither Diana Cheeseman nor Hilary van Beek had any idea that the Vavasor estate had slapped a veto on the whole thing.

'I'd need to know everything you know about Burgess and how he got involved with the Vavasor case,' I said. 'Also, I'd like an introduction to Isaac Vavasor.' Well, it was worth a try.

There was a long pause. 'Bring me the manuscript and I'll see what I can do,' she said eventually. 'One thing, though,' she added. 'Who are you and how will I get hold of you?'

'I have your number,' I said and as I hung up, I couldn't help punching the air. There was the minor issue of not actually having Burgess's case, but I was sure I'd get it back the following Monday, at which point the real fun could begin. It was only later that it occurred to me there was a decent chance that Diana Cheeseman now had me pegged as Burgess's killer. Still, I would cross that bridge when I came to it.

I'd also acquired one more bit of useful information as a result of the phone call, the full name of Burgess's editor. I googled Hilary van Beek and found she was the sole proprietor of Head Wind Publishing, a niche imprint specialising in paranoia porn, including books on how the moon landings were faked, the real truth about 9/11 and what to do if you wake up to find you've been anally probed by men from another world. The list also included Dinsdale Mazloumian's *Perpetual Pye*, along with a number of other Vavasor-related works that I hadn't previously come across. Burgess would have slotted in nicely there.

Head Wind turned out to be based in an industrial estate on the outskirts of Chippenham, well within easy driving distance, so I resolved to pay them a visit. I was sure Lucy wouldn't mind me borrowing her car again, but I thought it best to wait until tomorrow after I'd checked with her first. The odd atmosphere at breakfast had unsettled me and I didn't want to do anything to make things worse.

I spent the rest of the day making a desultory attempt at finding a job. After the excitement of the conversation with Diana Cheeseman, it all seemed a bit mundane and I knew my heart wasn't really in it. At around six I got a text from Lucy to say she was going to be working late and then maybe going for a drink with Shona. I was convinced Lucy had never mentioned Shona before. It was almost as if she was trying to avoid me. So I left another note on the kitchen table before I went to bed asking if I could borrow her car again, once more promising not to break it.

Chapter 10

I got to Head Wind Publications just after half past nine. They were located in a single-storey unit sandwiched between a manufacturer of novelty paperclips and the UK distributor for a brand of homoeopathic remedies for goldfish. I knocked on the door but there was no reply, so I pushed it open and went in.

The place was in a state of chaos. There were papers scattered everywhere and boxes turned over with books spilling out of them onto the floor. A young bloke with a straggly beard was kneeling down trying to sort one random pile into some kind of order.

'What's going on?' I said.

'It's awful,' said the beardie, throwing his arms around for emphasis. 'We've had a break-in. It's all a horrible mess. Why? Why? Why?' He seemed on the verge of tears.

A woman with wild, greying hair and large, red-rimmed glasses emerged from the back of the unit. She was wearing a shapeless, floor-length kaftan and a considerable amount of loud, clattery jewellery. She removed the cigarette that was in her mouth with a spectacular fit of coughing and examined me with some distaste. 'Can I help you?' she said in a rasping voice. I deduced that this was Hilary van Beek.

'I'm a friend of George Burgess,' I said, 'and—'

'Oh, not that little shit again,' she said. 'Well, you can bloody well sod off. I've had enough of him. Wretched man. Getting himself killed just when he was about to deliver.'

'I—'

'What do you want anyway? I take it you can see we're busy at the moment.' She waved the cigarette around her and a fine shower of ash fell on the books at her feet.

I decided to adopt a more emollient approach. 'I can see that,' I said. 'I was going to ask if you could answer a few questions about Burgess, but perhaps we could leave that for another time. Anything I can do to help?'

The young bloke looked up at this offer and gave me an eager puppy-like smile. 'That would be brill—'

'Quiet, Benjamin,' said Hilary van Beek. 'I'll handle this.' Benjamin looked crestfallen and returned to his sorting. 'Listen, you,' she said, pointing a gnarly finger at me. 'For all I know, you're one of the people responsible for this mess. You didn't find what you were looking for and you've come back for another go in broad daylight.'

'No, that's not true!'

She looked me up and down again and sniffed. 'No, I suppose not. You don't look the sort. You don't look much like a friend of George Burgess either.'

'He's more a sort of acquaintance.'

'And what's that supposed to mean?'

I noticed a copy of Dinsdale Mazloumian's *Perpetual Pye* on the floor. I bent down to pick it up. 'Mind if I take a look?'

'This isn't a sodding library, you know.'

I put it back.

'Look, I don't care who you are,' she said. 'Or what you want. Right now, I have a business to sort out and you, matey, are as much use as a marshmallow dildo.'

There was a snort from Benjamin.

'Oh, back to work, laddie,' she said, turning towards him. 'Good bloody grief. I could do that more quickly with one arm tied behind my back and the other one wearing a boxing glove.' She essayed a contemptuous laugh, which evolved with alarming speed into another grotesque bout of coughing. She stuck the cigarette back into her mouth and took a long drag before turning back to me. 'Are you still here? Christ on a bike.'

I was hovering there, trying and failing to think of a way of justifying my presence. She shook her head at me. 'Listen. The only possible way you could be any use to me right now is if you could furnish me with a copy of George Burgess's manuscript.'

'What manuscript?' I said, remembering to feign ignorance just in time.

'But I somehow – ' She suddenly clapped her hand to her head. 'Shit! That's it. That's what they were looking for. The bloody manuscript!'

'Sorry? But why would anyone else—'

'I bloody knew it. I bloody well knew it. Someone out there thinks the daft tit managed to deliver the thing to me and wants it back.'

'Do you mean a rival publisher?'

This set off another disconcerting bout of coughing. 'Good bloody grief, no. No one else out there would touch it. Cowards, the lot of 'em. More likely someone who wants to suppress it.'

'Surely not?'

'It's happened before. Look, I'm not discussing this now. I've wasted enough time with you already. Go home and play with yourself for the rest of the day.'

I put my hands up in mock defence. 'OK, I'll go,' I said. 'But here's my number. Call me when you're ready to talk.' I scribbled my number down on a scrap of paper and gave it to her.

'I very much doubt that's going to happen,' she said, putting it down on one of the piles of books.

I glanced down at Benjamin as I went out. 'Bye then,' I said.

'Bye,' said Benjamin, waving a hand vaguely in my direction.

I drove home feeling more confused than ever. If Hilary van Beek was right, I needed to be more careful than ever about who I told about the manuscript. Assuming, that is, that I possessed it in the first place. There was, after all, no guarantee whatsoever that it was in Burgess's case. But who would be trying to suppress the manuscript?

I was floundering. It was increasingly obvious that I was never going to solve this on my own. But I had no idea who to turn to. The only other Vavasorologist I'd met in the flesh so far was Rufus Fairbanks and I didn't feel comfortable with sharing any confidences with him.

In the absence of any better ideas, I logged onto *Vavasorology. com*.

I started a thread called 'Break-in at Head Wind', with a single post that simply read *Place ransacked. Anyone know anything?*

I set the flag to receive notifications and went and made myself a cup of coffee. When I came back I already had one e-mail from the forum, but it wasn't notifying me of a response to my post. It was telling me about a private message, from a user called *EulerIsGod*. I hadn't noticed him before, and when I checked out his profile, his posts were mainly in the 'Off Topic' area of the forum, usually discussing obscure aspects of online games.

EulerIsGod's message was terse and faintly disturbing. *Careful what you say*, it said. *People are getting hurt.*

What do you mean? I replied.

Just that. This place is getting dangerous.

What am I supposed to do then? I wrote. This time there wasn't a reply. I went back and took another look at my post. It looked pretty innocuous to me. I dismissed the conversation with *EulerIsGod* from my mind and returned to the important subject of what the hell I was going to do next.

I'd just finished my lunchtime sandwich when an irritating little noise started up somewhere. I eventually realised it was the ringtone for my crappy, little, new phone. I answered it.

'Oh, thank Christ,' said a breathless voice.

'What?' I said.

'Thank Christ you've answered. God, it's awful.'

'Who is this?'

'Benjamin. The intern. From Head Wind.'

'Oh yeah. Does she want to talk to me now then?'

'What? No, no. She doesn't want to do that. She can't do that.'

'Why?'

'She's dead, that's why. She's dead. Oh God, what am I going to do, she's dead.' He sounded utterly distraught.

'What?' This was an unexpected turn of events.

'She's dead. Mrs VB. She's on the floor. Dead. Not breathing. Dead.'

'Hey, calm down, it's OK,' I said, even though it clearly wasn't. 'Are you definitely sure she's dead?'

'I said, she's not breathing. I checked her pulse and everything. Oh God, oh God what am I going to do?'

'Look, have you called the police?'

'No. Mrs VB said never to call the police because they were a bunch of corrupt pigs serving the needs of the global military industrial complex.'

Ah. 'Well, you don't need to obey her every whim *now*, do you?' I said. 'Give them a call and they'll sort everything out.'

''Spose so,' said Benjamin. 'Still rather not.'

I have no idea why I said what I said next. 'Tell you what, I'll come over and maybe I'll call the police instead. Would you prefer that?'

'Yes. I think so, yes, I'd like that.'

What was I thinking of? Then I had an awful thought. 'There's no blood, is there?' I said. I wasn't sure I could cope with anything really unpleasant.

'No. She's more sort of strangled.'

'Sort of?'

'Yeah. It's a bit odd really.'

I had another awful thought. 'Did you do it, Benjamin?' It seemed unlikely, but I suppose it was possible that he'd finally had enough and flipped.

'Nooooooo. I went out to get something for lunch and when I came back she was—'

'OK, OK, I was just checking.' On reflection, it was a stupid question to ask. Benjamin looked like he would have found it a challenge to strangle a Beanie Baby. 'Stay there,' I said. 'Don't touch anything and I'll be right over.'

I felt an odd sense of elation. I was on a mission. I had no idea where it was going to end, but for the first time for months I had a sense of purpose.

When I got back to Head Wind, the front door was flapping backwards and forwards in the breeze. I poked my head inside and called out, 'Benjamin?' There was no reply. Surveying the scene, it was evident that any progress that Benjamin may have made in clearing up the aftermath of the previous night's break-in had been undone by the struggle between Hilary van Beek and her assailant. There was a bad smell in the air.

'Benjamin?'

There was still no answer, so with some trepidation I crossed the threshold into the unit. Hilary van Beek's body lay on the floor in the middle of the room, next to an uneven pile of books entitled *1001 Ways You Can Save YOUR Life*. Her head was at an odd angle to the rest of her body. It did indeed look as if she had been strangled, but I saw now what Benjamin had meant. The murder weapon was one of those flexible ruler things that mathematicians use for drawing curves.

What the hell was going on?

I bent down and touched her neck with the back of my finger. I'd seen people do this in films, but I couldn't feel any pulse.

'Benjamin!' I called, shaking slightly. 'Where the hell are you? It's OK, you can come out now.' But there was no response. Benjamin had disappeared off the face of the earth.

There was nothing else to do apart from call the police. I took out my mobile, hit the first nine and then had second thoughts. If I was the only person there when they arrived, there was every chance I'd be taken in, and I didn't feel that adding 'murder suspect' to my CV was a wise move right now, either from the point of view of my relationship with Lucy or indeed from the point of view of any prospective employers.

I could always scarper after calling them, but they probably had ways of tracking me down even if I withheld my number. So instead I used Head Wind's landline, taking care to pick up the handset with my hand wrapped round the tail of my shirt to avoid leaving any fingerprints.

'Emergency. Which service?'

'Police. Someone's dead here. Strangled.'

There was a sigh at the other end. 'Address, please?'

I gave it to them.

'Your name, sir?'

'Um… ' (Come on, think of something.) 'Dave.' (Jesus, why Dave?)

'Dave?'

'Dave Benjamin.' Well, full marks for inventiveness there, Tom.

'Please stay right where you are then, Mr Benjamin, and make sure you don't touch anything. Someone will be there very soon.'

'Thank you.' I put the phone down and raced out of the unit. As I drove away, I was sure I could hear the sound of a siren approaching.

Back home, I checked to see if there were any more notifications from the forum. There weren't. So I went back to my conversation with *EulerIsGod*.

What exactly did you mean when you said this place was getting dangerous? I wrote.

The answer came back almost straight away. *What's happened?*

Something bad.

Who's dead?

Burgess's publisher. I was being reckless, but I needed to talk to someone and part of me felt I could trust *EulerIsGod*.

Shit. How?

Strangled.

Christ. Let me guess. With a spline?

What's a spline?

Look it up.

It turned out that a spline was one of those flexible ruler things that mathematicians use for drawing curves. So that's what they were called. *How did you know?*

A hunch.

Who are you? I wrote.

Never mind, came the reply. *Rule no 1: no outing.*

Sure, but you're beginning to freak me out.

Trust me, I'm on your side. How about you tell me what you were doing at Head Wind?

A hunch, I wrote. Two could play at that game.

Come on, you can do better than that.

I was beginning to feel oddly emotional now. For the first time since I got involved in this thing, I was having a proper conversation about it with someone who understood my obsession. I was also only just coming to terms with the fact that I'd just seen my very first dead body. I was very close to telling this stranger everything – Burgess, the case, the running away guy in Swindon, Diana Cheeseman, getting sacked, even all my troubles with Lucy.

I desperately needed to talk to someone.

But then I remembered that for all I knew, *EulerIsGod* could yet turn out to be Rufus Fairbanks. Or, God help me, Isaac Vavasor. Yes, it was unlikely that either of them would be online gamers, but in the looking-glass world of Vavasorology anything was possible. I needed to proceed with caution.

I logged out and walked away from the computer. I had never felt so alone in my entire life.

Chapter 11

'What's that smell?' said Lucy when she arrived home that evening.

'What smell?' I said.

'The burnt smell.'

'Oh that. It's OK, I sorted everything out.' Actually, the saucepan in question was still in soak and might need to remain there for another few days. But a vigorous scrub with some wire wool and a bit of bleach would probably restore it to a useable state.

She eyed me suspiciously. 'You hardly ever cook,' she said.

'I thought I'd surprise you.'

'You've certainly done that.' She peered into the pot that was bubbling away on the cooker. 'What is it?'

'Bolognese sauce with home-made meatballs.'

She gave it a stir. 'I like the flecks of charcoal. Nice touch.'

'You're being unfair,' I said. 'I'm just out of practice.'

She shrugged and went to get changed, while I put the spaghetti on to boil, resolving to take especial care draining it. Last time I'd ended up spending several minutes fishing pasta out of the sink.

'So what gives?' said Lucy when she came back in to the kitchen. 'Are you considering retraining as a chef? It's not a career path I'd have thought of for you, but I guess it's worth exploring all the angles.'

'Stop it,' I said. 'I just felt like cooking.' I was being completely truthful here. My mind was buzzing with Archie and Pye and George Burgess and Hilary van Beek and I had to do something to distract myself before my head exploded. There was something very therapeutic about moulding mince into meatballs and it gave me a great sense of satisfaction, right up until the point where they had stuck fast to the bottom of the pan.

'Well, I guess there's a first time for everything,' said Lucy.

We sat down opposite each other and began eating. When I'd hit on the idea of doing meatballs, I'd planned to serve it all up on one plate between us so we could share. Perhaps this would do something to lighten the atmosphere in the flat. If things were going well, I'd even toyed with the idea of nudging a meatball towards Lucy with my nose in the style of *The Lady and the Tramp*. I'd done this once with a previous girlfriend and it had gone down quite well, right up to the point where some of the sauce went up my nose and I had a coughing fit.

In the event, we went for separate bowls.

'What do you think?' I said.

'Did you actually check the seasoning?'

'Um, no.' I always forgot to do this.

She nodded as if she'd suspected this all along. ''S'ok,' she said. 'It's actually not bad.'

This was praise indeed. 'So how was your day?' I said, sensing an opening.

'All right. Same old.' She put her fork down and tilted her head on one side. 'What about you, though? You're behaving very strangely.'

'I saw a dead body today.' I hadn't intended to say anything about that, but it just came out.

'What? In the street?'

'No, in Chippenham.'

'What were you doing in Chippenham?'

'Visiting a publisher.'

'What? Tom, you're not thinking about writing a book, are you? Because I think you've got more chance as a chef. Even on the basis of this.' She gestured at the last meatball on her plate with her fork.

'I thought you said it wasn't bad.'

'My point exactly. So why were you visiting a publisher?'

'Archie and Pye. The mathematicians. The bloke I met on the train. Who died. I did tell you, didn't I?'

'Some of it. I may not have been paying attention. Why are you so obsessed with it?'

'Obsessed? I'm not obsessed.'

'Yes you are. You're on about it all the time.'

'Believe me, that's nothing. You should meet some of the other Vavasorologists.'

'Other what? You're losing me, Tom.'

'People like Dorothy Chan at school. She used to talk about nothing else.' Shit. Why did I suddenly mention her?

'Who's Dorothy Chan?'

'Someone I… used to know.'

'Ha!' Lucy pointed her fork at me in accusation. 'You fancied her, didn't you? Don't deny it, because I can read you like a book.'

'Well, maybe a bit.'

'Gotcha.' She put the fork down, folded her arms and leaned back in her chair. 'You don't still fancy her, do you?'

'I haven't seen her for years.'

'Good thing too. So who's the stiff in Chippenham then? Also, why the hell weren't you looking for a job today? We have bills to pay, Tom.'

'I was going to do that as well, but—'

'But what?'

'Didn't get round to it. Wish I hadn't mentioned the dead body now. You're not being very helpful, Lucy.'

'To be fair, Tom, neither are you.' She got up from the table. 'Anyway, got to go.'

'Where are you off to now?'

'Zumba. Thursday night is Zumba night. Remember, Tom?'

'What exactly is Zumba?' I said.

She shook her head. 'You wouldn't like it.'

She disappeared to change into her leotard and I stole her last meatball. 'When are you back?' I called after her as she left.

'Don't wait up,' came the reply.

Lucy didn't return until the early hours of the morning. I was going to ask her about this at breakfast, but she'd already gone by the time I got up. I had no set plans for the day, so there was little incentive to haul myself out of bed and I didn't get up until well after ten o'clock.

Once I'd had breakfast I settled down at the computer to start a proper search for a job. No distractions, no chasing around after dead bodies, no nothing. Lucy was right. I was in thrall to an all-consuming obsession that was threatening to derail my life.

An e-mail pinged into my inbox announcing a new personal message from *EulerIsGod*. I hesitated. No, it was OK to go ahead and look. I just had to read it and then get on with what I'd planned to do. I didn't even have to respond.

We need to meet, said the message. *You posted twice yesterday either side of a trip to Chippenham. Let's assume both posts were sent from the same static PC, either at your home or your place of work. Probably home, given the apparent flexibility of your arrangements. So I'm guessing you don't live too far from Chippenham. Right?*

I hesitated again. *Bristol*, I typed eventually.

Perfect. I'm in town for the day. Let's meet for lunch and compare notes.

Well, why not? What was the worst that could happen? He wasn't going to jump me in a crowded pub, was he? Also, it would be good to step out of the flat for an hour or so. It would give me a break from the hard work of finding another job.

The hard work of finding another job had only been going for five minutes when my mobile rang. The number looked familiar and then I remembered that it was the one Benjamin had called me on yesterday afternoon. I picked it up.

'Benjamin!' I said. 'Where the devil are you?'

But the voice that answered wasn't Benjamin's. It belonged to a man, but one several decades older than him. 'Hello?' it said. 'Did you call me?'

'No, I think you called me,' I said.

'Ah yes, so I did. You see I was walking along by the Arnolfini gallery this morning – do you know the Arnolfini?'

'Sorry?'

'Lovely café. Always treat myself to some carrot cake. Although Marjorie used to say I'd put on weight if I'm not careful.'

'Excuse me, but—' What on earth was this man doing with Benjamin's phone?

'I don't look at the exhibitions, though. Marjorie used to say they were too modern, and I think I feel the same way.'

'What?'

'The exhibitions. Too modern. Pickled sheep and all that sort of nonsense.'

'What?'

'Pickled sheep. Look, if you can't keep up with me—'

'No, it's not that. It's… what are you doing with that phone?'

'I'm coming to that. Dear me, you are impatient. Still, everyone is these days I suppose. No time to sit down with a cup of coffee and a nice piece of cake and watch the world go by. Did I ask if you knew the Arnolfini?'

'I think you did, yes, but—'

'Peter, that's my son, he's always saying I repeat myself. He lives in Sydney, you know.'

'What?'

'He lives in Sydney. In Australia. But we talk to each other on Skype every weekend. It's wonderful, Skype. Although sometimes it goes all blocky.'

'What?'

'Blocky. Sort of freezes and the sound goes wobbly. Very annoying.'

'Yes,' I said. 'Now, about the phone—'

'You're trying to hurry me again, young man. You'll make me lose my thread. Now where was I?'

I bit my tongue.

'Ah yes,' he said eventually. 'Skype. That's what we were talking about. Marjorie would have liked Skype. Although I don't suppose I'd have ever got a look in.' He paused. 'I do miss her,' he said.

I suddenly felt very sorry for this man. He sounded so lonely. I had an idea. 'Shall I come over to the Arnolfini now?' I said. I could give him a bit of company and he could hand over Benjamin's mobile. Also, even though it wasn't long since I'd had breakfast, I quite liked the idea of cake.

'Good heavens, no,' he said. 'Why would you want to do that? I'll be long gone. There's a Russ Meyer retrospective at the Watershed starting in ten minutes. Special showing for seniors.'

'Oh.'

'Well, then. Don't you want to know how I came to have this phone?'

'What? Oh, the phone. Yes, of course I want to know.'

'It was lying on the pavement. It's a bit scratched, but I'm sure you can find someone who'll repair it. Although they don't repair things any more, do they? They just throw them away. Doesn't take much to fix things. I'm still using a toaster Marjorie and I bought in the seventies.'

'What?' The brief moment of focus had passed.

'I just sent off for a new element,' he said. 'Had to trim a couple of inches off after I'd finished wrapping it round, but it works right as rain.'

'Going back to the phone—'

'Ah yes. Yours was the last number dialled, so I thought I'd give you a call. Shall I leave it at the box office for you to collect?'

I was taken aback. I hadn't expected anything quite so practical. 'Well yes, that would be brilliant,' I said.

'It's no trouble. As Marjorie used to say to me, you should always do whatever you can to return something valuable to its owner.'

'Well, I'm not the owner—'

'Ah yes, but I'm sure you know them. Anyway, must be going. Been a pleasure talking to you.'

If I wanted to get to the pub in time to meet *EulerIsGod* after first picking up Benjamin's phone, I would have to leave the flat almost immediately. This meant I would have spent all of five minutes so far today job hunting, but I felt that these diversions were justified. I would still have plenty of time in the afternoon.

'Can I help you?' said the girl behind the desk at the Watershed.

'Yes,' I said. 'I've come to pick up a phone. I believe it's been handed in.'

'What sort of phone?'

I had absolutely no idea. 'Not sure. Bit scratched, I think.'

She gave me an odd look. 'Is it your phone, sir?'

'No, it belongs to a friend.' Of course it wasn't my phone. I'd have known what type it was, wouldn't I?

'What was your friend's name?'

'Benjamin... something,' I said. 'But he isn't the one who left it here.'

'So who did leave the phone here?'

'Someone else. An old man.'

'Well, what was his name?'

'I don't know,' I said. 'His wife was called Marjorie, but she's dead. I think his son was called Peter, but otherwise—' This wasn't going as well as I'd anticipated.

'Oh, hang on,' she said. 'The old bloke. I remember now.' A puzzled expression drifted across her face.

'What's the problem?' I said.

'Well, I've already given the phone back to your friend. He came in a quarter of an hour ago.'

'Ah, that's OK, then.' At least that meant Benjamin was unharmed. I'd been worrying about him. 'Weedy bloke? Wispy beard?'

She frowned. 'No, not him. He was more sort of muscular. Clean shaven. All in black. Sunglasses. Bit scary, really.'

'What?'

'Funny accent, too. Sort of Eastern European.'

Shit. I didn't like this at all. 'Do you know which way he went?' I said. Not that I had any intention of following him.

'No, sorry.'

'OK, thanks anyway.' I turned round and headed back out onto the Bristol waterfront. There was nothing more to be done about Benjamin's phone for now and I had a lunch appointment to get to.

I'd arranged with *EulerIsGod* that he should be sitting near the bar studying that day's *Racing Post*. I would be carrying a copy of *The Times*, a plan that I remembered at the precise moment I arrived at the pub without one. I immediately resolved to strike 'spy' from my list of potential new career directions, before spending the next ten minutes trying to find a newsagent.

Now armed with a prominent copy of the day's *Times* tucked ostentatiously under my arm, I strode into the lounge bar, which turned out to be almost empty. In fact the only other person in the place turned out to be female, a slight figure in her late twenties or early thirties. She was wearing a jaunty cloth cap and a leather jacket over a plain white T-shirt and jeans. More importantly, she was at this moment deeply immersed in the *Racing Post*.

I walked slowly over towards her and gave a slight cough. She looked up and saw me, and a look of horror passed over her face.

'Oh shit,' she said.

I burst out laughing. 'Hello, Dorothy,' I said.

Chapter 12

Dorothy Chan gaped at me. This was one of those rare occasions when the word 'speechless' was an entirely appropriate adjective.

'Well,' I said.

'Well indeed,' said Dorothy. 'I have to say I didn't expect this for one minute. You of all people.' She didn't seem terribly pleased to see me.

'Can I buy you a drink?' It was the least I could do.

She hesitated. 'Orange juice and tonic,' she said.

I got a pint of beer for myself and sat down again. 'How long is it? Ten years?'

'Probably.' She looked much the same as she used to, although there were a few subtle changes. The hair was clipped short and the body language was more confident than I remembered. 'Christ, you of all people, Tom.'

She really didn't seem pleased to see me. I racked my brains but I couldn't begin to think why. We continued drinking in silence.

'Look,' I said. 'We seem to have got off on the wrong foot here. Is there something I'm missing?'

She gave a deep sigh. 'No, no. Don't worry. Everything's fine.' She sipped her drink then glanced at her watch. 'OK, let's get on with it, then. I haven't got long. Running a workshop at the 'Women in Gaming' conference this afternoon. I saw that post of yours about George Burgess. Tell me what happened.'

'He was sitting next to me on the train. I didn't have any idea who he was apart from the fact that he was extremely annoying. Shouting and swearing about his book on his mobile in the quiet compartment. I complained and he got shitty with me and made me spill my drink.'

'Sounds like George Burgess.'

'You knew him?'

'Never met him, but I know people who have. He wasn't well liked.'

'Anyway, he felt guilty for spilling my drink and offered to buy me a replacement.'

'Weren't you the lucky one.'

'We got talking. He said Isaac Vavasor had just told him he couldn't use – what was it? – the Marginalia for his book. What is the Marginalia, anyway?'

'The Marginalia – plural – are a rambling series of notes made by the Vavasor twins in the margins of their mathematical papers. They've acquired something close to mythical status in the Vavasorology community, mainly because hardly anyone's been allowed to see them. Wait a second. Are you telling me Burgess had access to them?'

'Seems that way.'

'Good grief. How did the old fart manage that?'

'Well, that's it. Isaac Vavasor seems to have given him access. No one seems to know why. Did you see that post the other day about Burgess having been given the "crown jewels"?'

'Yeah, *UltimateTruth*. Usually pretty reliable. Oh my God, are you telling me that Burgess actually HAD them? So what happened to them when he died? This is humungously important.' Dorothy was leaning forward now and waving her hands about as if conducting the finale of the 1812 overture. 'Are you telling me the papers are still out there?'

'They could be.'

'No wonder people are dying.'

'What?'

'The Vavasor papers are dynamite. Surely you realise that?'

'I'm only just beginning to.' Over the last few days, the pond I'd gone for a bracing dip in was slowly revealing itself to be an alligator-filled swamp. On the plus side, it was at least possible that I'd now come across a lifeguard in the shape of Dorothy Chan. It was time to open up. 'Look, I may have an idea as to where the papers are.'

'You? How on earth would you have a clue?'

'Burgess had a security briefcase with him when I met him on the train.'

She frowned. 'So what?'

'I think they were in that case.'

She leaned back in her seat. 'Well, even if they were, it's no use if we don't have access to it. Chances are whoever murdered him ran off with it.'

'I don't think so.'

She leaned forward again. 'Why not?'

'Because he left it on the train,' I said.

Dorothy looked shocked. 'He did what? But what… oh my God.' She was bouncing up and down in her seat now. 'You've got it, haven't you?'

I didn't say anything.

'Jesus. This is mental. So what's in it? Have you read it all?' She was eagerly leaning forward now. All the previous awkwardness between us had dissipated.

'Ah.'

'What do you mean, "Ah"?' A note of suspicion had entered her voice.

'First of all, I haven't opened it yet. It's got a six-number combination lock.'

'That's only a million different options to go through.'

I stared at her.

'OK, maybe that would take a while,' she conceded.

'Also, I haven't got it right now.'

'WHAT?' Suspicion had now been replaced by a toxic compound made up of ninety per cent incredulity and ten per cent pure, unrefined rage. 'Please explain.'

'Well, first of all, I thought I'd better take it back to Burgess's house and hand it over to someone, but I didn't manage to do that because I left it in my car and lost the keys.'

'How…? No, never mind. Go on.'

'And then when I got the spare set of keys, I had to hand them over to work because I got sacked and I forgot to take the case out of the car first. And then the leasing company took the car back and they can't give me the case until Monday.'

Dorothy smacked her head with her fist and gave out an angry howl. Incredulity and pure, unrefined rage were now present in equal proportions. 'I don't know what to say, Tom. I really don't. You've come up with a whole load of words that sound like English, and you've put them together into a series of ostensibly correct English sentences. But none of it makes any sense whatsoever.'

'I think that's a bit harsh,' I said.

'No, it's about right,' she said. 'By a complete fluke, you – you of all people, Tom Winscombe – have somehow come into possession of the single most important set of documents in the history of mathematics but you've proceeded to lose the lot before you've even had time to look at them.'

I had to concede she had a point. 'I still think you're being a bit negative. I'm going to get the case back on Monday.'

'Are you, Tom? Given your track record so far, I'd rate it a pretty poor bet.'

'You sound just like Lucy,' I said.

'Who's Lucy?'

'My girlfriend.'

'Poor woman.' She took a sip of her drink. 'What was that about getting sacked? Was that anything to do with this?'

'No. It was… no, never mind. It's a long story.'

She looked at her watch. 'Yeah, well, maybe we can keep that for another time. I need to get moving soon. One more drink?'

'What were you saying about the single most important set of documents in the history of mathematics?' I said when she'd brought the drinks.

'Exactly that. Archimedes and Pythagoras Vavasor kept more secrets than GCHQ, and no one – but no one – knew what they were up to. Which of course led to rumours.'

'The Riemann hypothesis?'

'Oh, we have done our homework, haven't we?'

'Yeah, yeah.'

'Understand it?'

'No.'

'Not many people do. That wasn't the only thing they were working on.'

'There was something about the twin prime conjecture. And glühwein.' The detail about the careless Dolmetsches had stuck in my brain for some reason. Possibly because I felt a sense of kinship with them.

She tipped her head on one side and frowned at me. 'Wow, you really have been doing your research. Yes, the twin prime conjecture. Actually, there isn't a single unsolved problem in the whole of mathematics that they haven't been suspected of solving.'

'So why doesn't Isaac Vavasor just publish the papers for everyone to see?'

'A very good question. The obsession with secrecy seems to be genetic. Isaac keeps a vice-like grip on the twins' papers and no one's ever made copies. Very occasionally, he's allowed another mathematician to view the work, but only for very short periods and under close supervision.'

'Is that because he wants to keep it to himself?' I said. 'So he can finish the work and claim the credit?'

Dorothy laughed. 'Good heavens, no. Isaac's no mathematician. The word on the street is he's not terribly bright.'

I felt sorry for Isaac. I felt a sense of kinship with him too. 'What about Margot Evercreech? Burgess said something about her having had access to the Marginalia.'

'Ah yes. I'm glad you reminded me about her. Isaac made the mistake of giving her an interview for some daft magazine or other. She managed to persuade him to show the papers to her and she's built an entire career on the basis of that glimpse. I reckon she had half an hour at most.'

'Bloody hell. But what about Burgess? Why on earth was he given them? Why pick him?'

'I've absolutely no idea. And unfortunately, possibly thanks to your efforts, one of the people who might have given us a clue is now dead.'

'Sorry, what? Are you suggesting I was responsible for Hilary van Beek's death?' I rather resented this.

'Well, you were the one who posted about the break in at Head Wind, weren't you? Could have been construed as a signal she had something worth killing for.'

'Are you telling me she was murdered because someone thought she had the Vavasor papers?'

'It's possible.'

'That's ridiculous.'

'Stranger things have happened.'

Well, that was certainly true. 'How did you know about the murder weapon?' I said. That had been bothering me for a while.

'Like I said, a hunch. But a correct one, right?'

'Yes, but what made you…' (Was there a verb 'to hunch'? There ought to be one.) '…think of that?'

'Had to be something mathematical. And there aren't many mathematical instruments you can strangle someone with.'

I hadn't really confronted this yet. There was, obviously, some kind of pattern developing to the murders. 'But do you really think it's the same person who did both Burgess and van Beek?' I said.

'Don't forget Pye.'

'But whoever heard of a serial killer taking a ten year break?'

'Why not? Maybe there've been other deaths that no one's noticed. Maybe he kept things under control for a while. Certainly looks like he's getting the scent of blood now. I keep trying to imagine what the next one's going to look like. Could be you, you know.'

'Thanks.'

At that moment, my phone started ringing. I decided to ignore it.

'Aren't you going to answer that?' she said.

I sighed and pulled it out of my pocket. Dorothy stared at it, goggle-eyed.

'What in God's name is that?' she said.

'It's my phone,' I said.

'I can see that. It's adorable. Some kind of retro, hipster thing, or are you just a Luddite? Tom?'

I was ignoring her because I'd noticed the number that was calling. It was Benjamin's. I pressed the answer key.

'Hello?' I said.

There was no reply, although I thought I could hear someone breathing. I ended the call and sat back in my seat, trembling.

'Who was that?' said Dorothy.

'Don't know. It was Benjamin's phone. Hilary van Beek's intern. I know because he called me from that number yesterday to tell me about her death. He'd vanished by the time I got there, though.'

'But it wasn't him now?'

'Don't think so. Some old bloke found the phone this morning and called me because mine was the last number dialled. He was going to leave it at the Watershed but some other guy got there first. I'm a bit worried about Benjamin to be honest. I hardly knew the guy, but—'

'Turn it off,' said Dorothy, urgently. 'Seriously, turn it off now.'

'Why?'

'They could still be round here, listening for phones ringing when they call your number.'

'Shit.' I saw what she meant. I quickly turned the phone off. Dorothy was scanning the room. It had filled up a little since I'd come in, but the clientele didn't appear to be any dodgier than usual for a city centre pub in Bristol.

'I think we need to move,' she said, gathering her things.

'OK.' I wasn't going to argue with her. I drained my pint and we headed out into the street. Dorothy checked her watch again.

'Right. I need to head back to the conference.' She handed me a card. The word:

.chan

filled the entirety of one side, while the other listed a vast array of e-mail addresses, phone numbers and social media handles.

'Ignore the Twitter stuff. I'm on a break at the moment.'

'Why's that?'

'Never mind. Just text me if and when you get the case back and try not to get yourself killed in the meantime. If you don't get it back – or if you get yourself killed – it was... interesting... meeting you again.'

I stared at the card. 'Ah,' I said. 'I get it. Neat. Look, I haven't got any cards with me right now, but I'll write down my number for you.' I scrabbled in my pockets for a piece of paper and a pen but all I found was an old till receipt and a blunt pencil. My attempts at writing the first digit of my number merely succeeded in gouging a hole.

'It's OK,' said Dorothy, striding off with a shake of her head. 'I won't be needing it.'

Chapter 13

Lucy and I spent Saturday tidying the flat then preparing food for a dinner party that I'd forgotten about and Sunday clearing up afterwards while dealing with our respective hangovers. I didn't feel inclined to engage her in anything beyond the bare minimum of conversation and it was clear she felt the same way about me. We were both walking on eggshells.

On Monday morning, I remembered I'd forgotten to ask her if I could borrow her car again to go and fetch Burgess's case but I was sure it would all be fine. To be honest, I'd been using it more than she had this past week, and I was beginning to feel something approaching a sense of ownership. I still had the keys in my pocket, anyway. Obviously, I was the type of guy whose aspirations stretched further than a Nissan Micra, but it was a serviceable interim substitute until the next company car came along.

I arrived at Six Star Leasing at around half past nine. I went in and pressed the bell on the service desk. 'Africa' by Toto was still playing in the background.

After a couple of minutes, Terry appeared, wiping his hands on the same oily rag as last time. He squinted at me. 'Can I help you?' he said.

'I've come to pick up the case. From the BMW.'

A grim smile came over his face. 'Ah yes. The leased BMW. You're the bloke from that PR company with the daft name, aren't you?'

'Not any more,' I said. 'They let me go.'

Terry raised an eyebrow. 'So what does it take to get fired from a PR company, eh? Must take some doing.'

'Never mind. I've come for the case. You said Mikey might have it.'

'Indeed I did.'

'Well?'

Terry looked at his watch and tapped his nose. 'Word to the wise. You've been here five minutes now and I don't think you've once asked about how my good friend Mikey's wife and baby are getting along. Seems a bit previous to launch straight into demanding a favour from him.'

I stared at him. Terry stared back at me, then he shook his head. 'Mikey's picking the twins up from school. He'll be here in half an hour. Like a drink?'

I was taken aback by this. 'Well, yes, please. Thank you very much. Can I have a coffee? Black, no sugar.'

Terry shook his head. 'Listen, mate, this isn't bleeding Starbucks. Tea with milk and two sugars, take it or leave it.'

'Right, yes, that will be fine.'

Terry disappeared into the bowels of the service area and returned a couple of minutes later with a chipped bright red mug emblazoned with the slogan 'Keep calm and shut the fuck up', filled to the brim with tepid, sweet, milky tea.

'Thanks,' I said.

'Don't mention it,' said Terry.

While I was waiting for Mikey to arrive, the ten o'clock news came on the radio. I wasn't paying attention until one item leapt

111

out at me. Police were hunting for a white male in his twenties in connection with the death of the publisher Hilary van Beek. His name was given as Benjamin Unsworth, and members of the public were warned not to approach him as he might be dangerous. This bothered me. Quite apart from the fact that he was about as dangerous as a three-legged hamster, he wasn't the one the police should have been looking for. Perhaps I ought to let them know.

A while later, Mikey emerged from the service area. He had a severe five o'clock shadow and gave off a strong whiff of nappies and stale milk.

'Hi,' he said.

'Congratulations,' I said.

Mikey grimaced. 'Yeah,' he said. 'Yeah.'

'Um… did you bring—'

'Oh, yeah. That.' He disappeared back into the garage and returned with Burgess's case. 'Quite a lock you've got there. Hope you know the combination, mate.'

'Yeah, no worries,' I said, wondering how I was ever going to open the thing.

Mikey handed it over and I got back in Lucy's car. Right, I thought. This is where the real fun starts.

I pulled out of the garage and took the road back towards Bristol. After a couple of miles I noticed a car following me. A black Mercedes, driven by a guy wearing sunglasses. My heart skipped a beat. *Shit.* Were they coming for *me* this time?

We were on a single carriage A road, maintaining a steady fifty miles per hour. There wasn't any other traffic, so I increased my speed to sixty. So did the Merc. I put my foot down and eventually the little car managed to crawl up to seventy. So did he. I kept my foot down, but it appeared that the engine in Lucy's motor was already at its upper limit. If I still had my

BMW I might have been able to outrun them, or at least given them a decent chase, but in the Micra I was a sitting duck. I wondered what my best strategy might be.

Maybe he was just waiting for an opportunity to overtake me. However, for the time being he seemed to be maintaining a constant distance between us, occupying a position that was just slightly closer than one I felt comfortable with. Finally, we reached a long, straight stretch and I waited for him to overtake. He didn't. I slowed down to sixty again. So did he. I looked at him in the rear-view mirror. All I could see were his inscrutable sunglasses.

Time to take evasive action. There was a turning coming up that would take me back into Bristol via a twisty side road that went down through a valley. There were a few speed bumps to negotiate along the way but I reckoned I'd be able to use my local knowledge to my advantage. I held on until the last minute and then I yanked the steering wheel over to the left as hard as I could. The tyres shrieked in agony and the little car wobbled alarmingly but I just managed to keep it on the road. The irritating painted wooden Ganesh pendant that Lucy had dangled from the rear-view mirror swung frantically from side to side.

Under normal circumstances I would have reduced my speed at this point, but these were nothing like normal circumstances, and I continued hurtling down into the valley. I glanced behind to see if my antagonist was following me and I felt a sickening lurch in my stomach as I realised that he was. *Shit.* It now struck me that my spur of the moment change of tactics was significantly flawed. Down here he was much more likely to catch me up and there were fewer potential witnesses to whatever he had in mind when he eventually did. I should have stayed on the main road. However, it was too late to turn back now.

The twenty miles per hour sign up ahead signalled that the first speed bump was heading my way. This was no time for faint hearts. I crashed into it at full speed and there was a truly horrible thud from the underside of the car and a simultaneous yelp from myself as I cracked my head on the roof. This was followed by an ominous metallic tinkling as something detached itself and started bouncing away up the road behind me. I hoped it wasn't anything important that I might need later.

Having negotiated that obstacle with something approaching success, I now had to deal with the reason for its existence: a sudden narrowing of the road to a single lane. Fortunately there was nothing coming the other way so I steamed on through, swinging from side to side as I did so. Ganesh was now spinning around in wild circles and George Burgess's case had begun to slide backwards and forwards on the rear seat. Meanwhile, a whole slew of junk had apparently come loose in the boot and was clattering about as if an automotive poltergeist had been awoken from a hundred years' slumber.

My head was pounding from the combination of the tension of the moment and the bashing it had received when I went over the speed bump. I glanced in the rear-view mirror again. This time, there was no sign of my pursuer. At last! I had outrun the bastard. Yee hah! Thank God, I was safe. Or was I? No, I had to banish all feelings of complacency. I needed to maintain speed and keep powering through until I reached the bright lights of Bristol. I refocused my attention on the view ahead, at which point I caught sight of a sharp bend coming up. I stamped on the brakes but this time my manoeuvre was too late and the offside of the car lurched against a wall, establishing the kind of close contact that a limpet would establish if the limpet was made of metal and was being scraped along a wall at seventy miles an hour. *Shit shit shit.*

I managed to haul the car back into the middle of the road, but I still hadn't quite regained control because it now started bouncing against the wall that had inconveniently sprung up on the opposite side of the road. After a while I succeeded in stabilising the direction of travel, but unfortunately it was too close to the wall and the horrific banshee scraping filled the air once more. *Shit shit shit shit shit.* At last, however, the road straightened out again, and it was at this point that I hit the second set of speed bumps to indicate that we were leaving the twenty mile an hour zone.

The effects on the underside of the car and the top of my head were identical to those encountered at the first speed bump, except that in the case of my head, first blood had already been drawn and consequently the pain was even more acute than before. *Shit shit shit shit shit and arsing bollocks.*

I risked another rearwards glance and was relieved to note that the Mercedes was still nowhere in sight. But my attention was now grabbed by a loud horn coming towards me from the front. I looked forward again and jerked the wheel just in time to avoid a white van hurtling towards me on the opposite side of the road. I heaved it quickly back in the other direction to get round a tight corner and it was around about here that my luck ran out.

Up ahead a tractor pulling a trailer, piled high with large cylindrical bales of hay, had pulled up at the side of the road. Between me and the tractor, scattered randomly across the road, there were several bales that had evidently just fallen off. I slammed on the brakes but at my current speed there was no way I could either avoid them or stop before I hit one of them. There was a horrible crunch of metal from the bonnet as I ploughed into the nearest bale. Inside the car, Ganesh started dancing a mad bhangra and Burgess's case flew into the back of my seat at the exact same time as the airbag erupted from the steering column and squashed me against the other side of it. The car stalled and silence enveloped the scene like the morning after a battlefield massacre.

I heard the sound of another car pulling up behind me. I turned round and saw the black Mercedes. *Oh God, no.* The driver's door opened and a man in black wearing sunglasses got out. *Oh, please dear God, no.* He glanced around as if to see if there was anyone watching and then ambled over to my car. *Please, dear God, I haven't asked for much from you before apart from that time before my Geography GCSE and you probably weren't listening then but this time I really mean it, I'll even start going to church again, really I will, I'll do anything.* I went to open my door so I could make a run for it, but I got tangled up in the deflating airbag and didn't even get as far as undoing my safety belt. It was too late. *Pleeeease!* I squirmed into my seat in terror as my pursuer drew level with me and reached for the door handle.

Oh shit.

This was it. I was going to die and I hadn't even managed to open Burgess's sodding case yet.

Chapter 14

'You OK, mate?'

'W-what?'

'I said, you OK, mate?' The man was looking down at me with a puzzled expression. I saw now that he wasn't actually dressed all in black. It had just looked that way against the sun. His polo shirt was more a sort of dark purple and his trousers were dark green. There was a gold chain round his neck and he was wearing a fairly obvious toupée. His voice had the air of wide-boy-made-good.

'I... think so,' I said.

'Only you were driving like a bleeding maniac back there. Could have got yourself killed. Or anyone else for that matter. Are you pissed or something?'

Shit. Whoever this guy was, he didn't sound like a crazed Belarusian mobster. While this was undoubtedly good news in the immediate term, the longer term implications were not so good. 'No, I'm stone cold sober,' I said. 'Honestly. I just thought – ' No, telling him what I thought he was would have been a very silly thing to do. 'Never mind,' I said.

'Muppets like you shouldn't be allowed on the road,' said the man from the Mercedes, jabbing his finger at me. I could see his point. He seemed to be thinking about what to do next. 'Look, I need to get moving,' he said eventually. 'You sure you're all right?'

'I'm fine. Really I am.' Apart from a head that felt like it had been used for baseball practice and a deep groove across my chest where the seat belt had cut into it. Oh yes, and a sick feeling in the pit of my stomach because I'd just totalled my girlfriend's car for no good reason and I was going to have to discuss this with her in the very near future.

'OK, then. I'm going to leave you to it. I should probably call the filth, but me and the boys haven't always seen eye to eye. If you know what I mean.' He touched his index finger to the side of his head as he said this.

I didn't know what he meant, but I was very happy to go along with the sentiment. 'Thank you,' I said.

He shut my car door again and walked back to his Mercedes, shaking his head. I imagined him mouthing the word 'Twat' to himself as he turned the key in the ignition. He managed to negotiate his way through the bales, waved on by the farmer who was now heading my way. I decided I didn't want to get bogged down in another awkward conversation, so I tore the remains of the airbag away, turned the engine on again and prepared to get going. Remarkably it still seemed to work and after some crunching of gears I managed to engage reverse. I pulled back from the bale of hay, moved into first gear and turned the wheel to move out. I carefully picked a path through the scattered bales and past the farmer, who was now staring at me and scratching his head as if he'd never seen anything quite like it before. I guess there was every chance he hadn't, unless he spent his leisure hours at the local demolition derby circuit.

As I moved up the gears and picked up speed, there was an unpleasant clanking from the underside of the car which continued for a few minutes until the exhaust finally decided to seek a better life for itself as an independent entity and detached itself altogether. Fortunately, everything else stayed in place for the remainder of the journey and I limped back into Bristol just before lunchtime, giving me an entire afternoon to come up with a sensible explanation as to what had happened to Lucy's car since she had last seen it.

The full tally of the damage was impressive. The offside had very little paint left on it at all and there were a number of deep grooves along its entire length. The nearside had fared a little better, merely acquiring several go-faster stripes. There was, however, very little left of the rear light cluster apart from part of a bulb dangling uselessly from a length of wire. On the plus side, now that both wing mirrors were gone, the car was marginally more streamlined than it had been before.

The front was bent into an inverted V and there was a massive dent in the bonnet, to the extent that it wouldn't now open at all. This, incidentally, also meant that it was impossible for me to remove most of the hay that was poking out from underneath it.

Apart from a few patches where some vestiges of tread lingered on, all four tyres now boasted a perfectly smooth outer rim and would require immediate replacement.

Underneath, things were no better. The exhaust was missing and the sump had a hairline crack down the middle. Indeed, as I looked back along the road, I could see a telltale dotted line of oil that would probably lead me back to the first speed bump if I felt inclined to follow it.

There was no doubt about it. Lucy's car was a write-off.

I considered how we might present this to the insurance company and I eventually decided our best bet would be for Lucy to say it had been taken without her permission. Technically, this was true, although it did beg the question of whether the police would then get involved trying to track down the perpetrator. No, perhaps that wasn't such a good idea after all.

Realistically, the only viable way out of this godawful mess was to buy Lucy a new car, and this was a complete non-starter because of my lack of funds. If I wasn't going to be permitted to purchase a sofa the chances of me ponying up for even an ancient Micra were equivalent to being struck by lightning on the way to collect my EuroMillions lottery winnings. Right now, my funds would barely stretch to a pair of rusty roller skates.

And my head hurt.

And my shoulder.

This was not a good start to the week.

I was no closer to deciding what to say to Lucy when I heard her key turn in the lock. She walked in to the lounge, threw her bag on the floor and closed the door behind her. She remained standing, legs apart, arms folded. I stood up, took a step towards her and then thought better of it. There was some ground to be covered before we reached the hugging point.

Lucy's face was a picture, and if a picture was worth a thousand words, I was fairly sure I could guess a few hundred of them. To avoid any possibility of misunderstanding, though, she had evidently decided to go ahead and say them anyway.

'What,' she said, 'have you done to my car, Tom?'

'I—'

'My lovely, little car, Tom. It's smashed to pieces.'

'I—'

'What happened, Tom? Please tell me what happened.'

'I had an accident.'

'What sort of accident, Tom?'

There was a rising tone of anger underlying her voice and I formed a mental image of a needle on a seismometer somewhere near the Yellowstone supervolcano that was beginning to twitch a lot more than it was supposed to twitch.

'You could at least ask me how I am,' I said.

Lucy put her hands on her hips and appeared to be counting my limbs. 'You don't look hurt,' she said, after a moment's consideration. Too late, I remembered the golden rule: never ask for sympathy from a nurse, especially one you're in a relationship with.

'I've got a really bad bruise on my arm,' I said, before realising too late that I'd just triggered the eruption.

'MY LOVELY, LITTLE CAR HAS BEEN SMASHED TO PIECES,' she wailed. 'I DON'T CARE ABOUT YOUR ARM. I WANT TO KNOW WHAT'S HAPPENED TO MY CAR.' She looked as if she was about to burst into tears.

'I thought I was being chased by the Belarusian mafia,' I said. We were going to get to them at some stage, so I decided to go straight to the point.

'Belarusian?' She looked confused. The volcano had erupted, but for a moment it looked as if I might have managed to divert the flow of lava.

'Yes, the Belarusian mafia.'

'This isn't funny, Tom. Is this about Arkady?'

'Who's Arkady?' Now I was the one who was confused.

'My Zumba teacher,' said Lucy. There was a slight hesitation to her reply and I was sure I detected a slight colouring to her cheeks. This was all very odd.

'What about him?'

'He's from Minsk.'

'And?'

'That's the capital of Belarus. That means he's Belarusian.'

'I still don't know what this has to do with him, though,' I said. Was I missing something important?

'Isn't it obvious? You're jealous of him. As well as being a bit racist.'

'I'm not bloody racist! And why would I be jealous of your Zumba teacher? Unless...' Christ, I definitely *was* missing something. I stared at Lucy. Surely not?

'What really happened, Tom?'

'I told you. I thought I was being chased by the Belarusian—'

'SHUT UP ABOUT THE FUCKING BELARUSIAN MAFIA.' This was serious. Lucy hardly ever swore. The lava was back and heading straight for me now.

'But it's true. Why are you so touchy about it?'

'Never mind that, Tom. WHAT ABOUT MY CAR? WHAT ARE YOU GOING TO DO ABOUT IT?'

'No, hold on a minute. What's this about you and your Zumba teacher? Why should I be jealous of him?'

'Oh, Tom. He's just a friend. Don't be ridiculous. WHAT ABOUT MY CAR?'

'I don't care about your car. It's just a load of metal—'

'Well, it certainly is now.'

'Oh, for heavens' sake. Our relationship is far more important. If you've been shagging this Arkady bloke behind my back—'

'WHAT? Are you seriously suggesting…? I don't believe this. WHAT ABOUT MY CAR, TOM?'

This was going even worse than I'd anticipated. I always found it difficult arguing with Lucy because she was so good at remaining on topic. I had this uneasy feeling that something was going on with this Arkady bloke but of course every time I tried to bring him into the discussion it only provided more evidence for my paranoia.

'Look,' I said, moving forward and putting my hand on Lucy's shoulder.

She shook it away. 'No, Tom. I want to know the truth,' she said, quietly. 'What happened to my car? And what are you proposing to do about it?'

'I said already. I thought I was being chased by—'

'Oh, enough. You know what, Tom? I'm getting a bit tired of all this. I don't know what's got into your head lately but you've changed. You're not the man I used to know. We used to have a laugh. Go out and do stuff. But you've gone weird. Throwing your job away. All this stupid rubbish about dead mathematicians. And I bet you STILL haven't phoned the landlord about the leak in the bathroom, have you?'

'What?' My head was spinning now.

'And then you go and smash my lovely, little car up and don't even say sorry.'

'I did say sorry, didn't I?' Maybe I didn't. That was careless. 'Or if I didn't,' I said, 'it was only because you didn't give me the chance to.' No, that came out wrong.

'Oh, so it's *my* fault, is it?'

'No, that's not what I meant. You know that.'

'I don't know if I do, Tom. I don't know if I know anything about you any more.'

'Look,' I said again. 'I'll get your car fixed. I really will.'

'HOW? YOU CAN'T EVEN BUY A NEW SOFA!'

'OH, FOR CHRIST'S SAKE. I DIDN'T EVEN LIKE THAT FUCKING SOFA!'

'WHAT?'

'I said, I didn't even like that fucking sofa. The colour was horrible.' It was. Really horrible. Sort of peachy vomit.

'Well, why didn't you fucking say so?'

'Because you were so fucking dead set on fucking well buying the fucking thing.' The more I thought about it, the more I hated that sofa. It was the worst fucking sofa in the fucking history of the whole fucking world.

'Oh, I despair of you,' said Lucy.

'Look, I'll pay for the car to be fixed when I've got a new job.'

'BUT YOU'RE NOT EVEN LOOKING FOR A NEW JOB!' Lucy held her hands to her head.

'I'll start tomorrow. Promise.'

'You know what, Tom? I don't believe you. I don't believe a single word you say any more.'

'Oh, come on—'

'No. I've had enough, Tom. It's over.'

'WHAT?'

'I said it's over. You and me. It's over.'

'But, Lucy—'

'No, Tom. I'm sick of it all. I'm sick of you and I'm sick of your stupid obsessions. I'm sick of the way you slob around not looking for a new job. I'm—'

'Lucy—'

'I HAVEN'T FINISHED YET! I'M SICK OF YOU TREATING MY LOVELY, LITTLE CAR AS IF IT WAS YOUR OWN AND SMASHING IT UP AND I'M SICK OF YOU LEAVING THE WASHING UP IN THE SINK AND LEAVING THE TOILET SEAT UP ALL THE TIME AND SQUIRTING TOOTHPASTE EVERYWHERE AND I'M SICK OF THIS HORRIBLE SHITTY LITTLE FLAT WITH A NASTY, SMELLY LEAK IN THE BATHROOM AND ALL THIS TATTY, OLD FURNITURE. I HATE YOU!'

She flounced off into the bedroom without saying another word, slamming the door behind her.

I sat down in one of our tatty, second-hand armchairs, shaking. What now? How could Lucy say all that? None of it was true. Apart from the bit about the car, obviously. And the toilet seat, if I was to be entirely honest. And maybe the bit about the toothpaste. Once. But there was nothing wrong with the flat apart from the leak in the bathroom and the landlord was going to fix that once I got round to telling him, and the only thing we needed furniture-wise was – oh yes all right – a decent sofa. But there was nothing wrong with ME. Was there? It wasn't all MY fault. Was it?

I considered my options. I could crawl on my hands and knees and beg forgiveness. But why should I do that? What did

I need to be forgiven for? Apart from the car, yes, but to be fair I was being chased by a psychopathic killer, even if they turned out not to be one in the end. Alternatively I could wait for her to calm down and come out. This was definitely a non-starter because Lucy could sulk for England. I strongly suspected that, when she eventually did come out, the atmosphere would be no better than it was before. It was very likely that I would not be admitted to our bedroom tonight. And unfortunately, as Lucy had been very happy to remind me several times, there wasn't a sofa I could sleep on either.

Sod it. Lucy was right about one thing. We were over. It was time to clear out.

I grabbed an overnight bag and collected together a few things from the bathroom. While I was there I made sure the toilet seat was standing to attention and I squirted some toothpaste in the basin for good measure. I was just about to go when I remembered something important. I needed Burgess's case out of Lucy's car. I'd left her keys on the table but they seemed to have gone during our argument. Shit.

I went and knocked gently on the bedroom door. 'Lucy?' I said. 'Can I borrow your car keys?' No reply. 'Please?'

Lucy appeared at the door. She was holding her phone in her hand and she looked as if she was in the middle of texting someone.

'Can I borrow—?' I began again.

'I heard you the first time. Why? Do you want to finish the job off or something? Maybe kick the boot in? Smash the windscreen? Take a dump in the passenger seat?'

'No. I left something in the back.'

'What something?'

'Something important. Please.'

She gave a deep sigh and then went and fetched the keys to the Micra. I went back downstairs and tried to open the rear passenger door. It took quite a struggle and when it did finally come free, it helpfully decided to shear off at the hinge as well. I retrieved George Burgess's case and then spent a minute or two trying to decide what to do about the door. Eventually I chucked it in the back and hoped no one would notice.

I went back up to the flat to return the keys to Lucy.

'I'm going now,' I said. 'Can I get some stuff?'

She shrugged and walked back into the bedroom. I followed her and grabbed a change of socks and underwear.

'I'll be back for my things,' I said.

Lucy just shrugged and carried on texting.

'Bye then,' I said.

Chapter 15

It was early evening when I left the flat. I had no idea what I was going to do next. All I had with me were the clothes I was wearing, a rucksack containing a change of underwear and a toothbrush, and Burgess's impenetrable case. My bank account was heading due south and it was only a matter of time before it would be found frozen to death in a tent, somewhere in Antarctica a little way short of the Pole. I had forty quid in my wallet, plus two maxed-out credit cards and a fifteen per cent discount voucher on a coke and curry combo at Admiral Akhbar's.

I was hungry.

I looked at the voucher again and realised I knew exactly what I was going to do next. Admiral Akhbar's Tandoori Cantina was calling to me.

I was shown to a table in the corner beneath a poster advertising a Bollywood rip-off of *The Empire Strikes Back*. Mo came over and grinned at me.

'Tom, my man,' he said. 'Good to see you.' He gave me a conspiratorial look. 'Hey. Remember last week I said I had something to show you?'

'Did you?'

Mo went off and came back holding a framed picture. 'Look what Dad just went and bought,' he said. 'Jeremy Bulloch's signature. Look, he's wearing the full Boba Fett.'

I took it from him. 'Very good,' I said, with as much enthusiasm as I could muster. I didn't share Mo's mad fascination with the minor characters from Star Wars at the best of times and this was one of the worst of times.

Mo frowned at me. 'You all right, mate? Where's your lovely lady?'

'We split up,' I said.

Mo's face fell. 'Oh, mate, I am so sorry to hear that. She was well fit.'

'I know.'

'What happened?' said Mo, before quickly adding, 'No worries if you don't want to talk.'

'No, it's all right,' I said. 'I smashed her car up. Thought I was being chased by the Belarusian mafia.'

Mo stared at me. 'You what?' he said. Then he tilted his head on one side. 'Hold on, mate. This is about them mathematicians, innit? What did I tell you about them? I said it would come to no good.'

'Yeah, I know.'

'Believe me, what you need to do is get out and get out fast, mate. I have seen lives destroyed by that lot. It's like that Moby Dick, innit. Archie and Pye Vavasor are your great white whale, mate. Pull out now before you lose anything else. Leave it to the mentals on the internet, like I said. Because if you don't, you'll become one of them too.'

'I know.'

Mo peered at Burgess's case. 'What's that you've got there?' he said.

'It's a case.'

'I can see that. Got more locks than Fort Knox. You got the nuclear codes in there or something?'

'What? No—'

''Cos if you have, you'd better keep an eye on it, mate,' here, he snuck a glance from side to side, 'in case the Jihadi brethren take an interest.'

'Good grief, surely not?' Were they involved in this as well?

Mo laughed. 'Nah, mate. I was winding you up, innit.'

'Sorry. I'm not quite with it tonight.'

'No worries, mate. So what can I get you? The rogan josh is particularly fine tonight.'

'Yeah, that'll do,' I said, handing the menu back to him. I wanted to make as few decisions as possible.

Mo jotted down the order and then looked at me again. 'Mate, word to the wise. When you've finished here, go back to your lady. Tell her you love her and that you'll make everything better.'

'What if I can't?'

'That, my friend, is the gilded path that leads only to despair and defeat,' said Mo. 'Promise me you'll think again?'

'Suppose so,' I said.

For once, Mo was right about the food. It was so good, I decided to forego my fifteen per cent discount and upgrade to a pint of Kingfisher. And then another one. And maybe just one more for the road. I paid my bill and staggered out of the door.

If Mo was right about the food, maybe he was right about everything else. I should go back to Lucy and patch things up. What kind of a man was I? Was I just going to give up on us? No, I was better than that. And if I had to repair every single panel on Lucy's car myself, I'd bloody well whip out my hammer and get tapping. I headed back to the flat with a spring in my step. I bounded up the stairs, put my key in the lock and pushed against the door.

The door refused to open. Someone had put the chain across.

'Hello?' I called through the gap.

I heard footsteps padding back and forth, followed by Lucy's voice saying 'Shit!'

'Hello there?' I called again.

Lucy appeared on the other side of the door.

'What do you want?' she said. She was wearing a kimono and not a lot else. I didn't remember her owning a kimono before.

'I came back to... hang on, who's that?' I'd caught sight of someone mooching about in the flat behind her. Someone male. She moved to block my view. 'Lucy, who's that in the flat with you?'

'It's not what it looks like.' She seemed quite certain about this.

'Well, what is it then?'

She was temporarily stumped for something to say. 'Look, it's a bit late for this conversation, Tom,' she said eventually.

'Too bloody right it is.' Jesus, I was even more of an idiot than I'd previously thought. If there was a competition right now for South West Numpty of the Year, I'd win first, second and third prizes. I was the Victor Ludorum of numpties. Lucy and I stared at each other in silence through the gap in the door for several more seconds.

'I'd better be going then,' I said.

'Yes,' said Lucy, 'you probably should.' She paused. 'Sorry,' she added in a soft voice before shutting the door again.

So what now? I stood on the street outside the flat considering my options. I needed to find somewhere to stay until things sorted themselves out. Given the state of my finances, checking into even the sleaziest of hotels for the duration was out of the question. Most of the friends I could think of calling were mutual ones and it wasn't guaranteed they would see my side of the story. It was highly likely that Lucy had already updated most of them on what I had done to her lovely, little car.

There was only one avenue left to explore. I took out my phone and switched it on. I hadn't used it since I'd been with Dorothy Chan in the pub on Friday. There were two voice-mails. One was from Benjamin's number, timed at three fifteen on Friday, consisting of nothing more than heavy breathing. The other one was from Rufus Fairbanks, timed at half past six this evening. It simply said 'Fairbanks. Need to have another little chat.' I listened to it another couple of times, trying to establish whether the clipped tone was menacing or merely effi-cient. Either way, I decided to ignore him for now, at least until I'd found somewhere to stash Burgess's case.

I found the number in my contacts and called it. It rang a few times, then a tired voice answered.

'Hello?'

'Hello, Dad,' I said. 'It's me.'

'Ah. Hello, son.'

'So, then. How are things?'

'She's left me, Tom.'

'Oh dear,' I said, resisting the urge to ask him who had left him this time. 'Look, I was wondering if—'

'I loved her, you know.'

'I know you did, Dad, but I've got a bit of a problem myself—'

'I'm not very good with women, Tom.'

'No, Dad, I know.' He was so bad with women that at least one of them had emigrated to the other side of the world to get away from him.

'You're so much better at that sort of thing than I am. Dunno where you get it from.' He gave a bitter laugh. 'Maybe you can come over some time and give me a few tips.'

'Ah well, that might not be such a bad idea,' I said, sensing an opening. 'You see, I could do with a place to stay for the next few days and I was wondering if I could drop in on you.'

'Really?' His voice brightened slightly. 'That would be nice, Tom. Could do with a bit of company. Might be a bit cramped with the two of you, though.'

'It's just me,' I said.

'Oh.' He paused. 'Well. Anyway. It'll be good to have some company again. I've only had Wally to talk to lately.'

Wally was a large, hairy, flea-ridden dog of uncertain parentage whose favourite activities were scavenging, dribbling and crotch-sniffing. I'd forgotten I'd have to share the place with him as well. This was going to be pretty grim, but I didn't have any choice in the matter.

It was now getting on for eleven o'clock and I needed somewhere to sleep before heading off to my father's place. I reasoned that the cheapest plan would be to hold on for as long as I could before catching the milk train tomorrow morning. I could get some kip then. So I headed off to the station, where I bought a ticket before looking around for somewhere to spend the intervening hours. I found an all-night, chipped formica café populated by taxi drivers, shift workers and nocturnal drifters, and settled myself down with a mug of milky coffee in a seat by the corner.

Reflecting back on this majestically catastrophic day, I remembered that in the midst of it all, something truly significant had happened. I had George Burgess's case back in my possession. Quite unexpectedly, a warm glow began to envelop me. The mission was still alive. I had a purpose in life.

It struck me that I hadn't even told Dorothy Chan, so I found her card and texted her. *I've got the case.*

She replied immediately. *WHAT?*

Yup.

No way. Sorry ever doubted you. What's inside?

No idea.

Ah. Haven't opened it?

Course not.

Have you tried?

Are you kidding? This thing has 6 dials.

A million combinations. Yes, I know. But we can narrow them down.

How?

Using our brains.

How?

Not going to tell you.

Spoilsport.

I want to be there when it opens. My place, Wednesday morning.

Where's that?

I'll meet you here: Dorothy added a link to the address of a coffee bar in Hoxton.

OK

Pls try to stay alive.

Will do.

Switch yr phone off now. Pls.

I did as she said, glancing through the window at the deserted Bristol streets and wondering who might be lurking in the shadows. Surely I was safe here? Then I had a worrying thought. What about Lucy? What if they came looking for me and found her instead? Was I abandoning her now? Would that Zumba teacher bloke look after her? But the awful truth was he'd almost certainly look after her better than I ever could.

Around two o'clock in the morning, a van drew up to the station and delivered the papers. The driver dropped in to the café for a drink and left a couple of copies of the Western Daily

Press on the counter. I picked one up and started reading it to pass the time. My attention was immediately seized by the front page headline: Chippenham Publisher Suspect Still Missing.

The story described Benjamin Unsworth as a twenty-year-old English undergraduate at Bristol University who used to work for the deceased Ms van Beek, adding that the police were not currently looking for any other persons in connection with her death. There had been several unconfirmed sightings of him running through the streets of Bristol, and his clothing had been found in the river Avon. A computer had been removed from the flat he shared with some other students.

Poor Benjamin. I would have bet everything I had left that he had nothing whatsoever to do with Hilary van Beek's death. The longer he was missing, the more likely it was he would turn out to be another victim who was in the wrong place at the wrong time. But did that mean that Archimedes Vavasor was similarly unfortunate? It always seemed unlikely he could have killed his twin brother, although I guess there were biblical precedents.

It was getting murkier by the minute, and I couldn't wait until Wednesday came around and I could discuss things with Dorothy. Maybe we'd even manage to open Burgess's case and get our hands on the Vavasor papers at last. Things would get better. I was sure of it. There was, after all, no possible way in which they could get worse. Yesterday, I had reached rock bottom. The only way now was up.

Chapter 16

The train pulled into Paddington at around half past six in the morning. Exhausted and hungry, I found a restaurant that was open for breakfast and decided to treat myself to a full English. Given the prospect of spending some time with my father, it was unlikely that I was going to get anything like a nutritious meal for some time.

The previous occupant of my booth had left behind a copy of the *Daily Mail* and I scoured it for further news on Benjamin Unsworth. There wasn't a great deal more beyond what I'd already read apart from some lurid speculation as to what might have turned up on his computer. There was also a hastily-written rent-an-expert piece explaining the seven telltale signs that your exploited intern is becoming psychotic – this was already being referred to as 'Turning Worm Syndrome' – and what action you should take if this happened.

The breakfast was as comprehensive an English as I could have hoped for and I arose from my table a fatter but a happier man. It was time to head across London to St Pancras and thence to Park Street, where my father lived in a static caravan.

The first thing I noticed was that the small army of gnomes that used to greet visitors had been considerably reduced in number, evidently following some kind of skirmish. The remains of a couple of them could still be seen languishing underneath the home, awaiting a decent burial. The departure of my father's latest paramour had not passed without incident.

I knocked on the door, and my father appeared. He had bags under his eyes, his chin was bristly and his long, grey hair was yet to see a comb. He was wearing a pair of baggy, striped pyjama bottoms and a grubby, white T-shirt that bore the legend 'Honk if you think I'm sexy.'

'You're early,' he said.

I made to go in, but I was first subjected to an intense genital examination by Wally the dog. After a couple of minutes detailed analysis, my meat and two veg were eventually passed as satisfactory and I was allowed to proceed.

The interior of the caravan gave off a rich aroma made up of equal parts of Calor gas, pizza, dog fur and stale body odour. This was to be my pied-a-terre for the foreseeable future.

'Make yourself at home,' said my father, gesturing towards a moth–eaten bench seat covered in bills and old newspapers. I put my rucksack and Burgess's case down, moved the papers into a single pile and sat down. Wally came over and began to dribble on me. He had capacious salivary glands and was visibly anxious to share their contents. 'Be back in a minute. Put the kettle on,' said my father, disappearing off to the other end of the caravan.

Pushing Wally away, I stood up and found the kettle, filled it with water and placed it on a rickety two-ring stove, which whooshed into life alarmingly when I lit a match. When my father returned, his face looked marginally smoother and he had swapped the pyjama bottoms for a pair of jeans, but otherwise he didn't look a lot different. He located a couple of mugs and handed me one. It had a picture of a kitten on the side, a crack down the other and a sticky, brown residue in the bottom. I licked my finger and did my best to wipe the latter away.

'Tea bags are over there,' said my father, pointing to the cupboard over the sink. Then he went to the fridge, took out a pint of milk and sniffed it. He wrinkled his nose and passed it to me. 'Do you think this is off?' he said. I smelt it and nearly choked.

'Jesus!' I said.

'Black tea OK?' he said.

We sipped our tea in silence. 'Sorry about...' I began.

My father waved a hand. 'Magda? Nah. Forgotten her already.' He slurped noisily and smacked his lips. 'Good to see you, son. You're looking...' He searched for a word. 'You look tired, son. Are you all right?'

'Could be better. I've split up with Lucy, Dad.'

'No! But she was lovely. I thought she was the one.'

'Doesn't look like she is now. I made a bit of a mess of things. So did she. Still not entirely sure which one of us cocked it all up.'

'Women, eh?'

'Yeah.'

'Do you hear from your mother much?'

I always dreaded this question. 'She's doing OK,' I said, carefully. 'The herd's up to a couple of hundred now.'

'Well. Y'know, I wonder if I'd have made it as a farmer. Always fancied learning how to shear them. Sort of skill a man should have.'

'You'd have been awful, Dad.'

'Yeah. 'Spose you're right. So what happened with Lucy?' he said.

'Long story. First of all, I went and lost my job. So I had to hand my company car in. Then I borrowed hers. And I broke it. Then I found out she was seeing someone else. All a bit of a mess.'

'Ah,' said my father. 'That's a sad story, but maybe a serendipitous one.'

'What do you mean?'

'Well, I bet you're feeling less burdened now. Like a sixteen ton weight's been lifted from your shoulders.'

'Well...' I wouldn't have put it quite that way, no.

He raised a significant index finger. 'You, son, have just discovered one of the great truths of this life. Free yourself from the chains of oppression – employment, relationships, possessions, all that shit promulgated by the mass media – and you will find true happiness. Follow your dreams, son. Look at me.' He spread his arms wide. 'You are looking at the happiest man in the world. If the fancy takes me, I can be out of here in thirty minutes flat with everything I need. Like a lone wolf.'

I wanted to say he didn't sound very wolf-like when I called last night, but that would have been unkind. Even wolves had off-days.

'Right then,' he said, standing up. 'Going to get some bread and milk and stuff.'

'OK.'

He paused uncertainly by the door. 'Got a tenner I can borrow?' he said.

I sighed and pulled out my wallet. I'd topped up at a cashpoint in Paddington and the balance on the slip had been alarmingly low. I handed over a twenty, because past experience told me he probably needed more than he'd asked for.

'Cheers, son.'

When he came back, we went out and walked the dog. Then we had a sandwich for lunch before spending the afternoon playing cards and talking about old times. I began to wonder if, in a way, my father was right after all. There were more important things than careers and doomed relationships. There were more important things than money and possessions. There were more important things than computers and the world wide web.

The latter point was particularly relevant because my father didn't have any sort of connection and neither of our phones had internet capability. Right now I was disconnected from the outside world altogether. Still, there was something good, wholesome and innocent about just sitting down with my dad and playing a few hands of cards, leaving the world to get on with whatever it wanted to get on with. I was aware of a sense of calm that I hadn't felt since everything had kicked off two weeks previously.

Later on, we ordered pizza. Judging from the stack of boxes piled on the back of the delivery boy's moped, there were a substantial number of lone males with limited cookery skills living on this site. We cracked open a couple of cans of lager and tucked in. When we had both finished, there was a satisfied silence, until something wafted over the table and it became clear that farting dog was going to join the list of aromas for the rest of the evening. My father shook his head and grabbed the bottle of Jack Daniels, pouring us both a generous shot.

'OK, then,' he said. 'What's in that case of yours?'

'Just some papers.' I said. The last thing I wanted was to get my father involved. There was every chance he'd get us all killed.

'Papers eh? Bit of a secure lock, isn't it?'

'They're very important papers.'

'You're chasing something, aren't you, son? I can always tell when someone's chasing something they didn't ought to be chasing. Shadows. Phantoms. Things that go bumpity bumpity bumpity oh shit—' He was waving his arms about so much that he'd knocked over his glass. He picked it up again and poured another shot.

'It's real, Dad. I'm not wasting my time on this one. Honestly. It's no phantom.'

'Well, whatever it is, just don't be silly. Y'know all that crap about following your dreams?'

'Yes?'

''S'bollocks, son.' He put down his glass and looked at me full in the face, with an expression so honest and vulnerable I could hardly bear to look back. 'Don't end up like me, Tom,' he said. 'Please don't.' Then he drained his glass, picked up the bottle and left the table. 'I'm off to bed,' he said. 'Sort yourself out.'

Chapter 17

The next morning I woke up late, aching all over. Alcohol had provided an agreeable additional pillow for the first half of the night, but this had mutated without warning into a rough granite boulder around half past three. I got up and got dressed. Wally came over, wagging his tail.

'No, I'm not taking you with me,' I said. The look he gave me made it clear I had gone down a couple of hundred fathoms in his estimation, and he wandered back to his resting station with barely a backward glance. 'Bye then,' I called out as I left. There was no response from my father.

I caught the first off-peak train into London and found the Hoxton café where she had suggested we meet. I was about to order a straight-up, lactose-free, hyperskinny flat Americano as this seemed to be the closest thing to a black filter coffee on offer when Dorothy appeared.

'Hi,' she said, holding her hand up. She was wearing sunglasses, drainpipe jeans and a T-shirt advertising an online gaming convention from a couple of years earlier. 'Got the case?'

'Of course,' I said, reaching under the table.

She held up her hand. 'Keep it covered for the moment,' she said. 'You never know who's watching. Anyone follow you here?'

'Don't think so.'

'Good. OK, time to head off to Dot Chan World Central.'

'What about my coffee?'

'Way too expensive. Come on. Now, I should warn you we will be entering a secure facility and you must under no circumstances divulge its location to any third party. Neither should you make any permanent electronic or physical note of its address.'

'What if I need to go there again?'

'You won't.'

'Why all the secrecy? Is this because of the Archie and Pye stuff?'

Dorothy gave a bitter laugh. 'As if. No, it's because I'm a woman working in the game industry.'

'So?'

'There's an internet full of idiots – male idiots, to be precise – who'd prefer I wasn't.'

'But surely—'

Dorothy shook her head. 'Don't. You have no idea.'

'Yes, but not all men—'

Dorothy rolled her eyes and raised both hands in front of her, palms out. 'Seriously, please don't EVER use that phrase around me again. And don't even try to take part in this discussion until you yourself have endured regular threats of sexual violence, been forced off social media and had your personal details broadcast on the web. If and when these have happened to you – and to be honest, it's unlikely to given your gender – then I'll be happy to chat. Until then, please believe me when I say that you have NO IDEA.'

I was getting strong signals that I should leave the topic alone. So I did. I picked up the case and followed Dorothy out of the café. She crossed the road and turned right down a side street before turning left at the next junction. We continued on for a couple of blocks and eventually arrived at an anonymous, five-storey warehouse unit. Dorothy waved a card at the door and it buzzed open. She didn't bother with the lift and instead hurtled up the stairs, with me puffing along in her wake.

'You OK?' she said, when we reached the top.

'Yeah… fine,' I said, between wheezes.

She gave a slight smile and shook her head. Then she went over to a door which seemed to be pulsating slightly. She waved another card at it and it opened, at which point my ears met with a bracing full cannon broadside of thrash metal. We were in a vast, industrial cavern with whitewashed brick walls and a vinyl floor. There was hardly any furniture apart from a couple of workstations, one at either end. Illumination was provided by a series of bare fluorescent strips in the ceiling.

'COME ON IN!' bellowed Dorothy. We went in and the music immediately cut off. At the far side of the room, a woman with close-cropped, red hair and wire-rimmed glasses, wearing military fatigues was standing up and peering at us over a bank of half a dozen computer monitors.

'Hey, Dot,' said the woman. 'Found the memory leak.'

Dorothy went over and joined her behind the desk. 'Where?'

'In the tear-down between phase two and phase three. One of the tentacle objects.'

'Surely not. I double-checked the tentacle class.'

'It's not in the base class, Dot. It's one of the derived classes. Zombie tentacles. Dangling pointer to a putrefaction object.'

'Shit, of course. I added that in and forgot to delete it.'

'This is why I hate C++, Dot.'

'I know.'

'The sooner we go back to Java, the better. Who's the random?' she added, jerking her head in my direction.

'Him? That's Tom,' said Dorothy.

'Who's Tom?'

'He's Tom.'

'Yeah, I can see that.'

'He's brought the case.'

'Oh that. I take it you've brought him up to speed on the protocol?'

'Yeah, he's cool. Aren't you?'

'Er, yeah, I'm cool,' I said, anxious to join in the conversation. I walked over to where the two women were standing. 'What are you... er... developing?'

'Never you mind,' said the programmer. I snuck a look at the other side of the monitors, but before I could see anything in detail, she pressed a key and the displays changed, each one now showing a single letter in white on a black background. The letters on the top row read F U K, and the ones on the bottom read O F F.

'Right,' I said, moving back to the other side of the desk. 'I see what you're saying.' I hated it when techies did that sort of thing.

'This is Ali,' said Dorothy. 'I'd keep out of her way if I were you.'

'Don't worry, I will.'

'Hi,' said Ali, without looking up.

'Er, hi,' I said.

Ali plugged a pair of earphones in and started bashing away at her keyboard. I turned to Dorothy. 'So do you two develop everything here?'

'Nah. We outsource the grunt work to Chennai. We just do the fiddly stuff here. Now, shall we have a look at this case?'

'Yeah.' I followed her to the desk in the opposite corner of the room. Four pictures of women had been blu-tacked to the wall behind it: an etching of one in Victorian dress, a photograph of a severe-looking one in some kind of Naval uniform, another of one next to a pile of papers that towered over her head and finally a more recent picture of a young blonde woman.

Dorothy noticed my interest. 'From left to right,' she said, pointing, 'Ada Lovelace, colleague of Charles Babbage and inventor of the concept of programming. Admiral Grace Hopper, who wrote the very first compiler. Margaret Hamilton, chief software developer on the Apollo program. And finally Zoë Quinn, who had the temerity to develop a successful and well-received online game and was rewarded with an onslaught of harassment, abuse and death threats. Gamergate.'

'Oh, that.' I'd heard the word, even if the technicalities were sketchy.

'Yes, that. Progress, eh?'

I didn't know what to say.

'So,' she said, with a brief shake of the head. 'Six numbers. What do you reckon?'

'I thought you were the one with the ideas,' I said.

'I am. But I'm offering you the chance to participate.'

'I'm honoured.'

'Not that you deserve it.'

'What?'

'You still don't remember, do you?'

'What do you mean?' I had no idea what she was going on about. Obviously at some point in our shared past I had done her some deep wrong. The trouble was, our shared past had ended around ten years earlier, and the details were a bit vague now.

'Never mind,' said Dorothy. 'Look, you want to take the first guess?'

'I dunno. Something to do with a birthday, maybe?'

'Whose? Burgess's?'

'I was thinking more Archie's. Or Pye's.'

'They're the same.'

'I knew that.'

'It's Burgess's case.'

'Can't we try both?'

'As long as it doesn't jam up completely if we make too many wrong attempts.'

I hadn't thought of that. 'Is that possible?'

'Probably not. Actually, I might have been thinking of the TARDIS.'

I looked up at Dorothy. There was the faintest suspicion of a smile playing on her lips. It vanished.

'Do we even know Burgess's birthday?' I said. 'He said he'd been removed from Wikipedia.'

'Doesn't surprise me. OK, let's start with the Vavasors. Hold on. Think they were born in the fifties...' Dorothy was busy calling up Wikipedia on the screen on her desk. 'Ah yes, 1956. July 15th. So let's kick off with 150756.'

I set the numbers and tried to open the case. Nothing happened.

'OK, I've got a birthday for Burgess,' said Dorothy. 'Second of April, 1962.'

I tried 020462. This had no effect either.

'US style?' I said.

'Why?'

'No good reason.' I tried swapping the days and months around anyway, but this didn't do any good.

'Thought not,' said Dorothy, with a hint of triumph.

'Hey, it might have worked.'

'No. There's no possible reason for it working.'

'We could just attack it with an axe or something,' I said.

'Is that your standard approach to things?' Dorothy looked at me and tilted her head on one side. 'Wouldn't surprise me.'

'You're being unfair. Look, I'm a bit tired. I've had a bad couple of days.'

'Thought you looked rough.'

'Yeah, well, I split up with my girlfriend.'

Dorothy raised a questioning eyebrow.

'I crashed her car,' I added. 'Thought I was being chased by the Belarusian mafia.'

'The who?'

'The Belarusian mafia. From Belarus. You know, the one next to—'

'I know where Belarus is. I just don't understand why you thought they were chasing you.'

'You know they're after this case, right?'

'I have no idea what you're talking about.'

'You don't?'

'No. I've never heard of any Belarusian connection before,' said Dorothy. 'How did you hear of this?'

'It was on Vavasorology.com. Rufus Fairbanks told me it was rubbish, but—'

'Who's Rufus Fairbanks?'

'You don't know? I thought he was one of the key players in the community.'

'Could well be. But very few of us use our real names. So who is he?'

'Some kind of City bigwig. Claims Pye was working for some organization in the City when he died.'

'Are you sure?'

'That's what he said. He tried to explain what went on in the City, but I got a bit confused. I think he also offered to sell my grandmother.'

'Right,' said Dorothy, frowning. 'How did you get to meet him?'

'He tracked me down after I'd posted on the forum about meeting Burgess on the train.'

'How odd.'

'He seemed to be trying to find out if I had Burgess's case.'

'He wouldn't be the only one. Do you trust him?'

'Don't know,' I said. 'But he's not the killer, if that's what you're thinking. He says he was out of the country at the time of Pye's death.'

'Can he prove that?'

'I assume so. He said he was speaking at a conference in New York.'

Dorothy turned to her computer and fiddled with it for a minute or two. 'Investment strategies for shale oil extraction?' she said.

I shrugged. 'It's possible.'

'There can't be that many Rufus Fairbankses around. Looks like he was telling the truth. He's down for the keynote on the exact day that Pye Vavasor died.' She turned back to me. 'I'd still stay clear of him if I were you, though.'

'Well, I'm ignoring his calls for the time being.'

'He's been e-mailing you?'

'Don't know about that, but he's left voicemails and texts. E-mail's not an option where I am at the moment.'

'Where are you staying?'

'With my dad. He's pretty much off-grid.' And off quite a few other things, I thought to myself.

'Let's hope so. What about your girlfriend?'

'Some bloke's moved in with her already.'

'Whoa. Fast mover.'

'Yeah.'

Dorothy gave a deep sigh. 'Well, this is all very pleasant, but it isn't going to help us get this case open, is it?'

'No,' I said. 'So what are we going to do?'

Dorothy leaned back in her chair. 'I think we need to take a more mathematical approach.'

Chapter 18

'Mathematical?' I said. 'In what way?'

'e and π,' said Dorothy.

'What do you mean?'

'The two most important mathematical constants. e, the base of natural logarithms and π—'

'Yes, I've heard of that one, thanks. But you can run e past me again if you like.'

'The base of natural logarithms. If e to the power of x equals y, then the natural log of y will be x.'

I thought about this for a moment. 'No. Doesn't make any sense at all,' I said.

'Never mind,' said Dorothy. 'Just trust me, it's important.'

'What's it got to do with the Vavasors, anyway?'

'I'm coming to that. It's sort of a code. π stands for Pye – obviously – and e represents Archie.'

'Why?'

'As I've just said, e is the other important mathematical constant. And Archimedes has two e's in it. I know, it's tenuous, but there's an elegance to it. We like elegance in maths.'

'Right.' In truth, I had absolutely no idea how anything in mathematics could ever be described as elegant. Complicated, confusing and boring, yes. But elegant, no. However, it seemed easier to give the impression I was hanging on her every word than ask her to explain.

'Ever come across the ePis?' she continued.

'Oh, them. I think I applied to join their forum about a week ago. Still haven't heard back.'

'You won't. They're pretty exclusive.'

'That makes me feel a whole load better.'

'You're welcome. Anyway, the reason they call themselves the ePis is that epi is e and π together. Archimedes and Pythagoras. Also, epi in ancient Greek means "on top of". Which they like to think they are.'

'They sound a nice inclusive bunch. I bet you're one of them.'

Dorothy ignored this. 'So let's apply e and π to our current problem,' she said. 'What do you think?'

'Start with π?' I said.

'Won't work. It only represents one of the twins.'

'No harm in trying, though? First six digits?'

Dorothy shrugged. 'Go on, then,' she said, with a wave of her hand. I didn't do anything, and a smile slowly crept across her face. 'You don't know, do you?'

'Yes, I do. It's three point something.'

'Three point something. Jesus.'

'Oh, all right. I don't know and I don't care,' I said. Why would anyone need to know the value of π anyway?

Dorothy shook her head. 'How have you managed to get through life so far?'

'Are you going to tell me or aren't you?'

'Three one four one five nine.'

I tried this. It didn't work.

'No surprises there,' said Dorothy.

'What about e?' I said.

''Spose so.'

I looked at her expectantly. She didn't say anything.

'Oh come on,' I said. 'You can't expect me to know the value of e, can you? I don't even know what it does.'

'Well, you should do,' said Dorothy.

'You know what, I'm beginning to remember what annoyed me about you,' I said.

She shook her head again. 'Two seven one eight two eight,' she said.

That didn't work either.

'Well, no shit, Sherlock,' she said. She took a long hard look at me and frowned. 'How much do you know about Euler?' she said.

'Who's Oiler?' I said.

'Remember my user name?' said Dorothy, '*EulerIsGod*?'

'Oh. I thought it was pronounced "Youller".'

Dorothy sighed and shook her head. 'No,' she said. 'It's pronounced "Oiler". He was German.'

'Right.'

'So you've never heard of Euler's Identity, then?'

'No.'

'Only the single most important, mind-blowingly weird equation in the history of the universe?'

'No.'

Dorothy pulled up her left sleeve. It was an unexpectedly alluring action, or at least it might have been if it hadn't been for the overwhelmingly hostile atmosphere that had developed between us. Right at the top of her arm there was a tattoo of an equation. What kind of person tattoos an equation on their arm? 'Read it,' she said.

I peered at it. 'Um... e to the i π plus one equals zero. So?'

'Isn't that amazing?'

'I don't think I'm following this. You couldn't help me out a bit, could you?'

'OK, OK. Here goes.' She grabbed a pad of paper from her desk and wrote it out:

$$e^{i\pi} + 1 = 0$$

'e,' said Dorothy, 'is that number I was talking about just now. The 2.71828 one. It's an irrational number, meaning that you can't construct it from one integer divided by another. And it's also a transcendental number, meaning that… well, we'll leave that for now. It's a bit complicated.'

'e's the one that didn't work on the case, right?'

'Yes, that one.'

'And i is?'

'The square root of minus one.'

'What?'

'I said, the square root of minus one.'

'But that doesn't exist.'

'It does. But it isn't any number we know already. That's why we call it i.'

'That's cheating, isn't it? You can't just invent a new number just because you want to… can you?'

'Why not?'

'Well, what if you wanted to take the square root of i?' I had no idea why anyone would want to do this, although it struck me as the sort of pointless thing a mathematician would be keen to try. 'Do you need to make up another new number? j or something?'

Dorothy laughed. 'You don't need to invent any new numbers for that, and you wouldn't call it j anyway, because some mathematicians use j for the square root of minus one instead of i. The thing is, once you've added in the concept of i, you don't need anything else. The square root of i is i plus one divided by the square root of two.'

'What?'

'Look. I'll show you. Here.' She took the pad and wrote on it again:

$$(i + 1)^2 = (i + 1) \times (i + 1)$$

'OK?' she said.

'You've left off the divided-by-the-square-root-of-two bit.'

'We'll come back to that later. Now. Remember how to expand stuff in brackets?'

I thought back to my GCSE days and began to sweat slightly. 'Yes,' I lied.

'Good. We just multiply each term individually and add them up.'

Of course we do. Who's we, Dorothy?

She carried on writing:

$$i \times i + i \times 1 + 1 \times i + 1 \times 1$$

'OK?' She was talking to me in much the same way as a primary school teacher would talk to a particularly slow five-year-old.

'Yes, Miss.'

'Good boy. Now let's work out each of these terms, one by one. i times i?'

'Sorry?'

'I'm asking you a question, Tom. What's i times i?'

I had no idea.

'Tom, i times i is minus one. That's what "square root" means.'

'Oh yes. Of course.' She was making me feel really stupid now. I didn't like this at all.

'All right, let's try something simpler. Next one. i times one?'

'i?'

'Excellent. And one times i?'

'i again?'

'Wow. Gold star for you, Winscombe. And finally, one times one equals one.'

'I wanted to do that one too.'

'Tough. So let's see what we've got:'

$$-1 + i + i + 1$$

I stared at this. 'Hold on,' I said. 'Does that mean the one and minus one cancel each other out? Leaving—'

'Two times i. Which is pretty much where we want to be, except for a factor of two. Which is why we divide by the square root of two back at the beginning.'

'Just let me think about this for a while.' I thought about it for a while. My head began to hurt. I felt as if I'd just been shown a very clever magic trick but wasn't deemed trustworthy enough to be given the secret of how it had been done. 'Can we go back to opening the case, please?' I said eventually.

'In a moment. We just need to go back to Euler's Identity.'

'Oh God. That.'

'Yes, that. So we have that number e, raised to the power of i times π—'

'Hold on, can I stop you there? What do you mean by "raised to the power" again?'

'Multiplied by itself. Like if you square something, two times two. That's two raised to the power of two. Two cubed – two times two times two – that's two raised to the power of three.'

'Right… but what about – putting aside this square root of minus one shit to one side for a moment – raising something to the power of π?'

'Well, π is just over three, so two to the π would be two times two times two times a bit more.'

'A bit more?'

'Yeah. We just generalise the idea of raising to the power a bit.'

'Right. Why?'

'Because it's cool and it works. Look, we have the five most important numbers in mathematics here: e, π, one, zero and i. And they're all linked by this one amazingly simple equation. And – and – and the thing that gets me every time is that when you start studying maths—'

'As if I'd want to.'

'Well, yes, it is hard to imagine, but work with me here – you first come across e when you're studying probability theory, because it's really useful for stuff like the Poisson distribution.'

'Fish?'

'No. Nothing to do with fish. It was invented by some guy called Poisson. He was big in probability theory. Anyway, they used his distribution to predict the numbers of soldiers in the Prussian army who were kicked to death by horses.'

'So definitely not fish, then.'

'No. So that's e. And you know all about π because that's to do with circles and stuff.'

'Remind me again.'

'π is another irrational number like e. And also like e, it's a transcendental number. It gives the ratio of a circle's circumference to its diameter. You must remember that.'

'Any circle?'

'Any one.'

'Even a really big circle?'

'Any circle, Tom. That's why π is a constant.'

'Can you prove this? Have you tried every single circle ever?'

'Stop it, Tom.'

'I bet I could find a circle that it didn't work for.' I was getting annoyed by all this.

'Well, good luck with that.'

'Yeah. Well, try and stop me.' I wasn't entirely sure where I was going with my argument, but I felt better for saying it.

'It's OK, I won't. Anyway, that's π.'

'So you say.' Why did she annoy me so much? I didn't usually get this upset.

'So that's π,' she repeated. 'Then there's i, which is the imaginary numbers thing—'

'Imaginary numbers?' I had enough trouble with the ones I encountered in real life. My bank balance, for example.

'That's what the square roots of negative numbers are called.' Dorothy was now on her feet and walking around waving her hands in the air. 'And if you combine ordinary numbers and imaginary numbers together, they're called complex numbers. Anyway,' she said, 'that's by the by. The thing is, as a junior mathematician you think: all these constants come from COM-PLETELY SEPARATE branches of maths, don't they? Circle geometry, probability and imaginary numbers. They have nothing whatsoever to do with each other. Except it turns out that THEY ARE ALL SOMEHOW RELATED. By this one mad equation THAT MAKES NO SENSE WHATSOEVER!' Dorothy paused for breath. 'Isn't that TOTALLY AWESOME?'

At this point, Ali stood up, pulled her earphones out and came over. 'Don't suppose you guys could turn the noise down a little? I've got The Devil's Spleen turned up to eleven and I can still hear you arguing over it.'

'Sorry, Ali,' said Dorothy. 'How's it going?'

'Badly. I made the change but it's borked the UI. Can't press a key without a new tentacle sprouting from somewhere.'

'Go for a walk round the block. Usually works.'

'Might just do that. What are you doing, anyway?'

'I'm teaching Tom about Euler.'

This was apparently the funniest joke ever told in the history of mankind. When Ali had stopped laughing, she slapped Dorothy on the shoulder and said, 'Well, good luck with that, Dot. Good luck with that,' before going out.

I felt quite hurt. It was a lot to grasp in one go. 'Look, I'm sorry if I'm a bit too thick for all this,' I said, 'but—'

'It's OK, I'll do my best to work with the material provided.'

'Hey!'

Dorothy was laughing at me.

'So what's all this got to do with Archie and Pye?' I said.

'Remember that Archie was known as e and Pye as π?'

'I think so.'

'Each one was represented by a different transcendental number. A couple of years before they both died, there was a nice feature on them in the Guardian that described them as "The Transcendental Twins". Except some idiot sub-editor changed it to "The Irrational Twins". Which didn't make any sense whatsoever.'

Dorothy sighed. 'So if Archie is represented by e and Pye by π,' she continued, 'then we have an equation here that links the two.'

'That's nice. I'm very happy for them.'

'But don't you see? We need a six-figure number that incorporates them both. e and π.'

'So... what are you proposing?'

'Isn't it obvious?'

'No.'

'e to the power of π! Can't you see? We take out the i bit, because we can't do anything with that—'

'Obviously.'

'And that leaves us with... got a calculator on that Mickey Mouse phone of yours?' Dorothy looked at me. 'Ah, no. Silly question.'

'Can't you just do it in your head?' I said. I didn't like the way she was insulting my phone. What had it ever done to hurt her?

'Don't be ridiculous. OK, here goes.' She turned away to her computer. 'Put them in to seven sig figs… three point one four one five nine three times two point seven one eight two eight two… and the result is… twenty-three point one four oh seven.'

'Right.'

'Well? Go on then!'

My head was still spinning. 'Sorry, I didn't quite catch that.'

Dorothy sighed. 'Two.'

'Two.'

'Three.'

'Three.'

'One.'

'One.'

'Four.'

'Four.'

'Oh.'

'Oh.'

'Seven.'

'Seven.'

I pulled the levers to open the case.

Nothing happened.

'Shit,' said Dorothy.

'After all that,' I said. 'I feel quite let down.' I was grinning inside, though. Just a bit.

'Shut up, Tom.'

'Right-o.'

We sat in silence for a minute or two.

'What if… no,' I said.

'What?'

'No, it wouldn't work.'

'Probably not, but try me anyway.'

'What if we swapped them round so that it was π to the power of e?'

Dorothy stared at me and shook her head. 'That may well be the worst idea you've come up with today. It makes no sense mathematically.'

'Not even a little bit?'

'No. Not at all.'

'OK.'

Then I had another idea. I didn't even mention this one to Dorothy. I just got out a pad of paper and worked it out.

'What are you doing?' she said.

'Humour me. I'm just going to try something. Five… eight… five… nine… eight… seven… Right, here goes.'

Ping. The levers flipped out and the case clicked open.

Dorothy gawped at me. I gawped back at Dorothy.

'What did you do?' she said.

'I added them together.'

'You added what together?'

'e and π.'

'But that makes even less sense. There is nowhere, literally NOWHERE, in maths where you add e and π together. It's just stupid. Why would—'

'Why would Burgess use that for a code? Simple. Because Burgess wasn't a bloody mathematician. To him, e and π were just two numbers that happened to represent Archie and Pye. Archie and Pye to him meant Archie PLUS Pye.'

'I hate you,' said Dorothy. 'I really, really hate you.'

'Come on,' I said. 'Don't you want to look inside?'

Chapter 19

I carried the case over to an empty table and carefully lifted the lid. Sweet wrappers spilled out in all directions. I started scrunching them all up.

'Careful,' said Dorothy, following me over. 'Don't throw anything away yet. Might be useful.'

'You're kidding.'

'Burgess was the sort of bloke who'd scribble information down on the back of anything that came to hand. Such as this.' She waved a Bounty wrapper at me. It had an address on the back of it.

'Holy shit. It says "Standage" here. Wasn't that—'

'The Vavasors' housekeeper. He must have tracked her down.' Dorothy looked worried. 'I hope he didn't tell anyone else.'

'Why not?' I said. Then I realised. 'Shit. Someone needs to warn her. Is there a phone number anywhere?'

Dorothy went through the other wrappers, straightening them out and placing them in a neat pile. When she reached the end, she shook her head.

'Bugger,' I said. 'I'll have to go there myself then. Where is it again?' I peered at the address.

'Lewes,' said Dorothy.

'I thought she was rumoured to be hunkered down on the outskirts of Basingstoke?'

'Says Lewes here. Either way, you're not going until we've finished sorting through this stuff.' She gave me a stern look.

'Yes, miss.'

The next thing we found was the torn lower half of a twee 'Forever Friends' birthday card featuring a group of teddy bears dancing around a stationary badger. The tweeness was undermined by the cryptically suggestive message contained within:

I COULD FORNICATE
MY LOVELY VIXEN

'Classy,' I said. I was all for tossing it straight in the bin, but once again Dorothy restrained me.

'Oh come on,' I said. 'It's a poxy birthday card that Burgess had second thoughts about sending. It's nothing to do with us.'

'I still say we keep it.'

'If you insist.'

'I do.'

I placed the card underneath the pile of sweet papers and went back to the case. Next up was a bulging folder with the words 'Twins Book' scrawled on it in black magic marker. I took it out and laid it on the table.

'Oh Christ,' said Dorothy, looking back at the case. I hadn't noticed what was under the folder, and it was an unexpected discovery because I really hadn't pegged George Burgess as a subscriber to *Hot Asian Chicks* magazine. Without thinking I turned to look at Dorothy and realised, several aeons too late, that it was the wrong thing to do.

'Tom,' she said. 'Whatever you're about to say to me, please think very, very carefully before saying it.'

'I… no… what I mean is… I wasn't going to say anything. I really wasn't.' I really wasn't.

'Fine.' She picked up the well-thumbed magazine by the corner and dropped it, with great ceremony and not a little disdain, into the wastepaper basket. 'You passed the test. Well done. OK, Let's move on. What have you got there?'

The folder was bursting with sheets of A4, each one decorated with green spidery handwriting. 'Burgess's manuscript, I guess,' I said.

'Yeah,' said Dorothy with a sigh. 'Something else we could probably dispose of.'

'Not so sure. I think I know someone who might be interested. Assuming she's still alive.'

'Who's that?'

'His agent. Diana Cheeseman. I spoke to her – God, when was it? – a week ago. She was keen to get hold of it.'

'I bet. Especially now her client is dead.'

'Possibly less so now his publisher has joined him, but still.'

'Yeah.' Dorothy looked at me and tilted her head on one side. 'Does it ever bother you?'

'Does what bother me?'

'The way anyone who gets involved in this tends to get their life expectancy trimmed?'

'Good Lord, no,' I said. 'Actually, I'm lying. It bloody terrifies me.'

'Me too. Fun, though, isn't it?' Dorothy's eyes sparkled as she said this.

'For some definitions of fun.'

She laughed. 'I hope you extracted a good bargain out of Ms Cheeseman.'

'Yeah. I asked her to give me everything she knew about Burgess and how he got involved with the Vavasors. I also asked her if she could arrange access to Isaac Vavasor.'

'Really? Jeez. And what did she say to that?'

'She said she'd see what she could do.'

'Don't hold your breath. It's easier to get an audience with Howard Hughes's corpse. Still, if she can get you the full story of how Burgess got involved, that could be useful intel.'

'Let's hope she is still alive, then.'

'Well, I haven't noticed anything in the news, but the mainstream media aren't necessarily joining the dots.' She stuffed the manuscript back into the folder and passed it to me. 'OK, this one's your department, then. Give her a call when you've finished with Mrs Standage.'

'What's next?' I said, peering into the case.

'A half-used packet of tissues. A list of the Easter services for St Xavier's church, Swindon. A programme of events for "SWINdon: A Celebration!" – that's with "WIN" in fancy lettering in case you were wondering – with a couple of pages dogeared. A prescription for statins. A puzzle magazine.'

'No diary or anything like that?'

'Nah. That'd be way too easy. Ooh, here we are.' Dorothy removed a transparent wallet filled with paper. The top sheet was covered in mathematical formulae. Roughly three quarters of it was stained pink, as if someone had once spilled a glass of glühwein over it. 'Whoa.' I noticed that Dorothy's hands were trembling.

'Is that what I think it is?'

'Yep. The Vavasors' mathematical papers. I literally cannot believe I'm actually holding this.' Her voice had taken on a tone that was usually reserved for use in church.

'Cool. I'm very happy for you.'

'Don't take the piss, Tom. This is important.'

'I actually meant it. It looks like complete and utter bollocks to me, but I'm sure it's important to you.'

'Yeah, well, whatever.'

'So where are the Marginalia that Burgess was going on about?'

'Here.' She handed the top sheet to me and tapped the right-hand side with her finger. All I could see in the margin were a number of impenetrable remarks in red felt-tip pen. 'Insufficient iterations.' 'Try a higher order.' 'More sig figs?'

'Hang on,' I said. 'What about this one?' I pointed out a note that simply said 'Eat shit, π!'

'Yeah, well, when you get two people working closely like that, the mathematical commentary tends to get mixed up with verbal abuse. It's often tricky to tell which is which. For example, that "Try a higher order" comment is probably intended to be sarcastic.'

'How do you know?'

'Because maths.'

'That's a rubbish answer.'

'Works for me.'

'Pah.'

'It's a better answer than "Pah", anyway,' said Dorothy.

'Pah. Anyway, back to the Marginalia. Is this all just banter or did they genuinely fight?'

'Literally or figuratively?'

'Well, I meant figuratively,' I said. 'But remember, we're talking about set squares at dawn.'

'Dunno. A pair of twins can fall out like any pair of siblings. But what are you getting at? Whoever killed Pye has just struck again. Twice. Are you suggesting Archie's still alive?'

'Why not?'

'Because the autopsy confirmed beyond all possible doubt that the body in the woods was him. Anyway, it's pointless speculating. Better to work through this lot first.'

'But how long's that going to take?' I said.

'Couple of weeks, maybe.' Dorothy riffled through the pile of notes. 'Give or take a day or two.'

'TWO BLOODY WEEKS just to look at the Marginalia?!' She had to be kidding.

'Well, there's a lot to go through.' She had now adopted a distinctly defensive posture, with the notes held firmly against her chest.

'But... but... you don't need to look at all of it, do you? Just the stuff in the margins, right?'

'Well, it needs to be placed into context.'

'What? No, wait a minute. You're looking a bit shifty. Why are you looking shifty?'

'I don't know what you mean. I'm not looking shifty at all.'

'Yes, you are.' She so was looking shifty.

'Rubbish,' she said, turning away from me.

'Dorothy,' I said. 'Look at me. Come on, look at me. Admit it. You're not just thinking of the Marginalia, are you?'

There was a long silence.

'Dorothy,' I said. 'Don't go off-piste on me.'

There was another long silence.

'Look, Tom,' she said eventually. 'This could be dynamite. Think about it. The Millennium Prize!'

'What are you suggesting?'

'You know what I'm suggesting. This lot,' she smacked the sheaf of papers with the back of her hand, 'could contain the solution to one of the Millennium Prize problems. Maybe more than one of them. A million dollars a throw, Tom! Think of that.'

'And you're cool with stealing it?'

'Not stealing, Tom. I'd be building on their work. Shoulders of giants and all that.'

'But you're not a proper mathematician, Dorothy. You're a software developer.'

'Plenty of maths in game development, Tom.'

'But haven't you got a business to run?'

'The money could help the business!' She was waving the Vavasor papers around in the air with her right hand and gesturing at me with the left. 'We could delay calling on the second round funding and the year-on-year vencap leverage could be reduced by a significant percentage.'

'Sorry, you lost me there,' I said, holding up a hand. 'Do I understand from that burst of gobbledygook you're still looking for money? I thought if you were successful enough to have a place like this to work in—'

'We are successful, Tom. We'll be even more successful very soon. But we only got this place because it's the end of a lease after the previous tenants went bust.'

'And you're seriously suggesting you're going to waste time faffing around with some stupid mathematical problems?'

'They're not stupid, Tom.'

'At a time like this? I can't have you prejudicing this investigation.'

Dorothy stared at me. 'Tom, did you just say "I can't have you prejudicing this investigation"?'

'Yes. And?' Was there some kind of problem?

'Since when did you turn into Mr True Detective?'

'Well, someone's got to take charge.' Too bloody right they did.

'Take charge? I'm not sure I'm hearing this right.'

'I rather think you are.' She was definitely hearing it right.

'Tom, I've been following this story right from the damn beginning, and I'm BUGGERED if some upstart is going to muscle in and take it away from me just at the point when I'm just about to solve it.'

'Hold on, YOU'RE about to solve it? Who found the Vavasor papers? Who found the bloody Marginalia? Who found Mrs Standage's address? Ooh, I think I know! Miss! Miss! He's over here! He's over here!' I amplified this by waving my hand in the air and then pointing to myself in an exaggerated manner. It seemed a perfectly reasonable thing to do.

'That was a fluke, Tom, and you know it. If you hadn't bumped into Burgess on that train, you would never have got involved at all.' Dorothy was getting more and more agitated and was now smacking the Vavasor papers down on the table in front of me as she spoke.

'It may have been luck,' I said, 'But by God I was PRE-PARED. You would be NOWHERE without me. I repeat, NOWHERE.'

'Oh, stop being so bloody pompous.'

'I am NOT BEING POMPOUS. I AM JUST TRYING TO MAKE A POINT.'

We were suddenly aware there was a third person in the room. Ali had returned without us noticing.

'So how's Sarah Lund and her disposable sidekick?' she said, coming over to our table.

'Oh, piss off,' we both said in perfect unison. Then we stared at each other and burst out laughing.

'What?' said Ali. 'Have I missed something?'

'We were just—' said Dorothy.

'Sharing a joke,' I said.

'Yes, that's it,' said Dorothy. 'Sharing a joke.'

'Hey!' said Ali, suddenly noticing the case. 'You opened it! Nice work, Dot.'

Dorothy looked embarrassed. 'It… was… actually… Tom,' she said.

'It was a fluke,' I said. This wasn't the time to crow. I would obviously be doing some serious crowing at a later date, but not now.

'Well, there was a kind of a logic to it,' said Dorothy, unexpectedly establishing that she could be magnanimous too.

Ali looked at her, then at me, at her again and then back at me. Then she shook her head and frowned. 'OK, so what have you got?'

'Um… some sweet wrappers,' said Dorothy, 'A torn up birthday card, some racist porn, the manuscript of an unreadable book, oh, and probably the most important mathematical papers to have been produced in the last fifty years.' She underlined the last part of this by displaying the Vavasor papers in a way that would normally mandate the use of the phrase 'tada'.

'Wow,' said Ali. 'So what are you going to do?'

'Well, Tom here's going to go and see the Vavasors' housekeeper. Then he's going to speak to Burgess's agent so he can trade this masterpiece for access to their brother. And I'm going to be spending the rest of the day looking at equations.'

'Groovy,' said Ali. 'I take it you haven't forgotten about the conference call with the guys in Spokane this afternoon?' She seemed mildly peeved.

'Ah.' It seemed that Dorothy had forgotten.

'By the way, you know there's a shifty looking dude on a motorbike hanging around outside our building?'

'Oh shit,' said Dorothy. We all headed over to the window and crouched down so that our eyes were level with the ledge.

'See him?' said Ali.

We did. He was dressed in black leathers and was pacing up and down on the pavement next to a gleaming red motorbike. He'd taken his helmet off and he was talking into a mobile phone while waving his arms about. He looked familiar, although I couldn't place where I'd seen him before.

'Do you think he's phoning for back-up?' I said. I was beginning to sweat.

'Jesus,' said Dorothy.

'We need to get out of here,' I said. 'Is there a back way?'

'There's a rusty fire escape—'

'And we're five floors up, yes, I know. OK, let's think of something else. You don't have any weapons up here, do you?'

'Such as?'

'I dunno. Guns? Grenades? Big sticks?'

'Apart from the contents of the broom cupboard, nothing. So I'm afraid any idea of engaging in any kind of skirmish – even a boutique, Hoxton-appropriate one – is out of the question.'

'Shit,' I said. 'How did he find us, though? Did he follow me or something? I made sure no one was following me. I'm sure I did.'

'He wasn't following *you* exactly,' said Ali from behind us. Dorothy and I turned round and half-crawled, half-walked back to where we'd left the case. Ali was holding something up between her fingers. 'Think your inventory might be a little incomplete. I just found this in one of the inside pockets.'

'What is it?' I said.

'I'd say it was some kind of tracking device, wouldn't you?'

Chapter 20

'What?' I said.

'A tracking device,' said Ali.

'You're kidding.'

'Unless you know any better,' she said, handing it to me. I gave it a thorough examination. Given my limited knowledge of such things, largely drawn from the triumvirate of Bond, Bourne and Spooks, it was certainly possible it was some kind of bug. I passed it back to her.

'But why?' said Dorothy. 'And who?'

'It can't have been put there while I've had it,' I said. 'Unless it was by someone who knew the code.'

'And the only person who did was Burgess, surely?' said Dorothy.

'Maybe he put it there himself? In case he lost the case?'

'Yeah, right,' said Ali. 'We're talking about a man who writes books longhand in green ink. Doesn't compute. Also, how come he's posthumously managed to get biker boy out there on the case?'

'What if Isaac Vavasor wanted to make sure he got the papers back?' I said. 'Maybe he reckoned Burgess might accidentally leave them lying around somewhere.'

'So he attached a device to them?' said Dorothy. 'That came loose inside the case?'

'But why didn't they pick it up in Bristol?' I said.

'Because you were out of range,' said Ali. 'This little widget is designed to have a long battery life, which would mean compromising on signal strength. If the papers went missing while Burgess had them, they'd have a rough idea where to start from. It was never going to work in a more generalised scenario. The only reason matey in the leathers is on our tail is he was hanging around in London and he lucked out.'

'Fair enough,' I said. 'But it doesn't alter the fact that right now we are, to all intents and purposes, under siege.'

Both women looked at me.

'Aren't you being a little overdramatic?' said Dorothy.

'I'm not being dramatic at all. The guy might be armed. His reinforcements might have already arrived. They might be storming up in the lift EVEN AS WE SPEAK. In fact,' I said. 'Give me that tracking whatsit.' The thing was still transmitting away to all and sundry. It had to be destroyed. Why wasn't anyone doing anything about this?

I reached for it, but Ali held it away from me. I went round the side of the table and lunged again, but she backed away further. 'No,' she said, holding her hand up. 'I've got a better idea. One of us,' and she looked at me here, 'is going to take this device downstairs, sneak out the front door and attach it to a passing vehicle.'

'Nice idea,' said Dorothy. She turned to me. 'What do you reckon?'

'Um. Well, it might work. Except… why are you *both* looking at me? Oh, come on. You don't really think… no, no, no. Look, first of all, I'd have to get past that thug on the bike.'

'We don't know he's a thug,' said Dorothy.

'He looks thuggish to me.'

'It's just the leather. You'll be fine.'

'What if he's got a gun?'

'We're in Hoxton, Tom. If anyone found a gun in Hoxton, they'd use it in some kind of post-ironic artwork.'

Ali put her head on one side and gave me the hard stare. 'Tom, are you...?' She let the question hang. The two of them continued to look at me in silence for the entire duration of one of those minutes that actually lasts around six and a half hours.

I sighed. 'Oh, all right then.' Ali handed me the electronic tag and I headed for the door.

I reasoned that the lift might alert the man on the bike to my imminent appearance, so I jogged down the stairs as fast as I could go without making any noise until I reached the final flight. From there I crept down on tiptoe then walked forward to the double doors out into the street. I pressed the button to open the door and nudged it ajar. The biker was directly across the street, with – to my considerable surprise and relief – his back to me. I snuck out and made a dash for the corner. I continued down an alleyway until I came out on a street parallel to Dorothy's office. Now what?

There wasn't a single vehicle in sight. In fact the only traffic sound I could hear at that precise moment was the sound of a motorbike engine. I glanced down at the device in my hand. Shit. He must have spotted it moving.

I was now the target.

I dived into the nearest shop for cover and found myself admiring more accordions than I'd ever seen gathered together in one place. A youngish chap with a luxurious beard and a beret behind the counter was playing 'Non, je ne regrette rien' on one with delirious abandon. Right now, however, *je regrettais beaucoup de choses*. In fact, the list of things that I regretted would stretch most of the way to Swindon.

'Can I help you, man?' he called out, putting the instrument down on the counter. It wheezed out one last mournful note before subsiding into silence.

What I should have said was 'Help, I'm being chased by a thug on a motorbike! Would you mind awfully if I hid in your excellent boutique for a few minutes?' But that felt peremptory, so instead I opted for 'Um... do you sell anything other than...?'

'Accordions?' he said. He leaned back theatrically and looked under the counter. 'Sorry, man, nothing but accordions. We used to do ukes, but obviously... well, you know. They're so last year.'

'I can imagine. Look, I don't suppose I could just—' Out of the corner of my eye, I saw the motorbike pull up on the opposite side of the road. 'Actually, I'd like to have a look at those over there,' I said, pointing to the rack at the rear of the shop.

'Sure, cool.'

I shuffled over and cowered in the relative darkness, while the shop owner watched me curiously.

At that moment, the gloom darkened further as a lorry pulled up outside. I abandoned any pretence of looking at accordions and dashed out.

The lorry was a tautliner with the legend *¡Hola! Un plátano amarillo es un plátano feliz!* on the side, next to a bunch of smiling cartoon bananas. Without a moment's thought I stuffed the tracker under the canvas as far as I could without getting my hand stuck and stepped back.

A few seconds later the lorry moved off and for an instant the biker and I stared at each other across the street, my heart so close to my mouth I could taste it thumping. Then he glanced down at his handlebar and accomplished a perfect U-turn to follow the lorry wherever it went, which according to the writing on the back, was almost certainly Bilbao.

Yesssss!

I'd done it.

I'd actually done it.

I punched the air in triumph.

In fact I was so excited that I very nearly went back into the shop to buy a celebratory accordion. But then it struck me I'd already made enough bad life decisions in the last few weeks. Accordions would have to wait.

Back at the office block I pressed the buzzer to be let in again.

'Well?' said Dorothy's voice.

'Well what?'

'Did you do it? I'm not letting you back in if you didn't.'

'Yes, I did. I've bought you an accordion too.'

'What?'

'Never mind. Just let me in. We need to sort out what to do next.'

The door buzzed open and I took the lift to the fifth floor. Dorothy and Ali were looking through the Vavasors' papers. I spotted the programme for 'SWINdon – a celebration!' and remembered why the man on the bike seemed familiar.

'I saw him in Swindon,' I said. 'Or at least someone very like him.'

'Who?' said Dorothy.

'The biker. He was outside Burgess's house, trying to blag his way in. He was nervous. Shifty, even. When I tried to talk to him he ran off and got knocked down by a car. Then some blokes grabbed him and threw him in the back.'

'Where were you?'

'I was… hiding in someone's front garden.'

'Whoa. My hero.'

'Hey, that's not fair. There were four of them.'

Ali looked up at us. 'If you two are going to go off on one again, I've got other stuff to do.'

'OK, whatever,' said Dorothy, waving her away.

'Don't forget. Spokane. Two thirty.'

'I won't.'

Ali went back to her workstation.

'You guys OK?' I whispered. Dorothy waved a dismissive hand.

'So let's have a quick recap,' she said.

'Good plan.'

'I know it's a good plan, Tom.'

'Right.'

'So let's try this out for size. Isaac Vavasor – for reasons best known to him, although we can speculate – decides to call time on George Burgess. Later that day, Burgess is killed.'

'Serial killer style.'

'By person or persons unknown.'

'Got to be Vavasor, surely?'

'Why?'

It was a good question. 'Maybe Vavasor – or one of his henchmen—'

'Henchmen? Tom, did you really say HENCHMEN?'

'OK, maybe not henchmen.' I felt stupid. I wished Dorothy would stop making me feel stupid. 'Let's say one of Vavasor's men, hench or otherwise, turns up on Burgess's doorstep to pick up the papers – which, of course, he doesn't have – there's a scuffle and Burgess is killed.'

'All entirely plausible, except that if the death was accidental, I'm struggling to see how a mathematician's compass came to be involved. That smacks of deliberation to me.'

'Yeah.' I had to agree it was a good point. 'So what do you think happened?'

'I don't think Vavasor was directly involved in Burgess's death. From what you're saying, his man turned up much later, too late to retrieve the papers.'

'What about the guys who ran him over?'

'Probably circulating round waiting for him to show up. Find them and you'll be one step closer to Burgess's killer.'

'They didn't look like the kind of guys who'd use a compass. They looked like pros.'

'OK. Let's stick with Isaac's boys, then. Would you say our man today was exactly the same person as you saw in Swindon?'

'I can't say for sure. Perhaps they were just related.'

'That would take care of the awkward issue of resurrection.'

'He isn't necessarily dead,' I said.

'OK, but he wasn't even limping today, was he?'

'Good point.'

'I'm full of good points.'

'Hey, who planted the tracking device on the lorry? Eh?' I felt my contribution to the day's efforts was being glossed over.

'Yes, yes. Well done, Ethan Hunt. Good stuff.'

We sat in silence for a minute. Dorothy picked up a pen and started twiddling it between her fingers.

'So are we saying that Isaac Vavasor is definitely out of the frame for Burgess's murder?' I said.

'No. He's just not definitely in it.'

'Oh, good. So if I get an audience with him in return for delivering Burgess's manuscript to Diana Cheeseman, there's still no guarantee I'll get out alive.'

'No. But it's worth the risk.'

'Glad you feel that way.'

'Seriously, do you want to solve this?'

'Yes, but—'

'No buts, Tom. Full commitment. You haven't got a full schedule right now, have you?'

'I suppose not.'

'Do you want to get cracking on Mrs Standage and Diana Cheeseman then?'

'I'm on it. And what are you planning to do while I'm scouring the country for clues?'

'I'll be working on the software delivery and reading the Marginalia.'

'Just the Marginalia?'

'Yes, Tom. I promise. I'll save the juicy stuff for later.'

'Good girl. Listen, you couldn't lend me the price of a train ticket, could you? Save me going to a cash point.'

According to the timetable, I could be there soon after lunch. My stomach rumbled in anticipation, and I wondered if my finances would stretch to a pork pie.

Chapter 21

Lewes was one of those loopy English towns where the Reiki healers outnumber the dentists by a factor of five to one. This made it the perfect place for a woman – and a cat – in possession of dangerous knowledge to hunker down and wait a decade or so for the coast to clear.

Mrs Standage lived in a neat nineteen fifties bungalow tucked away on the outskirts of the town. The front garden was tidy and under twenty-four hour supervision by a small family of resin meerkats. More importantly, a large, fluorescent yellow ambulance was currently parked in her drive.

This didn't look good.

I ran to the open front door and rang the bell. There was no response. I called out 'Hello?' but again there was no response, although I did hear the sound of voices shouting instructions at each other. I crossed the threshold into the bungalow.

Through the doorway into the front room I could see a white-haired woman – presumably Mrs Standage – lying on the floor with a plastic tube stuffed down her throat. The furniture in the room – two armchairs and a coffee table – had all been pushed back against the wall. Her clothing had been torn open and a young, dark-haired paramedic was bent over her vigorously administering CPR.

This really didn't look good at all.

The paramedic's older, balding colleague was kneeling on the floor on the opposite side of their supine patient, peering hard over his glasses at a brightly coloured orange box. Cables ran from the box to a pair of paddles attached to opposite sides of Mrs Standage's chest. A perky female voice announced *Charging complete! Preparing to shock! Clear the area!*

The female paramedic stopped what she was doing and straightened up, wiping her brow. The orange box gave three beeps and Mrs Standage jerked into the air before landing awkwardly on the carpet again. There didn't seem to be any improvement in her condition. The female paramedic leant down and checked for breathing.

'No good, Bob,' she said, before lowering herself back to floor level to recommence pummelling Mrs Standage's inert chest.

Commence CPR!

'I know, I know,' said the paramedic, breathlessly.

Recharging!

'Think I'll give her another shot of adrenaline, Sonali,' said Bob. 'Poor dear's not looking good.'

Bob tore open a sealed package and cracked it open to reveal a pre-loaded hypodermic, which he emptied into a vein in Mrs Standage's arm. This didn't seem to have any effect.

Charging complete! said the defibrillator. *Preparing to shock! Clear the area!*

Sonali hauled herself upright and sat with her head bowed and hands on her knees, breathing heavily.

'You all right, love?' said Bob.

Sonali replied by nodding vigorously and holding a hand up. The defibrillator beeped three times and Mrs Standage's body writhed once more before collapsing back on the floor, unmoving. Sonali checked her again for any signs of life.

'No use,' said Sonali.

Commence CPR!

'How long have we been doing this?' said Bob. 'I reckon time's up. Poor love's not going to pull through, is she?'

Sonali shook her head and stood up. Bob bent down and listened for breathing, before shaking his head and switching off the machine. He peeled the paddles off and packed them neatly away before pulling the clothes back over Mrs Standage's body again.

'That's it, then,' said Sonali. 'She's gone.' She bent down to close Mrs Standage's eyes. 'Time of death,' she looked at her watch, 'fourteen hours twenty-seven.' Then at last she caught sight of me standing in the doorway. 'Can I help you?' she said, standing up again. Sweat glistened on her forehead.

I went into the room. 'Um…' I didn't really know what to say.

'You a relative?' said Bob, tearing off his rubber gloves.

'More of an acquaintance, really,' I said. I couldn't stop myself staring at Mrs Standage. This was only the second dead body I'd seen in my life, and even though my first one was less than a week ago, I still hadn't quite got used to it. 'What happened?' I said.

'Emergency call-out,' said Bob. 'Woman with chest pains. Still conscious when we arrived. Kept muttering "Bad pie" to herself.' Bob nodded towards an area of the carpet where the half-eaten remains of a meat pie lay scattered next to an upside-down plate. 'Steak and kidney, I reckon,' said Bob. He looked like a man who knew his way round a pie. 'Anyway,' he said, 'we did what we could, but she wasn't responding. Then she arrested and it all started getting hairy. Sorry, were you a friend of hers?'

'An acquaintance. Any idea what caused it? Something to do with the pie?'

'Could be. These oldies take any crap that's several years past its sell-by date from the back of the cupboard and just scrape off the mould. Then wonder why they suddenly feel a bit iffy. Trouble is, when you get to the age of Miss Evans here—'

'Standage,' I said.

Bob gave me a puzzled look.

'Standage,' I said again. 'She's called Mrs Standage.'

Bob continued to be confused. 'I'm sure it was Miss Evans,' he said. He turned to look at Sonali, who was busy packing the equipment away. 'Sonali, love? Who is the deceased again?'

She consulted her phone. 'It's a Miss Evans, Bob. Jennifer Evans.'

'Oh,' I said.

'You sure you've got the right place, mate?' said Bob.

'I… yes, actually,' I said. 'Thinking about it, that was her name before she married.' I hoped I sounded convincing.

Fortunately Bob didn't seem troubled. He seemed more concerned about getting on his way. 'Anyway,' he said, cracking his knuckles, 'whoever she is, we'll be needing a post-mortem. C'mon, love, let's get the trolley.'

Sonali got up and followed Bob out of the bungalow, lugging both bags. As they did so, I realised a small, black cat with white feet had entered the room and was peering hard into Mrs Standage's lifeless face. It was advanced in years and its tattered and leathery fur coat looked as if it had been bought at the Oxfam shop and didn't quite fit properly. There was no longer any doubt that this was indeed Mrs Standage lying on the floor in front of me.

'Hello, μ,' I said, bending down to scratch it behind the ear. It bent its head into my hand, mewing pathetically. 'What's going to happen to you now?'

The little cat disengaged itself and sauntered over to sniff at the discarded pie. 'I wouldn't eat that if I were you,' I said, suddenly realising that it might be necessary to intervene. But restraint proved unnecessary, as μ didn't give the dubious pie as much as a single exploratory lick before coming back to rub itself against my leg.

Bob and Sonali returned soon afterwards and lifted Mrs Standage onto a trolley, covering her over with a blanket.

'We'll be off now,' said Bob. 'Can we leave you to sort things out with the neighbours?'

Before I could reply, they had disappeared, taking Mrs Standage with them.

Now what? If only I hadn't spent the morning hiding in accordion shops, I might have got there in time to save her. This was all Ali's fault. I still wasn't sure if I liked her or not.

I decided to take a look round in case Mrs Standage had hidden any clues away in the backs of drawers, although I had a bad feeling that whatever secrets she might have had were already well on the way to the grave with her.

An urgent squeak from near my feet broke into my thoughts and reminded me I was now responsible for someone else's welfare. Where was the cat food?

I found a bowl and some treats in a cupboard and that seemed to keep μ happy. I rummaged through the kitchen cupboards and drawers and found nothing apart from a shopping list written in a neat, purposeful hand that betrayed nothing of the confused lifestyle that Bob had alluded to. All the food was in date and the fridge was immaculately clean.

But there was nothing anywhere in the house relating to Archie and Pye. The only connection remaining between the late Mrs Standage and her equally late former employers was small, four-legged, furry, and currently pestering me for food again. I made a decision there and then. I resolved to take μ back to London with me. I was sure Dorothy and Ali wouldn't mind. A cat was exactly what their office needed. A humanising influence. Or felinising. Or whatever. Everyone liked cats. So I rummaged around and found a carrier in the cupboard in the hall.

'What do you reckon, μ?' I said, stopping to pick the cat up. I took the tiny wail it gave by way of reply as agreement to the proposed plan. It was painfully light and offered no resistance to being bundled into its carrier. After one last check, I headed for the front door.

Chapter 22

μ and I were back outside Dot Chan World Central by late afternoon. Dorothy buzzed me in and we went up in the lift.

'Tom,' said Dorothy, 'what are you doing with a cat carrier?'

I shook my head and put it down on the table.

'What's wrong?' she said.

'This is μ,' I said.

'Oh my God. μ.' Dorothy bent down and peered in at the little cat. 'Aren't you gorgeous?' Then she looked at me and frowned. 'Tom, why have you got μ? Is Mrs Standage…?'

'She's dead, Dorothy. I got there just as the paramedics were calling time on her. If I hadn't wasted time chasing after—'

'Never mind that, what did she die of?'

'I dunno, some kind of heart attack. The paramedics were doing CPR and defibrillator stuff.' I sat down next to the table. Dorothy pulled up a chair opposite me.

'Are you trying to tell me it was natural causes?' She picked up a bent paperclip and started spinning it in between her thumb and forefinger.

'Well, she was quite old.'

'She was in her seventies, Tom. That's not old. Especially for a woman. Did she say anything before she died?'

'Not to me. I was too late. One of the paramedics said she kept muttering "Bad pie" over and over again.'

'Bad pie?'

'Yep. "Bad pie".'

Dorothy sat frowning and twiddling the paperclip for a moment. Then she threw it down and clasped both hands to her forehead. 'Shit! That's it!'

'What's it?'

'Pie! Don't you see? It's a pun. "π".'

'You just said "pie" again.'

'No, not "pie", "π"!'

'And again. This is getting annoying.'

'No, Tom, please listen to me. I'm talking about "π", OK?'

'I am listening to you. What I'm hearing is you saying "Pie" over and over again. It was a steak and kidney pie, if that helps—'

'Aaaaagh!' Dorothy threw up her hands in despair. 'Tom, I'm talking about the mathematical constant π. The one we talked about this morning.'

'Why didn't you say?'

'I did.'

'Oh. Sorry. I've had a difficult day. But what did you say it for?'

'Because it means Mrs Standage's death had a mathematical connection.'

'Oh Christ, I see what you mean.' I suddenly felt cold. I realised I was trembling.

'Exactly,' said Dorothy. 'First the stabbing with a set-square, then one with a compass, a strangulation with a spline and now this. A poisoned π. Four murders. And it's speeding up.'

'Bloody hell.'

We sat considering this for a while, until a squeak from the cat carrier broke the silence.

'Oh my God,' said Dorothy. 'We should let him – her – it – what is it? – out?'

'I think it's a her.' μ reminded me of an old lady in the careful but dignified way she moved.

'Have you got anything for it to eat?'

'I brought some stuff I found at Mrs Standage's.' I looked around. 'Is this place secure? It's not going to escape, is it?' I had another thought. 'Don't suppose you've got a litter tray, have you?'

'Can't imagine where it's going to escape to, so that's not a problem. Do you want to nip out and buy some cat litter?'

'In Hoxton? I'll only get artisan litter made from ethically-sourced organic teff. It'll cost a fortune.'

Dorothy's eyes lit up. 'Got a better idea.' She went over to the corner where some boxes had been piled up. She took one, grabbed a pair of scissors and cut a slot in the side. Then she poured in a load of polystyrene balls from another box. 'That should do it. OK, little one. Time to explore your new home.'

She placed the carrier on the floor and opened the door. A head emerged and peered myopically out.

'Come on out, my darling,' said Dorothy. 'Give me some of her food,' she added, holding out her hand and clicking her fingers. I removed the bowl from the carrier, filled it with some treats and passed it to her. She placed it just out of reach and μ slowly emerged. The cat nibbled at the food then stared up at us.

'Awwwwww,' said Dorothy. 'Isn't she sweet? But how old!'

'I know,' I said. I bent down to look straight into the cat's unfocused eyes. 'Hello,' I said. 'Remember me?'

μ cocked her head on one side as if to say 'You seem vaguely familiar, but remind me again exactly what you do?'

'I brought you here from Mrs Standage's house,' I explained. This seemed to satisfy the cat, who went back to her bowl and licked it clean. For such a tiny animal, she possessed an impressive appetite.

185

'Well, this is all very nice,' said Dorothy eventually, 'but it hasn't got us anywhere nearer solving the mystery. Not unless we can somehow interrogate μ. If anything, there are even more unanswered questions now.'

'Such as?'

'How did the pie get poisoned? How many more mathematical ways to die are there?'

'I'm struggling to think of any.'

'Well, obviously.'

I chose to ignore this. 'So what now?' I said.

'You need to call your agent person straight away and arrange to meet her as soon as possible. Assuming she's still alive, that is.'

'Can I borrow your phone? My battery's running low and I left my charger in Bristol.'

Dorothy sighed. 'Are you sure you'll be able to cope with anything this advanced?' she said as she passed it to me.

'Oh, piss off,' I said. I was beginning to feel protective about my Iron Age phone.

'Cheeseman,' said the voice.

'Thank God,' I said. 'You're still alive.'

'Of course I'm still alive, even if I am under virtual house arrest.'

'I'm sorry?'

'I'm under 24/7 armed protection.'

'Ah. That would explain why you're still alive.'

'I find that remark in considerably bad taste. Who in God's name is this?'

'I called you a week ago. About George Burgess.'

'Oh God, you. The nameless man who calls me a week after the murder of one of my clients dropping oblique hints he might have said client's final manuscript. The day before my late client's publisher – God rest her soul – is also murdered. Call me Miss Marple, but why shouldn't I regard you with anything less than complete suspicion?'

I could see where she was coming from. In her position, I'd be smelling a rat. Actually, I'd be gagging on a whole sewerful of the whiskery buggers. 'Honestly, I'm entirely innocent,' I said. 'I just happened to pick up Burgess's case when he left it on the train.'

She emitted a sort of harrumph. 'Well, we could debate this for hours and it won't get us any nearer to the truth. Look, what do you want? I'm in the middle of an auction and I don't want to be tied up on the phone.'

'I wanted to ask if the deal was still on.'

'What deal?'

'Burgess's manuscript in exchange for information on the Vavasors. Maybe an introduction to Isaac himself?'

The other end of the line went silent for a long time. Finally, she answered. 'Come to my house tomorrow morning at eleven.' She gave me her address. 'Who are you anyway? I'll need to warn security.'

'I'm…' Quick, think of something. Jack Daniels. No, that's terrible. Hang on. 'My name's Beam. Jim Beam.' Jesus. Was that really the best I could do?

There was a brief silence at the other end. 'R-i-i-ight. Eleven o'clock then, Mr Beam.'

I handed the phone back to Dorothy. 'Done,' I said. 'Where's Burgess's manuscript?'

'I put it in the safe,' she said. She went over to a cupboard behind her desk. I watched her spin a dial backwards and forwards before a loud clunk announced that the safe was open. She took out some papers and closed it again, spinning the lock to secure it.

'Here you go,' she said, handing me the manuscript. 'You'd better take this as well.' She passed Burgess's case to me.

'What was the combination again?' I said.

Dorothy sighed. 'e plus π, remember? I still can't believe it's that stupid.'

'I remember that, but I still have no idea.'

Dorothy shook her head. 'You're the world's worst pupil. OK, it's five eight five nine eight seven.' She wrote it down on a Post-It note and handed it to me. I opened the case up and stowed the manuscript safely in there, before closing it and spinning the dials again.

'I take it you still have the Vavasor papers locked away?' I said.

'Of course.'

'Have you had time to—?'

'No, she hasn't had time to do anything with that cack all afternoon,' said an angry voice behind us. Ali had returned, armed with a boxful of pizza and a coffee. 'And if she tries to do anything with it at any time during normal working hours for the next month – where normal working hours equates to seven a.m. through to eleven p.m. – I will shred the fucking lot. We do not need this level of distraction right now, Dot, do we?'

Dorothy winced. 'I can balance both strands of my work quite happily,' she said.

'Really?' said Ali. 'Spokane have given us an exceptionally aggressive schedule. As you are no doubt aware.'

'Leave that to me,' said Dorothy. 'You just sort out your last few bugs, I'll do mine and we'll be ready to go to beta next week, right?'

'I hope so.' There was a sharp intake of breath from Ali. 'Jesus! What the fuck is that?' She was staring down at μ, who was essaying an ineffective hiss back at her.

'It's a cat,' I said. 'She's called μ. She's famous. What's wrong?'

'First of all, if it bites me I'll probably turn into a zombie. That thing looks like one of the purring dead. Secondly, I'm allergic to cats.'

'Look, I'll see if I can find somewhere else,' said Dorothy.

'Don't look at me,' I said. 'I'm currently living in a static caravan with an aging, alcoholic hippy and a hairy dog called Wally for company.'

'Sorry, what?' said Dorothy. I hadn't got around to explaining my changed circumstances.

'Long story,' I said.

'Ah, sod it,' said Ali. 'Haven't got time to argue. I'm going to go back to work. One of us needs to.' She went off to her workstation and began constructing a cardboard box barricade around it.

Dorothy looked at me and shrugged.

'I'll let you know what happens tomorrow,' I said. 'Make sure you look after μ.'

'I will.'

I bent down to look at the tiny cat. 'Make sure she does, right?' I said. 'And don't worry about Ali. I think she's harmless.' She responded with a plaintive wail. 'If cats could talk, eh?' I called out as I headed for the door.

'If only,' replied Dorothy. 'Tom, are you really living in a caravan? Is your life always this much of a mess, or did I just catch you at a bad time?'

'No, it's not a permanent arrangement. I hope.' I was about to go, but something held me back. 'Been quite a day,' I said.

'Yeah.'

'What with opening the case and Mrs Standage and μ and all that.'

'Yeah.'

'Don't suppose you fancy a quick… drink or something?'

Dorothy looked back at me for a long time. Then she shook her head. 'No, Tom,' she said. 'I don't think so.'

I found my father sitting on the caravan step, plucking at a battered guitar, two strings of which were missing, leaving four that shared no common tuning. The level on the bottle of Jack Daniels by his side had dropped considerably since the last time I'd looked. It was hard to judge whether this had made his playing better or worse.

'Evening, son,' he said. Wally looked up from his position at my father's feet and gave me a disdainful look.

'Hi,' I said.

He wiped the top of the bottle and offered me a swig. I declined. 'You all right, son?' he said.

I looked for somewhere to sit down, eventually settling for an abandoned milk crate. 'I'm fine,' I said. 'Bit tired, that's all. Busy day.' I considered bringing my father up to speed on what I'd been up to, but decided against it. There was every chance he'd want to get involved himself, and I owed it to both of us to stop that happening.

'Nah,' he said, leaning forwards and tapping his nose. 'That's not it though, is it? That's not what's winding you up.'

'Oh?'

'Nah, it's a woman. Am I right?' He leant back against the caravan, arms folded in triumph.

I didn't know how to respond to this.

'Bet she's a Pisces,' he continued, rubbing his earlobe between his thumb and forefinger.

'What?'

'Obvious. You being a Sagittarius. Never going to happen.'

'Um…'

'Same thing with me and your mum. I'm an Aquarius and she's a Taurus. That's why we split up, Tom.'

This differed significantly from my mother's account of the marriage breakdown, which centred more on my father being a feckless, old, hippie drunkard. But I held my tongue. Whatever his faults, my father was at least providing me with somewhere to lay my head.

'See that up there?' He nodded towards the clear night sky. 'That's Sagittarius, right there.'

'It's Orion, Dad.'

He ignored me. 'And next to that is Gemini. That's where you should be looking for love, son.'

'What, with extra-terrestrials?' I said.

Once again, he ignored me. 'And, look, there goes the International Space Station,' pointing at an object crossing the sky above us. 'Always brings a lump to my throat.'

'It's a plane, Dad. We're right under the Heathrow flight path.'

He looked hard at me and shook his head. 'Your problem,' he said, 'is you've got no sense of romance.'

Chapter 23

Diana Cheeseman lived in an elegant Georgian townhouse in Highgate. A flight of steps led to the front door, in the centre of which a heavy ring hanging from a fierce lion's head dared me to knock. The door was answered by a close-cropped man who was either an enthusiastic connoisseur of steroids or wearing a stab vest. Or both.

'I've come to see Diana Cheeseman,' I said. 'Jim… Beam.'

'Case,' he said, without returning my smile.

I'd already unlocked the case, so I opened it and showed him the contents. He nodded and I closed it again. Then he scanned me with some kind of electronic tennis racket thing. Then he gave a slight nod and jerked his thumb towards the interior of the house.

'Back,' he said.

I headed off down the passage until I reached the door at the end. I knocked once and a voice called out, 'Come!'

I went in, closing the door behind me.

The room was bright, airy and high ceilinged with a vast fireplace at one end and a solid oak desk alongside a baby grand piano at the other. Several armchairs, a sofa and a chaise longue were scattered artfully around the room. Diana Cheeseman stood facing me, centre stage and silhouetted against the bright sunshine streaming through the French windows behind her.

She was, I guessed, in her early sixties. She was wearing a simple, black dress that probably cost more than I'd spent on clothes in my entire life. She held a lit cigarette in her hand and was fixing me with laser eyes. I went to shake her hand, but she didn't reciprocate. She just kept on looking at me.

Finally, she spoke. 'So, Mr Beam. Or whoever you really are. Give me one reason why I shouldn't hand you over to the authorities via my friend out there as a suspect in the murder of George Burgess and Hilary van Beek.'

I was expecting her to say this. For once in my life, I had actually taken the trouble to think through what was likely to happen and I had a plan. 'If you do that, I can guarantee you won't get your hands on Burgess's manuscript.'

'Oh, but I will. I assume that you have it in that revoltingly ostentatious case?'

'A reasonable assumption.'

'Well, then. I shall simply ask our man to relieve you of it.'

'But it's got a six number combination lock.' Which I'd already given a good spin to on my way through the house. I'd also taken care to place my hand over the setting while I'd shown the case to Mr Roid Rage by the front door.

'Ever heard of the Gordian Knot, Mr Beam? I'll just get someone to saw the bloody thing open.'

'Except for one thing. This type of case is usually used for transporting banknotes. If it is tampered with in any way, it will activate the internal ink spray and your precious manuscript will be ruined.' If you're going to tell a lie, best make it as outrageous as possible. I hoped Diana Cheeseman couldn't spot how much I was sweating at this point.

There was a long silence, during which my host took several long drags of her cigarette. The laser beams were now burning a neat pair of holes in the door behind my head.

'Hmmm,' she said. 'Hmmm.' She waved me over to one of a pair of armchairs looking out onto the back garden. The lawn had been trimmed with a pair of nail scissors and the flower beds exhibited a degree of discipline not usually seen outside a Pyongyang military parade. 'Coffee?' she said.

'So, then,' she said when we were both seated. 'How are we going to do this? I'll need to be sure of your part of the bargain before we start.'

'You want the manuscript before you tell me anything?'

'That would be a good starting point.'

'OK, then.' I was prepared for this as well. Two could play at this game, Diana Cheeseman.

I opened the case and handed her a thick wodge of hand-written papers before locking it again.

She gave the papers a cursory flick through, grimacing as she did so. Then she narrowed one eye and gave me the laser treatment again with the other. 'So tell me, Mr Beam, why should I bother giving you anything in return, now I have the manuscript?'

'Possibly because you only have the first half?' Touché! I was on *fire* today. 'I'll post the remainder through your letterbox when I leave the house.'

'Well, well,' said Diana Cheeseman. 'Aren't we the skilled negotiator?' She shuffled through the papers again. 'The question I should be asking at this point is "How do I know it's genuine?" but I have to say it does look horribly like the work of George Burgess.' She took a sip of coffee. 'Go on, then. Ask me a question. Let's get this over and done with.'

Finally.

'OK,' I said, 'How did you get involved with Burgess?'

She gave a deep sigh. 'I was contacted out of the blue by Isaac Vavasor a couple of years back. Phone only. He doesn't do e-mail and he doesn't turn up in person either. He wanted to know if I would represent a writer who was working on a biography of his brothers.'

'Archie and Pye.'

'Yes, Archie and Pye. So I asked him who it was, and why they didn't have representation already. When he said it was George Burgess, I had to admit I'd never heard of him. I asked around, but no one else seemed to know much about him either.'

'No one had heard of *Shroud of Ecstasy* then?'

Her expression suggested she had accidentally ingested a passing locust. 'It's not the kind of book that usually gets represented by,' she struggled for a phrase, 'let's just say, the kind of people *I* know.'

'It wasn't exactly mainstream.'

'It most certainly wasn't. Have you read it?'

'I tried once.' A lifetime ago.

'I must confess I was baffled as to why the Vavasor estate should have picked him of all people to represent their story. But Isaac was most insistent. It had to be Burgess. No one else would do. I already had several authors on my list who could have done a superb job, but he just wasn't interested.'

'But you still went ahead?'

'I could hardly turn him down. The more I thought about it, the more I felt that this could be massive. Even if Burgess didn't come up with the goods, I was confident I could find someone to ghost the book for him.'

'Had you actually met Burgess?'

There was a long silence. 'No,' she said.

'Ah,' I said.

'Greed makes fools of us all, Mr Beam.' She finished her coffee and reached for her cigarettes. 'Do you?'

I shook my head.

'I was in the middle of giving up when all this started getting messy. I suppose I should try one of those ghastly 'e' things.' She lit a cigarette, took a long drag and leant back in her chair, admiring the view. 'It's lovely at this time of year. You'd hardly know you were in the middle of a city. You know Coleridge is buried just down the road?'

'But you took Burgess on,' I said, wanting to nudge her back towards the subject.

'Yes, I did. Mr Beam, you must understand our business is not always driven by quality. We all love to imagine that every book that races to the top of the bestseller lists has been written by a genius who has honed their God-given talent over years of sweat and inner turmoil, but the sad truth is that what sells is what sells. I was being presented with a hugely saleable proposition that I simply could not ignore, whatever tangled rat's nest of strings might be attached. By the time I finally met Burgess, there was too much momentum behind the thing.'

'But why Head Wind?'

'Ah. Well, this was all very odd. It took some time to turn Burgess's green-ink ramblings into a serviceable proposal, but I really did feel I had something I could work with. I sent it out to some contacts at the Big Five who I was sure would lap it up.'

'What happened?'

'Nothing is what happened. Not a dicky bird. I heard every excuse under the sun. "Doesn't fit with our current direction." "We aren't taking on anyone without full-spectrum social media commitment." "Who wants to read a book about a couple of dead mathematicians?" I tried to probe, but everyone was stonewalling me. One or two indies showed interest then backed off suddenly when we were close to a deal. So we ended up with the fragrant Hilary. With a fraction of the advance we should have had.'

'I would have thought she and Burgess were made for each other.'

'That's a bit harsh, Mr Beam. She may have been a bit of a character, but that's publishing for you. Most people end up in it because they can't find reliable employment elsewhere.'

'You seem to have done all right,' I said, looking around.

'Well, a few of us know what we're doing. Although I confess this whole affair has shaken my confidence somewhat.' She stubbed out her cigarette and fumbled for another one.

'So what do *you* think is going on?' I said.

She lit her cigarette and stared out of the window for a good minute or so. 'You know what?' she said, turning back towards me. 'I think Burgess was deliberately set up to fail.'

'What?'

'It's the only plausible explanation. It's not the whole story by any means, but it's a good starting point.'

'But why?'

'Consider who's been permitted to view the papers. Initially, the only people allowed anywhere near them – under close supervision in a locked room – were maths professors. Why do you think that was?'

'Weren't they looking for a proof of the Riemann hypothesis or something? To somehow validate the twins' work?'

'Indeed. But the glühwein incident put paid to that.'

'Couldn't they have just used a copy?'

'I don't think it was the glühwein *per se*. It was more what it symbolised. The intrusion of the outside world. Remember Isaac Vavasor was recovering from an extreme and very public trauma. It would be unreasonable to expect him to behave in an entirely rational manner.'

'Which would also explain Margot Evercreech.'

'Ah yes. Margot Evercreech, who inveigled her way into the household on the pretext of an interview. Wouldn't surprise me if she didn't let him get his leg over.'

'Really?'

'Wouldn't surprise me at all. She's impressively shameless and Isaac was vulnerable. Do you know much about him?'

'Nothing at all.'

'No, hardly anyone does. Nothing like as clever as either of his brothers, but just as awkward. Anyway, Ms Evercreech persuaded him to let her have a look at his brothers' proverbial etchings and came out blabbering to the world about the bloody Marginalia.' She sighed. 'And that's where it all went horribly wrong.'

'In what way?'

'As you must have realised from a cursory scan of the various internet forums relating to, oh God, what I suppose I *must* refer to as Vavasorology,' she rolled her eyes at this. 'Margot's fevered reports about the Marginalia were catnip to every nutter and loon across the globe.'

'I bet.'

'And of course no one had a clue what it meant because neither of the buggers had remotely legible handwriting and most of it had nothing to do with mathematics anyway. Shopping lists. Things to do. Crossword solutions. Didn't stop all those ridiculous books being written, though.'

'I know. I've got several of them.'

'Have you read any?'

'I haven't got around to it.'

'Don't bother.'

'So was that why they brought in Burgess?' I said. 'It still seems unlikely.'

'Somewhere at the heart of this, there is a big secret. One Isaac would like to keep buried. Maybe Margot Evercreech really did see something. Maybe Isaac was desperately afraid the truth might get out one day. By hiring someone like Burgess to write the official account, giving him sole access to the Marginalia, perhaps Isaac was intending to muddy the waters and effectively shut the whole discussion down. He could legitimately say: "Look, he's seen the Marginalia, and they don't mean what you think they mean." I'm not saying it was a particularly well thought through plan, but it explains a few things.'

'Except Burgess went off at a completely different tangent.'

'That's the trouble with a loose cannon. They're hard to rein in once they're rolling.'

'But are you saying that Isaac Vavasor went so far as to have Burgess killed? Seems a bit over the top. And in that case, did he kill Archie? That's bonkers.'

'Maybe that's the big secret. Or maybe there's something else going on. There are a lot of parties involved in this who all want different things. What do *you* want, Mr Beam?'

'I don't know,' I said. 'The truth, I guess. Or at least *a* truth. Something true, anyway.'

She suddenly grasped my arm. 'Find out for me, Mr Beam. I can't stand living like this.'

I stood up. 'What are you going to do with the manuscript?' I said.

'I'll probably shred it. No one's going to want to publish it. They didn't want to when we first tried and they certainly won't touch it now. There might have been a window of opportunity when it looked like he was the only new victim, but it's well and truly closed.'

'So what was all the fuss about a deal?'

She gave a sad shrug. 'Indulge me, Mr Beam. I'm trapped here. Don't blame me for having a little fun. But one thing I'll say is that it proved you're a little more resourceful than you perhaps thought. Use that, Mr Beam. Use it well.'

Chapter 24

Dorothy was in a state of excitement when I got back. Before I could say a word about Diana Cheeseman, she started gabbling at me.

'Look,' she said. 'I think I know what the rest of it says.' She was holding up the torn lower half of the 'Forever Friends' monstrosity we'd come across when sorting through the contents of the case.

'What's Burgess's birthday card got to do with this?' I said.

'It's not from Burgess,' she said. 'It's nothing to do with him at all.'

'I expect you want me to say "Who's it from, then?" but I suspect you're not going to answer that straight away.'

'How did you guess?'

'It's that "Look at me, aren't I clever" expression you're wearing. Dead giveaway.'

'Spoilsport. I've half a mind not to tell you now.'

'Oh, go on then,' I sighed. 'This had better be good.'

'It's awesome. It changes everything.'

'Well, in that case, off you go.'

'OK,' said Dorothy, taking a deep breath, 'I think the missing part of the message is "HOW I WISH".'

'That's it? Look, I think you need to hear what Diana Cheeseman said, because that's far more—'

'No, wait. If you put the whole message together, you get "HOW I WISH I COULD FORNICATE MY LOVELY VIXEN".'

'Oddly enough, I'd worked that out already.'

'Count the letters.' Dorothy was beaming.

'Sorry?'

'Count them.'

'Why?'

'Just. Count. Them. Now.' She paused. 'Please.'

'OK, OK, I got it. Three. One. Four. One. Five. Nine. Two. Six. Five.' Something went 'ping' in my brain. 'Holy shit!' I said. 'That's π!'

'You see? It's a mnemonic.'

'Please don't tell me π mnemonics are a thing.'

'Yep. The most common one goes something like "How I wish I could recollect pi easily today", but there are others that are much longer. There's even a book based on the first ten thousand digits.'

'Jesus. But hold on, what does this mean?'

'It means that it was Pye who was intending to send this card. Secretly. What's more, the very fact of its existence probably means he was intending to send it on the day he died.'

'Because otherwise it would have just been thrown away.'

'Exactly. And – oh my God – I've just thought of something else. What if Mrs Standage didn't mean "Bad Pie" or even "Bad π" but "Bad Pye"?'

'Whoa there. Dorothy, I think we had a similar conversation yesterday. Except this one makes even less sense than that one did.'

'"Bad Pye", Tom. "Bad Pye".'

'You're at it again, Dorothy.'

'Oh, for God's sake. Do I have to spell it out? Bad Pythagoras, Tom.'

'Oh shit. I see what you mean. Bad Pye. She wasn't describing how she got murdered at all, was she? She was telling us her big secret. Bad Pye. Pye did something bad.'

'Ah, we got there eventually.'

'Hey, we aren't all bloody geniuses. So what did Pye do, then?'

'Good question,' said Dorothy. 'Something to do with a "vixen". Find her and maybe we'll find out what he did that was so bad.'

'Anything in the Marginalia?'

Dorothy glanced across at Ali, who was bashing away at her keyboard like a six-armed, mutant clone of Animal from The Muppets. 'Haven't looked yet,' she said, turning back in my direction.

'Hmmm,' I said. 'I wonder. Is it possible that Pye was killed because he was shagging someone he shouldn't have been shagging? Is it that simple?'

'That's what I've been wondering. It would certainly provide a motive, wouldn't it?'

'It's a bit odd, though. I'd sort of assumed they were celibate.'

'Why?'

'Um… because—'

'You're not really going to say "because they were a pair of geeks", are you? Because, believe it or not, geeks have sex too. That's where baby geeks come from, you know.'

'I wasn't saying that at all.' For some reason, I could feel myself reddening at this point.

'Go on, then. What were you going to say?' She seemed to be laughing at me.

'Look, it doesn't matter. The point is, it's entirely possible to imagine that one of them was involved with a woman.'

'We've got to find the vixen.'

'Yep. She's the key to everything.' I grimaced. 'Although on past form, there's every chance she's dead already.'

'Let's hope not. Did you get anything from Diana Cheese-man? Did you get an audience with Isaac?'

'Not as such.'

'Not as such?'

'All right, not at all. I didn't even ask. I don't think she's ever met him.' I gave a rough précis of my conversation with Diana Cheeseman, taking care to emphasise her closing remarks regarding my exceptional resourcefulness. Dorothy chose to ignore this.

'Ironic, isn't it?' I said. 'Burgess was closer than he thought.'

'In what way?'

'He thought it was all about sex. Maybe it was. Just not the way he imagined.'

'Poor guy. He was doomed from the start, wasn't he?'

There was a sudden commotion from the other side of the room.

'Will you just FUCK OFF?' shouted Ali, picking μ off her desk and dropping her onto the floor. The little cat gave Ali a hurt look but stayed close, biding her time and waiting for the next opportunity to climb up and annoy her.

'I see they're bonding well,' I whispered to Dorothy.

'Yes, μ is besotted with her,' she said. 'The feeling isn't entirely mutual yet, but I'm sure Ali will come round sooner or later.'

'I'm going with later,' I said. 'Where's the barricade gone?'

'Ah, that. μ wasn't sure which box to use for a litter tray last night and crapped in one of hers. Ali was less amused than I was.'

'I can see her point.'

Dorothy sighed. 'If only we could ask μ what happened to Archie.'

'Hang on, though,' I said. 'We can.'

'What? Sorry, Tom, are you proposing that we learn to talk cat?'

203

'Hear me out. Why don't we find some pictures of the main players and show them to μ to see how she reacts?'

'That's actually not quite as daft as it sounds,' said Dorothy.

'You're doing that surprised look again. I don't like it.'

'Yeah, well. OK, grab μ and I'll see if I can find some images.'

μ was wandering aimlessly around Ali's desk, every now and then straying within reach of either of Ali's feet, which responded by nudging her out of the way. I went over and picked her up. God, she was so light and bony! Poor thing.

Ali looked up. 'Euthanasia time?'

'No!'

'Ah, come on,' said Ali. 'You know it's just a question of when.'

'That's as maybe. Until that time comes, we have a moral duty to ensure she enjoys her twilight years with as much comfort and dignity as we can provide.'

'So you're proposing we should diversify into some kind of care home for elderly felines? Where they can lie all day in piss-soaked armchairs watching Jeremy Kyle and hurling racist abuse at the carers?'

'She's a special cat, Ali.'

'Yeah, right. Good word, "special".'

I hugged μ close to me. 'Don't listen to the nasty woman,' I said. For her part, μ hissed at Ali as if to say to me, 'Thank you, but I can look after myself.' Ali shook her head and went back to work.

'How are you doing?' I said to Dorothy.

'OK,' she said. 'I've got Pye Vavasor lined up already.'

'Pye? Wouldn't Archie be more appropriate?' I said.

'Tom.'

'What?'

'Tom.'

'Still not getting it.'

'Think about it, Tom.'

'Ah, right. Identical twins?'

'Yep.' Of course.

'But will μ understand that?'

'I don't think it will be an issue, Tom.' Dorothy's purse-lipped expression was one I recognised as having been used on many occasions by both my mother and several of my schoolteachers. And Lucy, now I came to think about it.

'Fair enough. Who else?'

'There's a blurry shot of Isaac Vavasor here. Hold on, are you sure μ isn't watching this? We need to make sure she comes to the process cold.'

'I'd already thought of that,' I said, indicating μ's face, which was firmly tucked into my armpit.

'Good. Who else?'

'Rufus Fairbanks?'

'Why?'

'Dunno. Can't help feeling there's some connection. Why was he so keen to see me?'

'OK, I'll see what I can do. One moment… ah yes, got him. Hmmm. Can't find any pictures of Mrs Standage. Be useful as a control.'

'Try Evans. Jennifer or Jenny. In Lewes.'

'Why?'

'That's the name she was using.'

'Ah, here we go. *Lewes Advertiser* report on a flower show. Jenny Evans. Third prize in the fuchsias. Right, we're good to go.'

'Cool. So how are we going to do this? Five seconds exposure to each image? Long enough for her to take it in and react.'

'She's half-blind, Tom. Might need a bit longer to work out who's who.'

'Ten seconds then.'

'Fifteen. Are you going to keep hold of her? That way you can measure how much she squirms.'

'Good point. Which raises the issue of what we're measuring. Squirms are definitely significant. Hissing?'

'Very significant, I'd say.'

'A squirm and a hiss?'

'Prima facie evidence for murder, I'd say.'

'Sounds good. Let's do it.'

'Right then,' said Dorothy. 'First image coming up. Are you ready?'

The first image was of Mrs Standage. I turned μ around to face the computer and she immediately tried to crawl out and sniff the screen. Then she sat on the desk pawing at the image, purring and making odd, little chirruping noises until Dorothy closed the image. I picked her up and settled her back on my lap.

'I think we have a workable baseline,' said Dorothy.

'Yup,' I said. 'You OK?' I said to μ, but she didn't seem overly troubled about her unexpected encounter with her previous owner. Cats clearly took this sort of thing in their stride.

'Ready for another?'

'We're hot to trot.'

μ's reaction to Rufus Fairbanks was very different. She squirmed. She hissed. She yowled. Her fur bristled. It was all I could do to stop her from scratching at the screen and we terminated the showing well short of fifteen seconds.

'Well,' I said, after μ had quietened down. 'That was unexpected.'

'It was.' Dorothy took a deep breath. 'How is she?'

μ's heart was still thumping. I looked down at her. She looked up at me, as if to say, 'Well, that wasn't very nice, was it?'

'I'm sorry, μ,' I said. 'But sometimes we have to revisit bad times if we're going to catch bad people.' μ didn't seem convinced by this argument.

'Wonder what cat-speak for "trigger warning" is?' said Dorothy.

'Yeah. I feel bad about this.'

'Let's carry on, though. We need to finish it.'

'I guess so. You ready?' I said to μ. μ didn't reply.

The next picture was Isaac Vavasor. μ didn't react at all, apart from rolling over on her side and trying to look cute.

'Probably never met him,' said Dorothy.

'Or just plain indifferent.'

'Yeah. Last one then.'

'OK.'

μ's reaction to Pye (or indeed Archie) was low key. She climbed onto the desk, sat there in front of the screen for a moment or two then climbed back onto my lap, before jumping down and wandering back towards Ali's desk.

'Not sure what that means,' I said.

'It's been ten years since she last saw either of them.'

'True. More than half a lifetime for her. Never mind, you did well, little one.' I'd brought a small box of treats with me and I put a handful down on the floor. μ turned round, peered at them and then ambled back. She hoovered up the treats before resuming her journey to the other end of the office.

'So where does that leave us?' said Dorothy.

'Rufus Fairbanks?' I said.

'Maybe, but why?'

'God knows. There's something we're missing, but I haven't a clue what it is.'

'If we had a clue, we wouldn't be missing it. Is Fairbanks still trying to get hold of you?'

'Don't know. My phone's out of battery and my charger's with my stuff in Bristol.'

Dorothy gave me a quizzical look.

'I left in a bit of a hurry,' I said. 'After crashing my girlfriend's car while not being chased by the Belarusian mafia and then finding out she was seeing someone else.'

'Ah.'

'Still, the only way is up.'

'I wouldn't bet on it. There's quite a lot more that could go wrong.'

'Thanks. Really appreciate that.'

'You're welcome.'

'Actually, I should go back and pick up some things. Maybe I'll think of something on the train.'

'Really?'

'No.'

Dorothy suddenly gave me an odd look.

'What?' I said.

'Just had an idea. Not sure if it's a good one or not.'

'Go on.'

'I've been wondering about those papers. Ever since we found that tracking device. Is it sensible to keep them here?'

'But don't you want to have access to them? Come on, you've got a safe.'

'Maybe I'll have to do without that for a while. The papers are more important than me. Safes can be broken into. Better to hide things sometimes. If you're going to Bristol, you must know somewhere discreet you can park them for a while.'

'I know somewhere even better. Where no one will ever think of going.'

'Where?'

'Trust me.' I tapped my nose.

'I can't believe I'm about to do precisely that,' said Dorothy.

'Cometh the hour, cometh the—'

'Don't overdo it, Tom.'

'Fair enough.' I watched as Dorothy went to the safe again and handed me the papers. I put them in Burgess's case and spun the wheels to lock it.

Something was nagging at the back of my mind. 'That picture of Fairbanks you found,' I said. 'Couple of other dudes in it. Any idea who they are?'

'Dunno. It just came up on Google images.'

'Find it again.'

Dorothy fiddled about on the computer. 'There it is. City A.M. Ten years ago.'

The picture showed a younger Fairbanks shaking hands with two heavy-set men in dark suits.

'Thought he looked slimmer. What's going on there?' I said.

'Something to do with a finance deal for shale oil extraction.'

'Anything about the other guys?'

'Nope. It's just a general article on shale oil investment. Fairbanks is the only one identified.'

'Bugger.'

Dorothy shook her head. 'What if μ wasn't hissing at Fairbanks at all?' she said. 'Maybe it was one of the other guys.'

For a brief hour or two, it had seemed as if we were making some kind of progress in unravelling the tangled ball of threads that made up this affair. But now it seemed as if μ had grabbed it and was rolling gleefully around with it in the corner.

Not only that, but things were about to get a whole load worse.

Chapter 25

After another uncomfortable night in the caravan, I got back to Bristol around lunchtime, having left Burgess's case safely stowed in the front offside wheel arch. It had been only three days since I left, but it seemed more like three lifetimes. I'd spent the journey trying to make sense of everything, but everywhere I looked there seemed to be one key detail that was eluding me.

I did briefly consider going to the police, but there was every chance I would be taken for a crank. It was even possible that I could end up being charged with stealing evidence, in the form of a small black and white cat.

I hadn't warned Lucy I'd be coming and she probably wouldn't be in. However I still had a key. All I needed to do was let myself in, grab my charger and clothes and head back to London.

The key didn't fit. She'd changed the bloody lock. Did she really not trust me? However, I was in luck, because I could hear movement inside: the clanking of machinery. I rang the bell. The clanking continued. I rang the bell again. Still nothing. I hammered on the door. Whatever it was, the machinery was still banging away.

Mercifully, it stopped. I rang the bell once more and this time I heard footsteps heading in my direction. There was a brief pause, then I heard the chain being taken off. The door opened to reveal a man standing there wearing nothing but a pair of orange boxer shorts.

Actually, the simple word 'man' didn't come close to doing justice to the primordial creature in front of me. His perfectly tanned body was the precise shade of brown identified as 'Adonis Bronze' on the Dulux paint chart. He had muscles for which the names hadn't been invented yet. His biceps were the size of an elephant's leg, as were his triceps and quadriceps. He probably had a few quinticeps lying around somewhere as well. If asked to choose a telephone directory to tear in half, he would most likely go for the London one. He could crack a walnut open with his earlobe.

'Can I help you?' he said. I recognised the accent – it was similar to one I'd heard a couple of weeks back, outside George Burgess's house in Swindon.

'Er, yes,' I said. 'I'm Tom.' After a moment's hesitation, I held out my hand. There was every chance it would end up being crushed to a bloody pulp if this monster reciprocated, but I felt I should be polite. Fortunately he didn't respond to my overture. Instead he frowned, as if trying to remember where he had heard the word 'Tom' before.

'Ah, Tom,' he said eventually, with a sad shake of the head. 'Tom Tom Tom Tom Tom.'

'Yes,' I said, 'Tom.'

'I am Arkady,' he said, gesturing for me to enter the flat.

Ah.

I imagine it's always awkward to be invited back into your erstwhile home by the very man who was the primary reason for your exit, but needs must. I went in, trying not to stray too close to Arkady. He was sufficiently massive to have his own gravitational field and I didn't want to end up stuck to him.

The place had changed since the last time I'd been there. For one thing, there was enough machinery lying around the place to equip a decent sized gym. Or possibly some kind of torture chamber – it was hard to tell with some of it. The centrepiece was a vast rowing machine that stretched all the way down the corridor and which had clearly been the source of the noise I had heard while hovering outside.

'So, Tom,' said Arkady, hauling a ripped T-shirt over his upper body. 'We meet.' Either he had trouble finding any shirts that fitted him or he suffered from a similar condition to the Incredible Hulk. He folded his arms and leant back against the kitchen work surface, which creaked slightly but stood its ground.

'Yes,' I said. There was an awkward silence. 'I came to pick up some things.'

'Ah. Some things.'

Another awkward silence.

'Lucy is very beautiful lady,' said Arkady.

'I know.'

'She very intelligent too.' He wagged a finger at me. 'I think maybe you not smart enough for her.'

WHAT?! This ape was telling me I was too thick for Lucy? I was speechless, which was a good thing because if I had said what I should have said there would not have been much of me left afterwards.

'Lucy needs – what is your English phrase? – intellectual stimulation. I don't think you give this to her.'

'I don't think—'

Arkady shrugged. 'Is just advice. Maybe next time you find someone closer to your level.'

'Now wait a minute, sunshine. I'm not going to take this from a bloody Zumba teacher.' Actually, on reflection, I probably was going to be taking it. There wasn't a lot I could do about it.

'Ha,' said Arkady. 'I am pathologist. I teach Zumba until I pass English exam. Lucy help me. She very good teacher.'

'Really?' The idea of Lucy teaching anyone anything struck me as bizarre. Maybe I had underestimated her as well.

Arkady reached into the fridge and came out with two bottles.

'Beer?' he said.

'Sorry?'

'Do you want beer? Is lunchtime. Is also cheese, rye bread, smoked sausage and beetroot.'

I considered this for a second or two and then hunger got the better of me. Breakfast had consisted of a couple of stale custard creams I'd found in the back of a cupboard, and one of them had the distinct smell of Wally about it.

I made myself a cheese and smoked sausage sandwich and took a mouthful to take the edge off my appetite. It wasn't at all bad. The beer, a Russian brand I hadn't come across before with the name of Летучая мышь моча сатаны, was also unexpectedly palatable.

'Sit,' said Arkady, who was now seated at the kitchen table. I sat down opposite him.

'Are my things still where I left them?' I said, glancing around. 'I'd like to charge my phone up.' I was feeling exposed without it.

Arkady shook his head. 'Eat first. Phone later.'

'Right,' I said. 'OK.'

We ate together in silence.

'So you're from Minsk?' I said.

'Yes.'

'And you're a pathologist?'

'Yes.'

'Is it easy to become a pathologist in Belarus?'

'No. Is difficult.'

'I see.'

'Is difficult everywhere to become pathologist.'

'Ah.'

There was a long pause. Arkady seemed deep in thought. 'Is easy to become PR man, no?'

'Well—'

'In Belarus we have no PR men.'

'Are you suggesting they need people like me?'

'No.'

'Oh.' I hadn't been anywhere near serious, but I felt more than a little deflated by his response. I finished my sandwich and drained my bottle of beer. I pushed my chair back and began to stand up.

'Sit,' said Arkady. 'I make coffee.'

'Actually, I don't—'

'I make coffee.'

'Fine. Fine. No sugar, though, please. And black.'

The coffee was delivered in a mug featuring a red and green flag with the legend I ♥ BELARUS. It was indeed entirely milk-free, but it did have half a dozen teaspoons of sugar in it. It took two hands to get the spoon turning. I could feel my teeth rotting away as I drank it. When we had finished, I was at last permitted to leave the table.

My phone charger was still plugged in where I'd left it, next to my laptop in the living room. I reached into my pocket for my phone and then I thought I might as well check some things on the computer first.

'Mind if I check my e-mails?' I said. I had no idea why I thought I needed his permission, but it felt more comfortable to make sure.

'Sure,' said Arkady. 'Go ahead.'

Then I remembered I hadn't been on *Vavasorology.com* for a few days.

I logged in.

The events of the last week or so had clearly had an energising effect on the Vavasorologist community, to judge by the number of new threads on the forum. I took particular delight in the half dozen devoted to speculation about the present whereabouts of μ. Poster *MsStandage2U* had apparently seen a cat answering μ's description wandering around a disused car park in Hove. The evidence for this was a blurred photograph reminiscent of the ones that tended to accompany stories of rural myths like the Beast of Bodmin. Further posts poured cold water on this, putting up pictures of other black and white cats of advanced years on, respectively, Brighton pier, the front at Peacehaven and the stage at Glyndebourne during an all-male production of *La Fanciulla del West*. She had become the Vavasorologists' Elvis.

There was, of course, much discussion about Mrs Standage's death and I was alarmed to read of the mysterious friend who had apparently turned up at the house while the paramedics were trying to resuscitate her. Fortunately, it was evident that neither Bob nor Sonali had taken much notice of me as neither of them had provided anything close to an accurate description. The general feeling was Mrs S had been living on borrowed time for the last decade and while it was all very sad, it had been horribly inevitable. I detected an undercurrent of resentment from several posters, as if she had spoiled their fun by going underground and keeping mum.

There was even less sympathy for Hilary van Beek, as it turned out that Benjamin Unsworth was a regular – if currently silent – poster on the forum, with the name *PoorIntern*, under which he had contributed a number of seemingly off-topic posts complaining about how he was treated in his job at a small publisher. It didn't take long for the rest of the forum to put two and two together and work out which small publisher he had been talking about.

The only thread that held out the promise of new information was one started by *UltimateTruth*, who I remembered Dorothy as saying was 'pretty reliable'. The thread had the enigmatic title 'Yes, but what about Viv?' This was the first post:

> *Was thinking about who might be next. Wondering about Viv.*

The first reply was from a poster called *Knobhead*, whose work I'd spotted elsewhere on the forum:

> *Who teh fucks Viv*

This was entirely typical of *Knobhead*, who seemed to spend most of his time on *Vavasorology.com* either making lame puns or indulging in small-scale flame wars of increasing venom until threatened with expulsion by the moderators.

But *UltimateTruth*'s response to this was curious, to say the least:

> *May be closer than you think, Knobby.*

I didn't understand this at all. Evidently, neither did *Knobhead*:

> *Your mental mate*

What the hell was that all about? That brief exchange seemed to be dangling some significant information in front of me about George Burgess's mysterious dedicatee – 'The Long-Suffering and Ever-Faithful Viv'. If only I could grasp what it actually was. I searched the board for any more references to Viv, but there was nothing remotely helpful. No one apart from *UltimateTruth* seemed to have a clue.

The more I thought about it, the more I became convinced that Viv was in fact the key to the entire mystery. Or was I clutching at straws? I decided to run it past Dorothy. She was bound to have a theory or two. I reached for my phone and at this point I remembered I hadn't charged it up yet. Cursing, I grabbed the lead that was dangling from the wall and plugged it in.

After a few minutes the screen flickered into life and then it started pinging to tell me that I had several texts, loads of missed calls and a couple of voicemails. Apart from a single text from Rufus Fairbanks, which I deleted without reading, all the texts and missed calls were from the same, unknown number:

> *Where are you Tom?*
> *Please call me*
> *Something bads happened*
> *This is Ali BTW*

Ali?! What did she want? Had she finally flipped and attacked µ? Or had something happened to Dorothy? Oh Christ. Something had happened to Dorothy.

I hit the button to listen to my voicemails. The voice was definitely Ali's, but with a level of emotion in it I hadn't heard before.

'Tom, it's Ali. She's… I mean Dot… I mean… oh shit, oh shit, oh fucking shit.'

The voice broke up completely and the first message ended. Trembling, I hit the button again.

'Tom. You've got to do something. I don't know what but you've got to. It's Dot. They've taken her, Tom. She's been fucking kidnapped.'

Chapter 26

I sat there for a whole minute, staring at my phone and trying to get my breathing back to normal. Then I listened to the voicemail again, just to make sure I hadn't imagined it.

I hadn't.

The messages were all from around eleven o'clock that morning. I cursed myself for not insisting on plugging the phone in earlier.

I called Ali. She answered before it rang even once.

'Where the fuck have you been?' she said.

'Never mind. What's happened?'

'Did you get my message? They've taken Dot.'

'Who?'

'I don't know. Some blokes in a big car. You've got to do something. We've got a fucking deadline to meet for these guys in Spokane and—'

'Never mind Spokane!'

'Easy for you to say that, pal.'

'Ali, this isn't about Spokane, it's about Dorothy.'

'I KNOW IT FUCKING IS. I'M JUST TRYING TO AVOID FUCKING THINKING ABOUT IT.'

There was an awkward silence.

'Sorry,' I said. 'What happened, then?'

'I went out to get a coffee and as I turned round the corner, there was this big, black car parked outside—'

'Mercedes?'

'How do I know? Yeah, probably. Anyway, before I get any closer, these heavy guys in dark glasses come out of the building, carrying Dot between them. I start to run after them but before I get halfway to the car, they've driven off.'

'Bastards.'

'Yeah, I know. So I go up to the office and the place has been fucking ransacked. Shit thrown everywhere.'

Oh God. I had a sudden thought. 'Is μ all right?'

'Oh yeah. That thing'll survive Armageddon. After the big one drops, it'll basically be cockroaches and μ. Found her cowering in a corner.'

'But what were they after?' I already knew the answer to that one.

'Probably that crap you and Dot are always going on about. The... you know... mathematical stuff. The stuff in the safe. The door was wide open and there was fuck all left in there.'

'Good thing I've hidden the papers then,' I said.

'What?'

'I hid them last night.'

'You did what?'

'I hid them.'

'You fucking numpty.'

'I may be a numpty, but it's probably the only reason Dorothy's still alive.'

There was a short pause.

'OK, So what do we do now?'

'I haven't a bloody clue, Ali.'

'Me neither. I'm scared, Tom.'

'Me too.' Then I had an idea. 'Hold on. I've just realised. I can ask Arkady.'

'Who the fuck's Arkady?'

'Belarusian bloke. Living with my ex-girlfriend. He's in my kitchen right now. Hang on.' I tried to stand up, but I'd forgotten that my phone was still attached to the wall and it jerked me back down again. 'Shit!' I said. 'Look, I'm going to have to put the phone down.'

I went back to the kitchen, where Arkady was still sitting at the table, a pair of headphones on his head, looking intently at a book and mouthing random English phrases to himself.

'Arkady?' I said.

There was no response. I waved a hand in front of his eyes. He looked up at me and took the headphones off.

'What?' he said.

'Arkady, we have a problem. What do you know about the Belarusian mafia?'

He narrowed his eyes. 'Why you want to know?'

'I think a friend of mine has been kidnapped by them.'

He shrugged. 'Your friend is dead.'

'No, that's not true! It can't be true. Please tell me it's not true.'

'Is true. They very bad people. He dead.'

'She. She's a she, Arkady.'

Arkady raised an eyebrow before shrugging again. 'She dead, then.'

'Don't say that. Please don't say that.'

'I am sorry. But nothing you can do. She dead.'

'Please stop saying that! Maybe life is cheap where you come from, but round here we like to think there is hope sometimes. We're a bit more civilised.'

'We civilised too. We have Svetlana Alexievich. She Nobel Prize winner in literature.'

'WHO? WHAT'S SHE GOT TO DO WITH DOROTHY?'

'She win Nobel Prize. We very proud of Svetlana.'

'I DON'T BLOODY CARE ABOUT SVETLANA. I WANT TO KNOW HOW TO GET DOROTHY BACK.'

'I am sorry. Your friend is dead. Sorry for your loss.'

'HOW CAN YOU SAY THAT?'

'I am pathologist. I see many dead bodies. Calm down, Mr Tom. Please. I need to finish my learning.'

'WHAT ABOUT DOROTHY?'

Arkady shook his head and put his headphones back on. I stomped back to the living room, fuming. I picked up the phone.

'Well, that went well,' I said. 'I said, THAT WENT WELL.' I looked at the phone. The connection to Ali had dropped while I'd been talking to Arkady. 'Oh, for fuck's sake,' I said to myself, just stopping myself in time from smashing the phone against the wall.

This was awful. Dorothy had been abducted by a bunch of goons from the Belarusian mafia and there was nothing I could do about it. For all I knew, Arkady could be right and she might already be dead.

Worst of all, deep down I knew it was my fault.

If I hadn't picked up Burgess's case and brought it to her, this would never have happened. Instead, right now she would be working with Ali on their game thing and generally getting on with her life. Like I should have been. We were in this way over our heads. A bunch of kids messing around in a grown-ups' world.

My phone went off. It was Ali. I grabbed it and fumbled for the answer button.

'Hi,' said Ali. 'It's me.'

'I know. Heard anything? Arkady thinks... well, never mind what he thinks, but—'

'Shut up for a moment. They called the office. I had trouble working out what they were saying but I'm pretty certain Dot's still alive. I think they want to do a swap. Dot in exchange for the Vavasor papers.'

'Oh God. Thank God for that. Arkady said she'd be dead.' I broke off and shouted, 'SHE'S NOT DEAD!' in the direction of the kitchen. There was no response, so I went back to Ali. 'Where?' I said. 'How? What?'

'Calm down. They want to meet somewhere down your way. Something like… Pilton Chumpsey?'

'Pilton Chumpsey?' I racked my brains. 'That's in the Levels, isn't it?'

'No idea. Best for you to talk to 'em. I'll text you the number.' There was a beep in my ear. 'Tell me where the papers are and I'll bring them down on the next train.'

'No,' I said. 'You need to look after μ. I'll handle this. Use a courier.'

There was a silence. 'Seriously? You want ME to look after μ?'

'Someone's got to. She's a key piece of evidence if this all goes tits up. I don't want to risk moving her again.'

'It better hadn't go tits up, sunshine.' There was another pause. 'You seriously want me to stay here with that moth-eaten freak while you swan around saving Dot?'

'Yes I do. I think you like her really.'

'No I fucking don't.' There was another, even longer pause. 'OK,' she said eventually. 'We'll do it your way. Tell me where I can find the papers and where you are right now.'

I gave the information to her and hung up.

I went back into the kitchen and thumped on the table. Arkady jerked out of his reverie and removed his headphones.

'She's alive.'

'Who?'

'My friend. The one being held by the mafia.'

He raised an eyebrow.

'Look,' I said. 'I need your help. I am going to talk to them now, but it might be better if it was someone who spoke Belarusian — is that a thing, by the way?'

'Yes, we speak Belarusian in Belarus. I also speak Russian and Ukrainian. And French. And German.'

It seemed gratuitous of him to mention this. I really could have done without being made to feel even more inadequate right now.

'OK, fine,' I said. 'I'm going to call them now.'

He didn't move.

'My phone's in the living room. Charging up.'

Arkady gave a deep sigh and followed me into the living room. 'You go after we do this?'

'Not quite. I need to wait for some papers to arrive so I can exchange them for my friend.'

'You go by seven o'clock?'

'I'm not sure. Why?'

'Is Friday night. Lucy and I watch film. Then we have sex.'

There wasn't an obvious response to this, so I didn't attempt one.

'Lucy very good at sex,' continued Arkady. 'She say I very good too.'

I decided to ignore this as well. 'Right,' I said. 'Here's my phone.'

'What kind of phone is this?' he said, regarding it with distaste. 'We have better phones in Belarus.'

'I'm sure you do, Arkady, but I prefer this one, thank you. Now listen. My friend is called Dorothy. The Belarusians wish to exchange her for some important papers that are being couriered here from London. I need to fix a time and place to do the swap. Also, I want to talk to Dorothy, to make sure she's safe.'

I found Ali's text with the number in it and passed the phone to Arkady. He pressed the number. I could hear it ringing at the other end then a peremptory voice answered. In response, Arkady launched into what sounded like a tirade of Slavic abuse. Something similar was batted back at him from the other end, before he replied in kind. The conversation went back and forth for several minutes, during which time Arkady became increasingly animated with much arm waving and stabbing at the air with his index finger. Finally he handed the phone over to me. I bent over.

'Hi, Tom,' said Dorothy. Her voice sounded unnaturally calm.

'Thank God you're OK,' I said. 'You are OK, right?'

'I'm fine.'

'They are treating you OK, aren't they?'

'Yes, I'm fine.' Her voice dropped to a shaky whisper. 'Tom, listen to me. I don't want you to do this.'

'Do what?'

'The exchange.'

'What? Why ever not?'

'The papers are more important than me. These people mustn't get their hands on them.'

'No they're not! That's ridiculous.'

'I mean it, Tom. You mustn't do this. I'm expendable.'

'NO!'

'Seriously, Tom. These are dangerous men. They mustn't have those papers. Promise me that, Tom.'

'NO! I WON'T!'

'Don't let me down again, Tom.'

'NOOOOOOOOOOOOO!'

There was a scuffle at the other end and a new voice came on the line, badgering me in a language I didn't understand. It was an ugly, brutal, male voice.

'You look after her!' I said. 'YOU LOOK AFTER HER!'

The line went dead.

I looked at Arkady.

'It's the Gretzkys,' he said. 'They very bad people.'

I sighed. 'I know that, but—'

'The Gretzkys are the worst. They will – how do you say – do the double cross.'

'What do you mean?'

'You give them the papers, they kill your Dorothy anyway. Kill you too.'

'But didn't you make an agreement with them?'

'Is worth nothing.'

'What else can I do?'

'Forget everything. I hear your Dorothy telling you not do it. She right. She very brave woman.'

'I know.' What did she mean about letting her down again, anyway? When had I let her down before?

No.

Whatever that was about, I wouldn't let her down this time.

I was going to bloody save her.

Whatever it took.

'Arkady,' I said. 'Just tell me where and when. I'm going to do the exchange and to hell with the consequences.'

He gave me a pitying smile. 'You think you brave like your Dorothy,' he said. 'But you just idiot.'

'Where and when, Arkady?'

'One mile out on west road out of the Pilton Chumpsey. Two o'clock tomorrow morning.'

Burgess's case arrived just after six o'clock. I placed it on the kitchen table.

'This is it?' said Arkady.

'Yes.'

226

'A case.'

'Yes.'

'So how you get your friend back?'

'I'm glad you asked me that,' I said. I really was. I'd been through this in my mind a thousand times during the afternoon, and I was quite pleased with the plan I'd put together. 'One moment.' I nipped into the living room and came out with a stuffed purple hippopotamus belonging to Lucy. I put this on the table. Then I took several paces back towards the door of the flat, taking the case with me. Arkady made to follow me but I put my hand up to indicate he should stay where he was.

'Right,' I said, pointing to the hippo. 'You have Dorothy. I have the case.'

'OK. She nice?' He looked at the hippo. 'Maybe I keep her instead.'

'No, Arkady. Please try to take this seriously. Watch.' I picked up the case and placed it roughly halfway between us. 'OK, you come forward now to the halfway point, bringing Dorothy with you.'

Arkady obliged.

'Now you release Dorothy and pick up the case.'

Arkady put the hippo down and picked up Burgess's case. Then he shrugged and mimed pulling a gun out of his pocket with two fingers. Then he cocked it and blew the hippo's head off, before aiming the same two fingers at me.

'No, Arkady, you wouldn't do that.'

'Why not? I have case.'

'But you don't know the combination. You see? I did something similar with Diana Cheeseman. It worked brilliantly.'

'Is she mafia?'

'I don't think so.'

'She much easier then. I think he threaten kill your Dorothy so you give him combination. You give him combination then he kill her anyway.'

'OK, OK. I'll tell him I won't give him the combination until he's back at his car.'

Arkady considered this. 'Maybe. Or maybe he shoot Dorothy anyway and he get heavy man to break open case. If you lucky, he take Dorothy with him.'

I had to admit he had a point, and I suddenly felt deflated. Then I remembered something. 'What if we were to attach some kind of tracking device to the case? That way we could keep them in our sights until we get back-up.'

I expected Arkady to laugh at this, but he gave me a grudging nod. 'Is not bad idea. I have friend who has devices. He in security.'

'What?' I said. 'You're kidding!'

'No. Is true. Sergei very clever man. He doctor of electronics from Vitebsk State Technological University.'

'Well, that's brilliant! Bit of a long way to Vitebsk, though.' Actually, I had no idea where Vitebsk was, but it definitely sounded like it was a good distance away.

'He live in Bedminster.'

'But that's just up the road! Can you… I mean, would you mind awfully if—'

'Is no problem. I go now.'

Arkady picked up the case and headed past me to go out. As he reached the door, he turned and said, 'You tell me combination?'

'Of course.' I got out Dorothy's Post-It note and copied the combination onto a scrap of paper. He looked at it, nodded and put it in his pocket. Then he left. Everything was beginning to fall into place. I had a plan and it was going to work.

Chapter 27

I called Ali. It rang once before she picked it up.

'What's wrong?' she said. She sounded anxious.

'Nothing's wrong.' I said. I resented the implication that any communication from me meant some kind of catastrophe had occurred. 'I just wanted to let you know the case has arrived.'

'I know. I checked the courier's website. By the way, any tips for getting the smell of that dog out of your clothes?' I could hear the clicking of keys in the background. Did she ever go home? Where was home? Or did she sleep on the floor in the office? I'd never really considered this.

'I spoke to Dorothy,' I said.

'Oh my God.'

'She's fine. Well, as fine as she can be in the circumstances. Which isn't that fine at all, now I come to think of it. Oh God, I'm blabbering. Sorry.'

'It's OK. I'm feeling a bit blabbery myself. When's the swap going to happen?'

'Two o'clock in the morning. At this Pilton Chumpsey place.'

'Cool. You've got a plan worked out? I'd like my business partner back as soon as possible.'

'Yeah. Everything's sorted. I've gone through it all with Arkady.'

'Isn't that the Belarusian bloke?'

'Yeah. He handled the negotiations. He was very helpful.'

'I bet he was. I don't like the sound of him.'

'He's OK. At least I think he is. Even if he did nick my girlfriend.'

'Well, as long as you haven't done anything really stupid, like hand the case over to him.'

I didn't answer this immediately.

'Tom,' said Ali. 'What have you done?'

I still couldn't think of anything to say.

'Please tell me you haven't handed the case over to Arkady. Because if you have—'

'Look, he said this mate of his could attach a tracking device to it. You know, like the one that... oh, shit. You don't think—?'

'I'm thinking lots of things, matey. Starting with "Who the fuck is this fucking idiot that I was persuaded to leave in charge of rescuing Dot from the fucking Belarusian mafia?"'

'You're being a bit melodramatic, Ali.'

'Am I fuck. Didn't the phrase "tracking device" ring any bells?'

'Yes but... no but... hold on, wasn't the tracking device guy something to do with Isaac Vavasor? I don't think he was with the Belarusians. No, I'm sure he... oh shit.'

'It's a bit of a coincidence, Tom.'

'I just thought it was really convenient. Arkady hadn't been particularly helpful up until then. Apart from talking to the Belarusians, that is.'

'I take it you understood every word he said to them?'

'Well, no. Obviously.'

'So you're sure he wasn't saying something like "Don't worry about staying up late tonight for the rendezvous, this dickhead's going to hand the case over to me anyway"?'

'I'm sure he wasn't saying anything of the sort.'

'How fucking sure?'

'Ninety-nine point nine nine nine, oh I dunno, nine?' Actually, the more I considered it, the more my level of certainty tumbled. Closer to fifty per cent. Twenty-five. Ten. One. Oh God. 'Ali, what have I done?'

'Fucked up. Badly. Dot's being held by a bunch of psychos and you've just thrown away our only bargaining chip.'

'Please tell me I haven't. Please?'

The phone went dead. I picked the purple hippopotamus up and sat down at the table cuddling it while rocking gently backwards and forwards. I was still in this position when Lucy walked in half an hour later.

Lucy stared at me, arms folded. 'What are you doing here?' she said. 'More importantly, what are you doing with Henrietta Hippo?'

I put Henrietta Hippo down on the table and stood up. 'You could say "hello",' I said.

'Yes, hello. Whatever.'

'You changed the lock.'

'And your problem is? Tom, you don't live here any more.'

'But it's like you didn't trust me.'

'Tom, why is everything about you? We changed the locks because we had a break in.'

'What? Arkady never said. Did anything—?'

'No, nothing of yours got taken, if that's what you're worried about. Nothing got taken at all. They just turned the place upside down. Obviously didn't find anything valuable, or maybe someone disturbed them.'

'Well, that's good.'

'It's not good the place got turned over. Took us ages to sort everything out again.'

'They were probably looking for my case.'

'Good God, you really do think everything's about you, don't you?'

'No, that's not true. They probably really were looking for it. Which reminds me, I need to ask you something. Is Arkady entirely kosher?'

Lucy's eyes narrowed. 'What do you mean?'

'Well, I've just given the case to him and I wanted to be sure he's not in the Belarusian mafia or something.'

'Oh, for crying out loud,' she said, gesturing at me. 'God, you're still the same, aren't you? Still living on your own little planet, floating off in outer space somewhere. You know, I look at you now and I wonder what ever I saw in you.' She went into the bedroom, closed the door and then opened it up again. 'You still didn't tell me what you're doing here,' she said.

'I came to pick up some stuff. Then a friend of mine got kidnapped and—'

The door slammed. I looked at Henrietta Hippo. Henrietta Hippo looked back at me. 'You don't know how lucky you are,' I said to her. Henrietta Hippo didn't say anything, but carried on looking smug.

A few minutes later, Lucy emerged. She had changed into a pair of skinny jeans and a T-shirt. I looked at her and for a moment I wondered if I still fancied her. She was certainly very easy on the eye. But then reality broke in and all the unpleasant stuff that was going on lurched back into my brain.

'Where's Arkady, anyway?' said Lucy.

'I was trying to explain. He's taken my case to a friend of his. Sergei something or other.'

'Why?'

'To get a tracking device attached to it. Like the one that was originally attached to it. I'm going to trade it for my friend who's been kidnapped.'

'He's what?'

232

'Like I said, he's—'

'Listen, Tom, if I find out you've enlisted Arkady into your stupid little games, you are not going to hear the last of it.'

'It was Arkady's idea.'

'Oh God, are you ALL like this? Is this what men are like?'

I shrugged. It all made perfect sense to me.

'I thought he was different,' said Lucy. 'He's a pathologist, you know.'

'He told me.'

'He's only teaching Zumba until his English gets better.'

'He told me that too.'

A dreamy look had come into her eyes. 'I'm teaching him, you know.'

'Yes, that as well.'

The dreamy look vanished. 'My car's a complete write-off.'

Whoa there. I didn't see that one coming. In my head I'd established some kind of moral – and hence financial – equivalence between the hurt caused by my destruction of her car and the hurt caused by her running off with Arkady, so I'd sort of assumed that we didn't need to discuss the matter further. Apparently I'd used an over-simplistic accounting model.

'Ah.'

'The estimate from the garage was about three times what the car's worth.'

'Right.'

'So I'm going to have to buy a new car.'

'Oh.'

'I can't afford a new car.'

'Hmmm.'

'Are you listening to anything I'm saying, Tom? You've gone all monosyllabic.'

'I'm listening to every word, and I'm really, really sorry but I can't think of anything to say. I have no money. I have no job.

I am currently living with my dissolute father and his malodorous dog in a static caravan.'

'Well, that's your problem.'

'Dad sends his love, by the way.'

'Great.'

'More importantly, someone I know really has been kidnapped by a bunch of psychotic Belarusians. Arkady says they are a very bad bunch. He spoke to them.'

Lucy waved her hands in the air. 'I can't deal with this now. I need to get supper ready.' She started to bustle about, chopping onions up and throwing them into a frying pan.

'Smells good,' I said. I always liked the smell of frying onions. 'What is it?'

'*Draniki*. Belarusian potato pancake,' said Lucy, 'and don't think you're getting any. In fact, why are you still here?'

'I'm waiting for Arkady to come back with my case.'

'I thought he wasn't going to.'

But at that precise moment, he appeared, although my joy was tempered by the fact that he wasn't carrying my case. When he had finished embracing Lucy – and the simple word 'embracing' fails to deliver the full impact of the performance that unfolded between them, stopping a couple of femtometres short of full penetration – I asked him what had happened.

'Sergei need more time to fix track device. Is good. He bring later tonight.'

'Oh God. Are you sure?'

'Of course. Sergei very good man.' Arkady sniffed the air and clapped his hands. 'My clever Lucy, she make *Draniki*. You eat with us?'

'What?' said Lucy. 'You're not suggesting he should sit down with us?'

'Why not? In Belarus, we always invite guests to eat. Is hospitable.'

'But this is Tom. I kicked him out of this very flat on Monday.'

'He not your guest. He my guest.' Arkady gave me a conspiratorial wink. 'I insist my guest sit down with us to eat.' This was most unexpected. Had I somehow impressed him with my brave and heroic plan to save Dorothy? Lucy, however, was still not happy.

'I hope you're not going to make a habit of this,' she said.

'Of course not. Mr Tom is my special guest. We eat *Draniki*, then we watch film.'

'I'll even join you for the sex afterwards,' I said, before instantly regretting it. Fortunately, Arkady found this hilarious and burst out laughing, slapping my back with gleeful abandon. I made a mental note not to say anything funny in future when Arkady was about.

Lucy looked at us with a mixture of disgust and contempt, before turning back to the cooker with a snort.

Arkady smirked at me. 'Oops,' he said.

Lucy continued cooking in silence, her every move conveying suppressed violence. Oil splashed over the cooker as she threw ingredients into the frying pan, and when she had finished, she hurled the pan into the sink, where it sizzled malevolently under the cold tap.

'There,' she said, chucking a plate at me. 'Eat.' She did the same at Arkady, without saying a word. He had clearly disappointed her.

Arkady took a few mouthfuls. 'Is good,' he said, nodding at it.

'You sure?' said Lucy, preening. 'I wasn't sure if…'

'No, is very good.'

'It's very nice,' I said.

'You keep out of this,' said Lucy. 'Some more?' she said to Arkady.

'Please.' He paused. 'I sorry for laughing at sex joke. We not have sex tonight.'

'What?' said Lucy, putting his plate back. 'Why not?'

'I take Tom to the Pilton Chumpsey. He not have car I think.'

'You're kidding me. Arkady, what on earth are you thinking? I'm not having you gallivanting off with this idiot. You're staying here with me. It's Friday night, I've had a difficult week and I want some time with you myself.'

She was slightly less than half his size, but she already had Arkady in her power. He relented immediately. 'OK. Tom will borrow car instead,' he said.

'Are you mad?' said Lucy. 'He destroys cars. You've seen what he did to my lovely little Micra.'

'Is OK. He break my car, I remove his head.'

I wasn't sure he was joking. It was entirely possible that head removal was part of his core skill set.

'I'll be careful,' I said.

'That's what you said to me,' said Lucy.

'Yes, but I thought I was being chased by the Belarusian mafia.'

'Well, this time it might actually be true.'

'Ah, so you believe me now!' I said.

'I DON'T KNOW WHAT TO BELIEVE. I just want to stay here with my Arkady.' She started sobbing, and Arkady put his arm round her. I got up from the table and did the washing-up. It was the least I could do.

Then we all sat down to watch Arkady's film, a four-hour black and white Belarusian mythical epic involving a cursed child that changed into a magical winged squirrel. I may have got some of the details wrong, but I wasn't entirely concentrating. It was getting very late and there was still no sign of Sergei.

Chapter 28

At thirteen minutes past midnight, the doorbell rang. Arkady got up and I followed him out of the living room. He motioned to me to stay back before going to the front door. He opened it a few inches and I could hear a brief, mumbled conversation in a language I didn't understand with someone I couldn't see. Then he shut the door and brandished the case at me. I began to feel excited.

'OK, Mr Tom. Let's go kick arse.'

I followed him down the stairs and out into the street. There was no one about, apart from a couple of lads coming home from a night's drinking, taking turns to shout, snigger and then hiss at the other one to be quiet. Arkady's car was a lovingly-preserved cold-war era Škoda. He placed Burgess's case on the passenger seat, then handed me the keys.

'Good luck, my friend. I go have my sex with Lucy now.' Then he hit me on the shoulder. I assumed he meant it to be playful, because he pulled the punch. I knew this because the shoulder was still correctly located in its socket when I rubbed it afterwards.

The roads were clear and I arrived at the rendezvous location a little after half past one in the morning. Things were looking up. It was all going to go just fine. Pilton Chumpsey was a tiny hamlet with only a couple of farmhouses, both of which were shrouded in darkness. The westerly road out of the village was an undulating, single-track affair with treacherous rhynes on either side. It was a clear night with a full moon.

I turned the engine off, got out of the car and nudged the door closed. They'd said they'd be coming from the opposite direction, but I wanted to make sure I wasn't taken by surprise. However, the landscape was as flat and featureless as Milton Keynes on a Tuesday night in February, and the only things in the way of a three-sixty-degree panorama were a rusting trailer and a bunch of cows, who were studying me with some interest.

'Bugger off,' I muttered to them.

Somewhere in the distance, a fox yowled, sounding like the screams of a newborn baby being slowly dismembered. I shivered and got back into the car.

I still had plenty of time, so I decided to check that everything was in order with the ransom. I reached for the case, took Dorothy's Post-It note out of my pocket and turned the dials to the correct combination. To my horror, it failed to open. I checked I'd set the right number. I had. I spun the wheels and selected the combination again. It still wouldn't open.

Shit.

If it wouldn't open, the Belarusians would go ballistic. We'd never get out alive.

I got my phone out and called Arkady. There was no signal. Jesus.

I got out of the car and began walking away from the village. Still no signal.

I walked the other way a few yards and finally one bar wobbled into view.

I called Arkady again. Please answer, please answer.

Arkady answered.

'Arkady!' I yelled.

'What is this?' His voice was drowsy or post-coital or, probably, both.

'That idiot Sergei has broken the case! It won't open!'

'What you mean?'

'I MEAN IT WON'T FUCKING OPEN!'

'Ah, yes. Sorry. I forget. He change combination.'

'HE DID WHAT?'

'He change combination. He tell me why but I not understand. He say it for your safety.'

'HE CHANGED THE COMBINATION FOR MY SAFETY? IS HE INSANE?'

'Please speak quiet, Mr Tom. Is late.'

'OK, OK,' I said, lowering my voice and taking a deep breath. 'Tell me the new combination.' I reached into my pocket for paper and a pen.

'I not know,' said Arkady.

'You what?'

'Sergei not tell me new combination.'

'R-i-i-ight. So let's get this straight. I'm sitting here waiting to hand this case over in exchange for my friend and it now turns out I can't actually reveal the combination.'

'Is OK, is OK—'

'Listen, mate. If I can't tell them the combination, we're dead.'

'Is OK. Sergei send you text.'

'WHAT?'

'Sergei say he send you text at two o'clock. Is OK.'

'Arkady, is not OK. IS VERY NOT OK. I am not happy with this. I am on my own on a scary road in the dead of night with only a few cows for company and I am about to have to deal with a bunch of very angry Mafiosi. I WANT TO KNOW THE COMBINATION.'

'I sorry.'

'Can you at least give me Sergei's number?'

'He say no. Sorry. Sergei very clever man. He has plan.'

'WHAT ABOUT MY PLAN, ARKADY?'

'Sorry, you cracking up. Signal bad. Good luck.'

The line went dead. I tried calling Arkady back straight away, but this time it went straight to voicemail.

'Urgh!' I said, biting my knuckles in an attempt to resist the urge to hurl the phone in the direction of the cows. Instead, I took the Post-It note and tore it into tiny shreds and scattered them over the car footwell. Why did nothing ever work out as planned? It was now ten to two. The one good thing about this whole situation was that it was going to be over very soon. Unfortunately, the very worst thing about this whole situation was also that it was going to be over very soon.

I paced up and down the road, trying to get my breathing close to somewhere near normal. I'd never felt this anxious in my entire life.

Finally, with five minutes to go and still no word from Sergei, I heard an engine in the distance and then soon after that, the headlights of a car appeared. It stopped a hundred yards away, with the engine still running and the headlights still on. I squinted at it with my hand over my eyes and deduced that it was a black Mercedes. I would have placed good money on it being the same one I'd seen in Swindon.

My phone rang. Evidently their phone had a better aerial than mine.

'Hello?' I said.

'Where is papers?' said a gruff voice.

'Show me Dorothy.'

A large man emerged from the rear of the Mercedes, pulling a much smaller figure after him.

'Tom!' cried a woman's voice. 'You don't have to do this! Run away now!'

Oh God. I was so close to her now. I had to keep calm somehow. I gulped several lungfuls of air and tried to stay focused.

'OK,' I said. 'I have the papers in a locked case with a six-number combination.'

'You hand over case. You give me combination. Then I hand over girl.'

'No, I'll bring the case to the middle. Then you bring Dorothy to the same point. OK?'

There was no reply.

'Then you can take the case back with you. When I'm happy Dorothy's safe, I'll give you the combination. If you try to break open the case without the combination, anything inside will be automatically destroyed.'

There was no harm in using the same bluff I'd used with Diana Cheeseman. I still didn't have the combination, of course, but that was a minor detail.

There was a long silence while they processed the details of the swap. Then the voice came back on.

'OK.'

I dropped the call. I was going to lose signal anyway so it was pointless keeping the channel open. I went back to the car and pulled the case out. I noticed that the driver's door of the Mercedes had now opened and a chap was standing behind it balancing a rifle on top. He was aiming the rifle straight at me as I walked towards the halfway point. I knew this because if I looked down I could see a little red spot of light twitching around my chest.

I was now way past the point of no return. If I gave the slightest hint of turning and running, I was as good as dead. I had to go through with it now. I continued towards the halfway point.

Something was nagging at the back of my mind, though. Something wasn't quite right. I tried to work out what it was, but I banished the thought to the back of my mind. I had to keep concentrating on looking straight ahead.

When I reached halfway, I placed the case on the ground and began to back away carefully to the Škoda, never once taking my eyes off the guy with the rifle. Then I continued on towards the village, back to where I could get a signal.

Still no word from Sergei, and it was almost two o'clock.

The front passenger door of the Mercedes opened and a tall guy wearing sunglasses came out and began walking towards the case.

This wasn't what we'd agreed.

The bastards weren't sticking to the script.

Panicking, I phoned their number and I could hear it ringing in the guy's pocket. He didn't answer. He just kept on walking.

'Hey!' I shouted.

He ignored me.

'That's not what we agreed!'

I ran forwards then caught a glimpse of the red dot playing around my torso.

'OK, OK,' I shouted, putting my hands up and moving back to where I'd been standing.

When he had retrieved the case, he took it back to the car. Then he called me.

'Sorry,' he said. 'We change plan. You give combination now or we kill her.'

Shit.

'No deal,' I said, after a moment's hesitation. They were going to kill Dorothy anyway and in any case I still didn't have the sodding combination.

'You will regret this.'

'I don't care. No deal.' I tried very hard to keep my voice steady, but it contrived an odd loop-the-loop as I said the last word. 'No deal,' I repeated.

Still no text.

Somewhere overhead an owl hooted. Bats flitted round. The hedgerow rustled. A cow wandered close to me and emptied its bowels. A warm, rural smell wafted over.

My phone was filled with the sound of heavy breathing.

My mind raced through alternative scenarios. Maybe they would stick to the deal and release Dorothy when I'd given them the combination. No, that wasn't going to happen. What the hell could I do instead? Perhaps I could just get in the car and drive at them? If I ducked down, I might avoid being shot and Dorothy might break free in the middle of the confusion.

That was a really terrible idea.

What if I insisted on giving them the combination face to face and somehow managed to take them all on in hand-to-hand combat?

That was even worse.

No. There were no solutions. I was out of options. The only card I had left was the combination.

Except that until Sergei came through – and it seemed increasingly unlikely he would – I didn't even have that.

'No deal,' I said again, mentally crossing my fingers, toes and every single other organ in my body.

The heavy breathing continued, broken by an angry, Belarusian imprecation. Then he gesticulated at his comrade. The man released his hold on Dorothy and she stepped forward.

The loudest sound for miles around was now the beating of my heart.

Dorothy took another step.

And another.

'Come on, come on,' I muttered under my breath. 'Come on!'

Dorothy kept walking. The guy with the rifle now had her in his sights, and there was still every chance that as soon as I released the combination he would fire.

But every second that passed by was another second during which we were both still alive.

Dorothy reached the halfway point and the angry voice barked into my ear. 'Combination, please.'

I waited as long as I could before responding. 'One moment,' I said.

'Combination NOW, please.' The man nodded towards his colleague with the rifle. The other man nodded back.

There was a loud beep in my ear and I jumped six feet into the air.

A text.

From an unknown number.

Containing six digits.

My brain froze.

Six digits.

I stared at them again.

Then I heard a tinny voice coming out of the phone's speaker, demanding the combination for the last time.

I jerked back into life and studied the six digits again. Then I read them out.

The man opened the case and at that exact moment I knew for sure that something was wrong. I couldn't see his expression, but there was something off about his body language. And finally I worked out what it was. The case had been way too heavy.

Oh shit.

'Run!' I shouted to Dorothy. 'For God's sake, RUN!'

Then for an instant, night turned to day, and a millisecond after that there was a cataclysmic boom that sounded as if a bomb had gone off. A millisecond after that, there was a second explosion as the Mercedes's petrol tank blew up. And a further millisecond after that, I realised that the reason the first noise sounded like a bomb going off was because some kind of bomb had indeed just gone off.

Chapter 29

Someone had stuffed my ears full of cotton wool.

'Dorothy!' I shouted, stumbling back to the Škoda, although all I could hear was 'Woowooffy!'

Dorothy was lying prone on the road just ahead of the car. As I reached her, she lifted her head and staggered to her knees. I reached out a hand, but she ignored it and hauled herself to her feet on her own.

'You OK?' I shouted ('Yooo oh-ay?')

'Yeh mfie! Mfie!' she replied. She shook her head and tried again. 'Fie!'

'Need to get going,' I said ('Neeoo geggo'). I jerked my thumb back towards the car in clarification. 'Geggo!'

Dorothy nodded. 'Oh-ay!'

We scrambled back to the car. I turned on the ignition and effected an untidy three-point turn before heading back towards the village. There was a light on in the upstairs window of one of the farmhouses and I hoped they didn't manage to glimpse the number plate as we sped through.

'Wha-appen?' said Dorothy, but I shook my head. I didn't want to embark on any complicated explanations until either my hearing had returned or I'd picked up a smattering of sign language.

'Oh-ay,' said Dorothy.

We drove on in silence. Halfway back to Bristol, Dorothy spoke again and this time I could just about make out what she was saying, although it was modulated with a distinct buzzing, as if someone had dumped a hive full of angry bees in the back seat.

'So. Feel like giving me a few pointers as to what just happened?'

'I'm not a hundred per cent sure.'

'Why am I not surprised.'

'Still, the good news is you're alive and well. I mean, you're OK, right? Did they treat you OK?'

'Yeah, I'm fine. I can look after myself, you know.'

'I know.'

Before I could say anything else, my phone started ringing. I fished it out of my pocket and handed it to Dorothy.

'It's Ali,' she said. 'She's still up.'

'Of course,' I said. But she was already talking.

'Hi... yes, it's me... yes, it really is... yes, I know, it's... I know... I'm fine... no, really, I'm fine... yes, yes, OK, I will... yes, yes, he's fine too... I know, I'm surprised myself... yes, sure... ah, OK... have you tried... what about the... have you downloaded the new patch... 5.1.3... not that one, that's the beta... too flaky... revert to the 3... of course I'm sure... I'll show you tomorrow... or what day is it...? Or Monday or something...? OK? Is μ OK...? You looking after her...? I'm sure, I'm sure... yes, I'm fine, honestly... dead, I think... yes, all of them... I'm not sure either... I know, the signal's going in and out... OK, see you soon.'

Dorothy ended the call. 'That phone of yours,' she said. 'Find a nice museum for it, will you?'

I ignored this.

'Do me a favour,' I said. 'See the number that texted me last? Give it a call, will you?'

'Why?'

'Please?'

Dorothy found the number and called it.

'Straight to voicemail,' she said, shaking her head. 'Strong accent. Who is it?'

'Guy called Sergei. Chap who planted the bomb.'

'Friend of yours?'

'Do I look like the kind of guy who hangs out with bombers?'

'Nothing would surprise me. But on balance, no.'

'He's a friend of Arkady. Lucy's new boyfriend.'

'How did that happen? Actually, I'm not interested in that right now. Just tell me what's happened to the Vavasor papers.'

Shit. I hadn't even thought about that.

'Um…'

'You do realise I never got round to making a copy, don't you?'

'Oh,' I said.

'So please tell me the papers weren't in the case when it blew up.'

'I'm not sure.'

'What do you mean, "not sure"? Either they were or they weren't.'

'I mean I have no idea. I just gave it to Arkady to pass on to Sergei so he could insert a tracking device. It all happened a bit quickly.'

'Oh my God, Tom. Those are the most important mathematical papers in history. *Were* the most important mathematical papers in history.'

'Surely you must have made a copy? Didn't you scan them or something?'

Dorothy was very quiet.

'What?' I said.

'They wouldn't scan,' she said.

'What?'

'I said they wouldn't scan. Something odd about the paper itself. Some kind of watermark or something. There's a thing they put on banknotes called a EURion to stop you copying them – it triggers something in the scanner – and I think they did something like that. I was going to try to work out a hack, but I didn't have time.'

'Shit. Still, I think we may be overlooking something here. The fact is, you're still alive.'

'Think of the bigger picture, though.'

'That may be easier for you to do than me.'

Dorothy yawned. 'I'm tired. We can talk about this tomorrow.'

'You might at least say—'

But she was asleep already. We didn't exchange another word for the rest of the journey back to Bristol.

We got back to the flat at a quarter past three. I had to ring the bell several times before Arkady appeared, sporting the kimono I'd last seen Lucy wearing on the night of my ignominious departure. It fitted her better.

He seemed surprised to see us.

'You're alive!' he said.

'Apparently so,' I said. 'This is Dorothy. Dorothy, this is Arkady.'

'Hello Dorothy,' said Arkady.

'Yeah, whatever,' said Dorothy, pushing past him and sitting down at the kitchen table. The sleep had done little to mollify her.

'Arkady,' I said. 'There's something important I need to ask. Your friend Sergei, what does he do, exactly?'

'Sergei? He do security work.'

'Government?'

'Not government any more. Private. Why you ask?'

'He put a bomb in my case.'

Arkady looked shocked. 'A bomb?'

'Yes. A bomb,' said Dorothy.

'Ah. So this is what he means. Sergei say "They killed my brother" to me. I not understand why, but now I do. Also this why he change combination. For your safety, as he say.'

'So I didn't blow myself up on the way there, yes. Very thoughtful of him.'

'What happened to Gretzkys?'

'Dead, I think.'

'Hmm. There may be – what is word – repercussions?'

I hadn't considered this. 'What do you mean?'

'I go to Sergei,' said Arkady. He rushed into the bedroom. I heard a muffled, heated discussion and then a minute later he reappeared, fully dressed.

'Keys?' he said, holding out his hand. I gave them to him. 'You not break car?'

'No,' I said. 'I didn't.'

'You good man,' he said, smacking my shoulder. The grin seemed less confident than it usually did.

'Are you going to be OK?' I said.

'Yes,' said Arkady. 'I hope.'

Then he left. Afterwards, I realised there were a whole load of other questions I should have asked, but the cotton wool from my ears had seeped into my brain and I wasn't operating on full power. I suddenly felt very tired indeed.

I ushered Dorothy into the living room and indicated the two armchairs. 'One for you,' I said, 'and one for me.'

'You could do with a sofa,' she said.

'Yeah, I know.'

I woke up around ten. Dorothy was sitting at the kitchen table tapping away at my laptop. Sun was streaming in through the window. I could smell coffee, although the pot was empty.

'Where's Lucy?' I said.

'She's on shift today,' said Dorothy. 'She said you're to make sure you're out of here by the time she gets back.'

'That's nice.'

'Well, you're not too fussed, are you? How did you meet her anyway?'

'At a party. I'd just come down to Bristol and a friend of a friend invited me along. Steampunk thing. We were the only two who hadn't bothered to dress up.'

'So that was what you had in common.'

'Basically yes. Seemed as good a basis for a relationship as any other. I suppose we drifted into it really. I'm pretty good at drifting.'

'So are a lot of people. Even the ones who look as if they know what they're doing.'

'Except, right now I actually feel as if, oh I dunno…'

'I know,' said Dorothy. 'I know. Look', she said, waving a hand at the laptop, 'been doing some digging. I was wondering how what happened yesterday might tie into the Vavasors. So I was thinking about Belarusian mathematicians. Which led me to look into Belarusian prizes for mathematics, and I found this thing called the Litvinchuk Medallion of Honour. It's awarded every year by some university or other. Very prestigious. Anyway, turns out there's only ever been one pair of brothers who've both won it and, guess what, the older one is called Sergei. Not conclusive in itself, but it turns out the younger brother, Maxim, did post-doctoral work on the twin prime conjecture, which should ring a few bells, as that's one of the problems the

Vavasor twins were rumoured to have found a proof for. By the way, thanks for yesterday.'

'Sorry?'

'Thanks. For, you know. I should have said so last night. I was so pissed off about losing the papers, I didn't even think.'

'Well, I mean, gosh, yes, I… it was nothing really.'

'No, it wasn't nothing. And you know it. I am actually very pleased to be alive and free. So, just to let you know, I do appreciate it.'

'Thank you for saying so.'

'It's nothing.'

There was an awkward silence between us.

'Anyway, going back to Maxim,' I said. 'Are you saying there's a connection with the Vavasors?'

'It's beginning to look like a possibility.'

'Right. Right. Look, I need to eat something before we go any further.' I felt as if I'd just got off the red-eye from New York. My balance was poor and my blood sugar was out of whack. I poured myself a large bowl of granola and devoured it in seconds. Dorothy regarded me with some curiosity, as if I were one of the more exotic residents in a zoo.

'What?' I said. 'I'm starving. It's hungry work saving people from the Belarusian mafia.'

'Yeah, OK,' said Dorothy. 'Don't overdo it.' But she said it with a smile.

I made more coffee and sat down again. 'OK, what now,' I said.

'First, we need to verify all this with Sergei.'

'Sounds like a plan. I'll give him a call.'

I selected Sergei's number from my history. As before, it went straight to voicemail. I shook my head.

'Too easy,' said Dorothy. 'What about Arkady?'

'I'm on it.' But Arkady's phone went straight to voicemail, too.

'Any idea where he lives?'

'No. Sergei's somewhere in Bedminster, but short of wandering around there looking for Arkady's Škoda, I'm not sure we're going to get very far.'

'True.'

'Anything on the news about last night? I'd like to know if we're likely to get a visit from the plods.'

Dorothy pulled up the BBC news website. 'There's a brief mention of an incident in the Somerset levels. Rumoured to be a gangland hit.'

'Right.' I waited a moment, then added, 'I feel a bit odd about that, you know. Should I feel guilty? I'm not sure I do, but I'm wondering if I ought to.'

Dorothy shook her head. 'I wouldn't. They were fully intending to kill both of us. Even if you'd given them the papers.'

'Fair point. OK, back to Maxim and Sergei. Sergei said they'd killed Maxim, so was he the guy I bumped into outside Burgess's place in Swindon? Before he was run down by a bunch of goons in a black Mercedes? The same bunch who kidnapped you?'

'I wonder where Maxim did his post-doctoral research. What if he was given access to the Vavasor papers—'

'Because his elder brother happened to be helping out with security for Isaac Vavasor? Bet it was Sergei who planted the tracking device in Burgess's case,' I said. 'Which means, incidentally, that it definitely *was* him hanging around outside the office that time. I'm guessing it wasn't the Gretzkys he was talking to on his mobile.'

'Makes sense. But how did the Gretzkys find the office?'

'Maxim's phone.'

'Sorry?' said Dorothy.

'Bet you anything Maxim and Sergei had their phones set up to track each other. It's the sort of thing they'd do. In case anything happened.'

'Trouble is, something did happen, and it worked to the Gretzky's advantage.'

'Yeah, well, techies don't always think things through…'

I raised an eyebrow. She ignored me.

'Anyway,' she continued, 'Maxim's there when the papers get lent to Burgess '

'Why did they do that, I wonder? They'd never let them out of the house before.'

'Would you want him hanging around your place like a bad smell?' said Dorothy.

'Fair point. But they were obviously concerned – hence the bug.'

'Yep. Anyway, Maxim hears about what happens to Burgess and goes to the house to try and retrieve the case before anyone else gets to it first.'

'Bingo. Still doesn't explain how the Gretzkys got involved in the first place though. And we're no nearer finding the Vixen. Or Viv.'

'Who's Viv?' said Dorothy.

'You know, the person that Burgess dedicated *Shroud of Ecstasy* to.'

'Oh, that Viv. The long-suffering and ever-faithful one.'

'Yes. There was an odd reference to Viv the other day on *Vavasorology*.' I hunted around for the post I'd seen the previous day, but it seemed to have been deleted.

'Bugger,' I said. 'More coffee?'

'Good idea.'

I put some coffee on and paced around the kitchen for a while.

'I'm going to regret this, but what is this twin prime thing anyway?' I said.

'Ha,' said Dorothy. 'Well, if it's unsolved problems you're interested in, it's one of the easier ones to formulate.' She held up her mug for a refill. 'First of all, you know what a prime number is?'

'Um.' I was sure I knew this. 'A number that's only divisible by itself and one?'

'Excellent,' said Dorothy, beaming at me in an unnecessarily patronising manner. 'Now a twin prime is a prime that's either two more or two less than another one. Such as three and five. Five and seven. Eleven and thirteen.'

Dorothy took a sip of coffee and looked at me expectantly. My brain churned. 'OK, fourteen and... no, not fourteen, because that divides by two... fifteen and... no, not fifteen... seventeen and nineteen!'

'Good boy. So the twin prime conjecture states that there are an infinite number of twin primes.'

'That's it?'

'Yes. There's a more general formulation where the gap between each prime in the pair is widened from two to n, where n is any positive even number. That's Polignac's conjecture.'

'Good for Polignac. But how would you ever prove that? More to the point, why would you want to?'

'The how is a very long and incomplete story. I could spend the rest of the day – actually most of the rest of the year – talking about that. But the why is interesting. There are loads of unsolved problems to do with prime numbers. Goldbach's conjecture, for example.'

'Go on, amaze me.'

'Goldbach's conjecture states that any even number greater than two can be expressed as the sum of two primes.'

'That's even less useful.'

'But it's interesting, isn't it? And a bit weird. There's no reason why it should be true, but it seems to be.'

'OK, what about, I dunno, sixteen?'

'Three plus thirteen.'

'Forty-two?'

'Five plus thirty-seven.'

'Twenty-three thousand, four hundred and sixty-eight?'

Dorothy laughed. 'Not a clue.'

'Jeez. Call yourself a mathematician. What is it about prime numbers?' I said.

'Maybe it's because they're a sequence that anyone can sit down and work out, but one that obeys no laws. There's no pattern. You can't say, OK, X is a prime number, therefore X plus n will also be one. They might as well be completely random.'

'I bet that really annoys you guys.'

'What?'

'The randomness. It must really upset you.'

'OK, I see where you're going.'

'But it's true, isn't it?' I said. 'It must be so annoying to a mathematician to have a bunch of numbers out there you can't pin down. It's nothing to do with it being beautiful or interesting. It's all about control.'

'Oh, stop it. It's about truth. Why stuff is the way it is. You're no better. Sure, you're not trying to solve a long-standing mathematical mystery. But you're trying to solve a ten-year-old murder that has nothing to do with you.'

'That's different.'

'Is it? Sounds pretty similar to me.'

I had a sudden horrible thought. 'What if it turned out that none of this was connected at all, and all these deaths were coincidental? What if we're just trying to impose our own stupid narrative on a series of random events?'

Dorothy looked at me. 'Please don't say that. I'd hate to think I nearly got killed over nothing.'

I shrugged. 'You've got to admit it's a possibility.'

In the silence that followed, I really did wonder where we were going to go from here.

Chapter 30

Dorothy paced around the kitchen, taking care not to trip over the various items of gymnastic equipment that Arkady had left scattered around.

'I wonder,' she said eventually. 'Ever heard of the three body problem?'

'No, but you're going to tell me about it, aren't you?'

'Yep. Not my field, really – more of a physics kind of thing – but it goes like this. If you've got a single body on its own in the middle of space and you know its initial velocity, you can predict where it's going to end up. Nice simple equation.'

'Don't you need to know which direction it's going in?'

'Velocity means speed in a particular direction.'

'I knew that.' I really did.

'Good. So if you've got two bodies, it's more complicated, because each one exerts a gravitational effect on the other. But you can still solve the problem. However, once you go to three or more bodies, you're stuffed. You can solve it for some special cases, but there's no general solution. The way the bodies move might just as well be completely random.'

'I see where you're going,' I said, momentarily feeling quite clever. 'We've got three different bodies in our problem: Isaac Vavasor, the Gretzkys and Rufus Fairbanks.'

'We're observing their movements around each other and seeing a load of random stuff that doesn't make any sense. But deep down, there's still a logic to it. What we've been missing all along is that each of them wants something different. Vavasor wants to hide whatever really happened with Archie and Pye – maybe some sex scandal. The Gretzkys – for whatever reason – wanted to get their hands on the mathematical papers. I have no idea what Rufus Fairbanks wants.'

'Me neither. But you're saying it isn't random after all.'

'Exactly. There's a method to this madness, but we just don't know what it is yet.' She sat down and slapped the table with the palm of her hand. 'Right,' she said. 'Come on, let's try harder. Think, Tom. Think.'

I thought. Then I thought a bit more.

'OK,' I said. 'Let's check if we've exhausted our existing channels.' I scribbled down a list on a scrap of paper. Then I started reading them out.

'*Vavasorology.com*?'

'Not safe to ask questions,' said Dorothy. 'I suppose we could search for something if we knew what it was we were searching for.'

'The Belarusians?'

'Dead or uncontactable. Arkady might turn up again, but don't hold your breath.'

'You didn't pick anything up from the Gretzkys while you were with them?'

'No. They only spoke in Belarusian, or whatever language it is—'

'It's Belarusian,' I said. 'I know these things.'

Dorothy raised an eyebrow. 'Anyway,' she continued, 'I've just remembered now. The only word I recognised was "Fairbanks".'

'Fairbanks?'

'Yes. Then they all laughed. As if they were just about to put one over him.' Dorothy got up and started pacing up and down again. She caught sight of the rowing machine in the hallway. 'How does this thing work?'

'No idea. Nothing to do with me.'

'No. I sort of assumed you weren't the fitness fanatic.' She sat down on the seat and began rolling gently backwards and forwards. 'OK, carry on.'

'Hilary van Beek? I can answer that one. Dead. Diana Cheeseman?'

'You tell me.'

'Can't think of anything I didn't ask her that might help, and that meeting with Isaac isn't going to happen.'

'Next?' Dorothy had lifted her feet onto the machine and was idly pulling on the handle.

'Fairbanks?'

Dorothy shook her head.

'Mrs Standage? Dead. μ?'

'Sad as it is,' said Dorothy, 'I think we've exhausted μ as an information source.'

'So that's it? No more existing channels?'

'I think that's the lot.'

'Who haven't we tried yet?'

'Hold on, I'm just writing them down.' I scribbled down some more names. 'OK, here we go. Isaac Vavasor.'

'Forget it.'

'Margot Evercreech.'

'Only as an absolutely final resort. You've seen her website?'

'Oh yes.'

'So you know exactly what I'm talking about.'

'Dinsdale Mazloumian?'

'Same.' Dorothy was now pulling hard on the rowing machine and the noise level was rising.

'Viv?' I called out.

'We don't even know who they are. Any more?'

'The Vixen?'

'Don't know who they are either. Any more?'

'That's about it.'

Dorothy stopped the machine and stood up. 'So basically we're left with Viv and the Vixen,' she said.

'Sounds like the worst cop show ever,' I said.

Dorothy was deep in thought and didn't react. 'What was it Burgess said about Viv?' she said. '"My Fellow Explorer, the Long-suffering"—'

'"And Ever-Faithful." Got to be some kind of partner, surely? Hard as it is to imagine with Burgess.'

'Everyone has someone,' said Dorothy, sitting down again opposite me. 'Even him.' Then she tipped her head on one side. 'Unless – '

'Unless what?'

'Unless Viv was someone who helped him with the book.'

'Some kind of researcher, you mean?'

'Dunno. It's possible.'

'God, what a thought.'

'Let's think about this a minute. *Shroud of Ecstasy* was about the Turin thing, wasn't it? So which areas do you think Burgess might have needed help with?'

I considered this. 'Well, I wouldn't have seen him as much of a theologian.'

'I can imagine. So who would he have turned to?'

'Someone in the church. Wait a minute. Wasn't there a thing about Easter services in Burgess's case?'

'You're right, there was. Saint… Saint—'

'Xavier! Saint Xavier's. Find out who the vicar is.'

Dorothy was back at my laptop already. 'A-ha! Got him. The vicar of St Xavier's, Swindon, is the Reverend Colin Fuchs.'

'Sorry?' Did Dorothy really say that?

'Fuchs. As in the polar explorer.'

'Who?'

'You know, Sir Vivian Fu—' Dorothy stopped in mid-sentence and raised her hands in the air in triumph. 'OH MY GOD, THAT'S HIM! THE EXPLORER!' she cried.

'Sorry, am I being a bit thick, or…?'

From the look on her face, it was clear that I was. 'Tom,' she said, 'it's a nickname. Colin Fuchs. Vivian Fuchs. Colin "Viv" Fuchs.' She emphasised this with air quotes.

'Ah,' I said. 'Got it now. Wow. That's brilliant.'

'Sure is. Even better, we've got his phone number and address.'

I reached for my phone.

'No,' said Dorothy. 'He might not want to talk about Burgess. Better to doorstep him, don't you think?'

It was a good point. I just hoped he'd still be alive when we got there. On past form, there was every chance we'd find him sliced apart with a protractor or something.

The vicarage for St Xavier's was an undistinguished nineteen thirties semi with a fifteen-year-old Honda in the drive. There was no sign of the emergency services, so it was possible we were in luck. The door was opened by a woman in her forties wearing a blue velour tracksuit.

'Can I help you?' she said. Her breath smelt of alcohol.

'We've come to see the vicar,' said Dorothy.

'Oh God, if I see another fresh-faced pair of lovebirds come in here to talk about their bloody wedding plans, I'm going to puke.'

'No, we're—' began Dorothy.

'Well, you'd better come in,' continued the woman, oblivious. 'He's out ministering to his bloody flock.' She ushered us into the tiny kitchen, which, judging from the smell, had recently been the scene for an impromptu vegetable cremation. A rickety sheila maid hung down from the ceiling, draping tights and underwear over our heads.

'If I had my time again,' she said, 'I'd have spent my youth royally shagging around instead of getting myself hitched. Gin?'

'Er, no thanks,' I said. Dorothy just shook her head.

'Mind if I pour myself another one?' said the woman, not bothering to wait for a reply before filling a tumbler with Beefeater. She had a bag under each eye the size of a Louis Vuitton weekend tote, and her skin was sallow and sun-starved. Her greying hair looked as if she'd tried to do something with it before giving up when it started to fight back. Underneath it all, there was a strong impression of someone who might once have been a beauty, but who had lost the will to stay that way.

'Thought he had money, you know,' she continued. 'Family's bloody loaded. But muggins here had to go and pick the one with the principles. Just you watch,' she said to Dorothy. 'You think he's going to be providing for you forever and – whoosh! – he's caught religion or poetry or some such thing and suddenly we don't need nice things any more.'

'Please,' said Dorothy, trying very hard to remain calm, 'We're not here to talk about marriage. Are we Tom?'

'No,' I said, fervently shaking my head.

'Oh,' said Mrs Fuchs, sounding almost disappointed. 'What the bloody hell are you doing here, then?'

'We just wanted to talk to Mr… Reverend… Fuchs about something else,' said Dorothy, but Mrs Fuchs wasn't paying her any attention.

'It's the people I can't stand,' she said. 'I do try to play the nice Mrs Vicar role, but some of them are just bloody awful. They bleat on about their petty problems and I'm standing there with a sympathetic smile when all I really want to do is give them a damn good slap and tell them to try living on a vicar's stipend. Ungrateful little toads. Count your sodding blessings, because sure as hell you've got a few dozen more than I have.' She took a swig at the gin. 'I went to Cheltenham Ladies, you know.'

We were spared having to respond to this because just then there was a clattering at the front door. Reverend Fuchs was home.

He walked into the kitchen and went straight up to his wife, grabbing the tumbler of gin from her in one easy movement and emptying it down the sink. Then he turned back and said, 'Time to lie down, Marcia.' She shrank to half her previous size and slunk out of the room without saying another word.

'I'm so sorry,' said the Reverend Fuchs, turning to us. 'Now what can I do for you?'

Dorothy and I exchanged glances.

'It's about George Burgess,' said Dorothy.

Fuchs peered at us over his glasses for a moment. 'You'd better come into my office,' he said.

The Reverend Fuchs was of a similar age to his wife. He was bald, apart from a couple of areas on top of each ear where some tufts were still holding out. He had a plummy, earnest voice that managed to sound sympathetic and judgemental at the same time. His office was marginally smaller than the kitchen, but at least it smelt of old books rather than burnt food.

He sat down at a desk that was piled high with papers and dust and indicated a couple of chairs. A crucified Jesus on the wall behind the Reverend Fuchs looked down at us with disdain.

'Poor old George,' said Fuchs. 'They still haven't released the body, you know. Still running tests.'

'Did you know him very well?' I said.

'Haven't seen a lot of him these last few years. Not since that book of his came out.'

'*Shroud of Ecstasy*?' I said.

The rictus that spread over his face told its own story. 'Yes,' he said eventually. 'That one.'

'So your relationship was purely professional?'

'Entirely. He needed an expert on the Turin Shroud, and quite by chance it turned out one of the world's leading authorities lived a few streets away.'

'That was you, I take it?' said Dorothy.

'Indeed. Fortunately very few people in the world of the Shroud know of my connection to the blasted book. The one good thing about that dedication was its anonymity. Viv the explorer. That's what he used to call me in the days before I realised what he was actually up to.' He paused for a moment. 'But I really don't know why anyone might have wanted to do the poor man in. Yes, there were times when I – ' here he glanced upwards, 'God help me – might have wished for something to happen to him, but I never in a million years imagined it would.'

'Do you know how he got involved with Isaac Vavasor?' said Dorothy.

'Who?' said Fuchs.

'The brother of the Vavasor twins?' I said. 'Mathematicians? Archie and Pye?'

Fuchs's face remained blank.

'There was a murder,' said Dorothy. 'Big mystery. You must have read about it.'

'I'm afraid I'm not a terribly worldly man. If I was, perhaps I would never have got involved with Mr Burgess. It looks very much as if I'm not going to be able to help you.' He made to stand up and Dorothy cast an anxious glance at me.

'But have you any idea how Isaac Vavasor might have come across Burgess? Might he have read his book?'

'It's possible, I suppose. Although despite the hoo-ha, it didn't sell a lot of copies. Most of them were given to friends by my sister. I think she did it to embarrass me.'

'Your sister?' said Dorothy, frowning.

'Yes. Cressida.'

'Would that be Cressida Fuchs, then?' I said.

'She spells it Fox, but yes.'

Dorothy shot me a glance, the significance of which escaped me for the moment.

'Reverend Fuchs, I don't suppose you have any contact details for your sister, do you?' she said.

'Why on earth would you want to speak to her?' he said.

'I don't know. I just wonder if she might be able to help.'

'Well. I don't suppose it can do any harm.' Reverend Fuchs took out a piece of paper from his desk and wrote an address and phone number on it in fine copperplate handwriting.

We stood up, shook hands and made our farewells. As we left the house, I noticed Dorothy was trembling.

'What is it?' I said.

'Wait until we're clear of the house,' said Dorothy.

We walked on to the end of the road.

'Don't you see?' she said. 'Cressida Fox! It's her. She's the bloody vixen!'

265

Chapter 31

I stared at Dorothy for a full twenty seconds. Then I grabbed her and hugged her hard. She clearly wasn't entirely expecting this, because the brief, awkward, clinch ended after a second or two with us separating and trying to avoid catching each other's eye.

We still had work to do.

'Well,' I said.

'Well,' said Dorothy.

'Next stop… where exactly is the next stop?'

Dorothy glanced at Fuchs's note.

'She lives in somewhere called Winkfield Row,' she said.

'Where the hell's that?'

'Not a clue. If I had my phone I could Google it.'

'I'd offer you mine, but—'

'It's OK, I'd already thought of that. Hang on. Give me your laptop.'

'Why? It's no use without – '

'Let me try something.'

I took it out of my rucksack and handed it over. She ran to a nearby bus shelter and sat down. I followed her and watched as she opened the laptop and started hunting for Wi-Fi connections.

'Bound to be someone around who forgot to set up a password,' she said.

'Is that legal?'

'Probably not. But needs must. Aha! Here we go.' She was pointing at a list of local Wi-Fi hotspots:

Pete and Sharon's Whiffy
The Midgleys
Fix your sodding fence you wanker
I'll fix it when I'm good and ready
Wallybobs
Base station 2

I peered at the houses opposite. 'Reckon it's that fence over there?' I said.

'No idea. Look. Base station 2 is unprotected. Here we go.' She clicked a couple of times. 'We're in.'

I glanced around nervously. There wasn't anyone about on the streets of Swindon and I didn't notice any curtain-twitchers either. But I still didn't fancy being caught red-handed stealing a stranger's bandwidth.

'Are you sure about this?' I said.

'If they're stupid enough to leave their Wi-Fi unprotected, they deserve everything they get. I hope they haven't got any smart appliances in there, or they'll come home one day to find some spotty kid's been hacking their freezer.'

'Is that possible?'

'Anything's possible in the Internet of Things, Tom. Right, here we are. Turns out Winkfield Row's a place, not a road. And there's where she lives.'

'Whoa.' The image on Google Streetview had been deliberately blurred, but you could still tell it was a monster. 'How much did that place cost?'

'I'll tell you.' Dorothy was now on a property site, which revealed that 'The Manse', a newly-built architect-designed property with ten bedrooms and six bathrooms, had recently been on the market for a cool twenty million.

'Bloody hell,' I said. 'So the Rev's wife wasn't kidding when she said the family had money. Where is this place, though? Is it far away?'

'Not a million miles. Nearest mainline station's Reading. Then we'll need a branch line. Look, there.'

'Let me scribble some directions in case we can't get a signal there.' I found a scrap of paper in my pocket. 'When's the next train?' I said.

'Hold on.' She pulled up a train schedule before glancing at her watch. 'If we get a move on, we can be there in just over an hour.'

We hot-footed it back to Swindon station and we were about to grab a couple of tickets when my mobile went off.

'It's Ali,' I said. Dorothy took the phone.

'Hi, how's… Ah, OK. No, no, the 5.1.3. Not the beta, it's borked. What? You sure? But… OK, maybe it's… Well, what version are you running of that? 4.2.5…? With or without the extensions…? OK, I'm sorry… Yes, I know we're close to the deadline… I'll be in tomorrow… What…? Swindon… No, I'm getting off at Reading first… This Fox woman… Long story… Yes, but can't you…? No, but… Yes, but… Look, I'll see what I can do… Are you sure it's not picking up an old version? The 4.2.3 is horribly buggy… OK OK I WAS JUST CHECKING.' Dorothy gave out a big sigh. 'Look, it's OK, Tom can handle this on his own… Well, he'll have to, won't he…? No, it's fine… Honestly, it's fine… Don't worry, this is more important… Yeah, yeah… See you in a couple of hours.' She ended the call and thrust the phone back at me with a groan.

'Problems?' I said.

'You could say that. Integration testing isn't going well and Ali can't fix all the bugs on her own.' She turned to me. 'Look,

I'm sorry. I'm not going to be able to come with you this time.
Are you going to be OK?'

I frowned. 'Why shouldn't I be?'

'No reason. I wish I could be there though. Maybe we should
postpone it for another day.'

'No. We need to keep the momentum going. I can cope. You
need to get back. μ needs you, too.'

We bought our tickets and caught the five thirty London
bound train with minutes to spare.

'Can I hang on to your laptop?' said Dorothy as we took our
seats. 'I'd like to do a bit more research on the way.'

'Sure.'

I stared out of the window at the passing countryside, my
mind going back to that encounter with George Burgess three
weeks earlier. I was in a state of nervous elation. I was nearing
the end of the journey. The truth would be revealed and the
story would be over. I'd come a long way in those three weeks.
I'd lost my job, my girlfriend and my home. I'd come close to
death on at least one occasion. But right now I felt more alive
than I'd ever felt in my entire life. For the first time, I was actually doing something.

I'd stopped drifting.

Also, there was Dorothy.

I turned to her. 'What did you mean about letting you
down?'

'Sorry?' She was frowning at the laptop, trying to get the
Wi-Fi sorted out.

'When I spoke to you, when you were with the Gretzkys,
you said something about not letting you down again.'

She shook her head. 'Let's not talk about that now.'

I leant back against the window and I realised that as well as
feeling excited, I was also completely knackered. It wasn't long
before I had drifted off into a dream where I was chasing a herd

of outsize π's that were running away down a long corridor. While I was doing this, I was being buzzed by a flock of winged e's that shrieked at me from every direction.

'Oi!' Dorothy was nudging me. 'We're coming into Reading.'

'Wha –? Oh.' Dorothy got up to let me out of my seat. She gave me a look of concern, then said, 'Take care of yourself, Tom,' before kissing me lightly on the lips.

I hesitated. I suddenly wanted to stay here forever.

'Go,' said Dorothy with a sad smile.

'OK.'

I made my way to the door as the train slowed, then stepped off onto the platform. I tried to catch a glimpse of Dorothy as the train moved off, but she had her head down, her hands bashing away at the laptop.

I looked across at the westbound platform. Three weeks ago, I was standing there, surrounded by commuters, tweeting libels and indulging in juvenile Wiki vandalism. I hardly recognised the man I used to be.

I raced over the bridge and found my way to the branch line. Six minutes to go until the train arrived, half an hour until we got to the other end and then another half hour or so on foot.

My whole body was trembling. There were butterflies in my stomach, along with several rare species of tropical moth.

I paced up and down for a minute.

Then I bounced up and down on my heels.

Then I paced up and down a bit more.

Fortunately, the train was on time. When I arrived at the other end, I set off towards Winkfield Row. According to Google Maps, the journey would take around forty minutes on foot. It was now a little after six thirty and there were a few people out walking their dogs. I took out my map and tried it in several different orientations until I found one that looked viable.

My route initially took me through an estate of modern, functional dwellings probably occupied by project managers, salesmen and – God help me – PR executives. Soon I was in open country – or as close to open country as the Berkshire commuter belt got. Try carrying out a rendezvous with a bunch of crazed Belarusians around here, I thought.

Did that really happen?

Was this really happening?

I was feeling increasingly giddy as I walked along. Was it excitement? Was it fear? Or was I just still short of sleep?

Eventually I reached another built up area and finally I turned into the road I was looking for where the homes suddenly ballooned in size to five times their previous proportions. I suddenly felt like a six-year-old kid about to ring the bell of the big house next door to get his football back.

I looked at my watch. It was a quarter past seven. Dusk was gathering.

Come on, Winscombe.

Time to find out what's been going on.

'The Manse' was hidden behind two vast, solid metal gates that wouldn't have looked out of place at a high-security gaol. There was an entryphone at the right hand side, and as I walked over to speak into it, I noticed a pair of security cameras tracking my every move.

I pressed the button.

After a pause that lasted several years, the speaker crackled.

'Hello?' said a perky voice.

'Hello,' I said. 'I'd like to speak to Cressida Fox, please.'

'What is this about, please?'

'Archie and Pye. Vavasor. She'll understand.'

'I go and check. Wait one moment, please.'

The speaker crackled again and then there was another interminable pause, roughly paralleling the time between the

Russian revolution and the fall of the Berlin Wall. Then the speaker crackled again.

'Who is this?' said the voice.

'My name's Beam,' I said. 'Jim Beam.' I felt it prudent to continue using a pseudonym for the time being.

'Wait one moment, please, Mr Beam.'

Another millennium passed. *Come on, come on, let's get this over and done with.* Finally, the gate clunked twice and slowly began to swing open.

My phone rang. It was Dorothy.

'Hi,' I said. 'I'm in! I'm just about to—'

'Tom,' said Dorothy. 'Wait. I've found something important.' She sounded anxious.

'No, honestly. I'm in. She's agreed to talk to me. This is brilliant.'

'Tom, you really need to hear what I have to say—'

But I wasn't listening any more. The gates were open wide and I was walking down the drive to 'The Manse'. I switched my phone off and put it back in my pocket.

I was finally going to learn the truth about Archie and Pye.

As I neared 'The Manse', I heard the soft hum of a motor as the front door opened in a gentle, even arc. At the exact same time, I heard a clang behind me and I turned round to see that the gates to the drive were once more shut. An array of dazzling security lights clicked on overhead, temporarily disorienting me. When my eyes readjusted, I became aware of a Filipina woman standing in the doorway, waiting for me in a posture of mild subservience.

'This way,' she said, motioning for me to enter. I followed her in and the door eased shut behind me without any apparent human intervention. We were now in a galleried hallway with staircases on either side with a tiled floor featuring an outsize segment of the Botticelli Venus in the centre. The woman continued to a door at the back and we found ourselves in a kitchen that was half the size of Alexandra Palace. The polished granite work surfaces had a combined length equivalent to an Olympic running track and they were host to an array of highly-specialised appliances. I struggled to divine the function of most of them, although I counted half a dozen different coffee machines.

'Take seat,' said my guide, indicating the opposite side of the vast table that occupied the centre space. Then she bowed and left the room. I took out a pad of paper and a pen and arranged them in front of me. After a while I got bored and started idly tapping away on the tabletop with the pen. Then I started doodling a picture. I'd got to the point where I was just considering hunting around for coloured crayons so I could finish my work off when the kitchen door opened again.

But it wasn't Cressida Fox who entered the room.

It was Rufus Fairbanks.

Chapter 32

My brain performed a complex backflip. If Cressida Fox was married to Fairbanks, he was connected to the Vavasors and if he was connected to the Vavasors he knew about everything that had happened and if he knew about everything that had happened, he was in this up to his neck. No wonder μ had been so terrified of him, because he had almost certainly been involved in several deaths. Burgess, certainly. Hilary van Beek and Mrs Standage, too. Maybe even Pythagoras Vavasor – but he was away when that happened, wasn't he?

And in any case, why?

What the hell was this all about?

A brief tussle erupted in my brain between the part that was still desperate to know the truth, and the older, more primitive part that was trying to point out that I was with a guy who probably had every intention of killing me and it might be a nice idea to get out as soon as possible. The older, more primitive part of my brain won. I pushed my chair back and began to stand up.

'I do apologise,' I said, 'but I think I may have come here by mistake.'

'Stay right there, Tom,' said Fairbanks. 'You're not going anywhere.'

Something in his voice made me stay put. He tapped his phone a few times and the kitchen door clunked shut. A few more taps and the blinds came down over the windows. A few more and the lights went up. Finally, the television screen on the far wall flickered into life, showing a patchwork quilt of CCTV images. In one of them I saw the maid walking off and the gates closing behind her.

Fairbanks tossed the phone aside and eased himself into the seat opposite. I started to tremble. This didn't look like it was going to end well, particularly when he took a gun out of his inside pocket and laid it out in front of him, the barrel pointing in my direction. 'Jim Beam, indeed,' he said with a sprinkling of indignation, 'I buy you lunch and you repay me by coming to my house unannounced to chat up my wife.'

'That wasn't—'

'Oh, be quiet. I know why you're here. The question is: what do we do now?'

I thought back to our lunch meeting. I realised now he hadn't been sharing information at all. He'd been trying to steer me away from him. He'd also been trying to find out how much I knew. To see if I was worth killing. And who else might be.

'Look—'

'Shut up, Tom. It was a rhetorical question, you moron.' He seemed to be weighing up his options. 'Coffee?' he said eventually.

'I'm sorry?'

'Do. You. Want. A. Cup. Of. Coffee?'

I was nonplussed by this.

'Don't worry,' said Fairbanks. 'I'm not going to poison you. Yet.'

'Um… yes, please, then. Black, no sugar.'

Fairbanks reached for a mug and placed it under one of the coffee machines. He tapped his phone again and the machine began to emit a grinding noise. This was followed by a long sequence of swooshes, clicks and burbles and then finally a jet of boiling black liquid hissed into the mug, which Fairbanks passed over to me. For a brief instant I considered the dynamics of hurling it in his face, before dismissing the idea as too risky.

Besides, I felt in need of caffeine.

'It's good,' I said, taking a nervous sip.

'Of course it bloody is.' He paused again. 'Who's helping you, Tom?'

I was taken aback, but fortunately realised the intent behind the question before I replied. 'No one,' I said. 'It's just me.' Whatever happened, I had to protect Dorothy.

'Really? Have you had some kind of brain transplant?'

'What? No, it's—'

'Oh, don't get me wrong, Tom. I like you. As I said when we last met, you seem to have more of your marbles present and correct than most of the Vavasor groupies lurking at the proverbial stage door. But when it comes to detective work, you have the skill and insight of a freshwater bivalve.'

'That's not fair!' I said. 'Is it?' What was a bivalve anyway? Were they like molluscs?

'I think so.' He fixed me with a beady eye. 'So who is it, Tom? Who's your partner in crime?'

'I haven't got one. It's just me, Fairbanks.'

He leaned back and stroked his chin. 'Prove it.'

'Prove what?'

'Prove you worked it out by yourself. If you can answer a few simple questions, you can prove you're the genius you're pretending to be. Biscuit?'

'N-no thanks.'

'Wise move,' said Fairbanks. 'Awfully fattening. Cress keeps telling me to give up.'

I took another sip of coffee and tried to calm down. If I could keep him talking, maybe I might lull him into a false sense of security and somehow overpower him. Right on cue, Fairbanks picked up his gun and started examining it, as if checking the paintwork was all in order.

'Don't even think about trying to make any clever moves, Tom,' he said. 'And don't imagine anyone's going to help you, either. The staff have all gone home and Cress is out with her girlfriends. It's just you and me here, Tom.'

'Right,' I said. 'Right.'

'Right indeed.'

I sat back and wondered how I was going to get out of this. Perhaps I wasn't. Perhaps the best I could hope for was to find out the truth then die happy.

No, that was absurd.

I was young. I had my life ahead of me.

I had Dorothy.

Actually, did I have Dorothy?

I still wasn't too sure about that one.

But it would be nice to find out.

Oh God, Dorothy. If only you were here with me. We wouldn't have cocked it up like I had. Two of us could have taken him on.

'So,' said Fairbanks. 'First question. How did you crack open Burgess's case? Don't tell me you don't know what I'm talking about. My sources told me Isaac Vavasor had given Burgess the papers in a security briefcase. I searched all over Burgess's house, but I couldn't find the damn thing. Couldn't find it at your place either, but you'd buggered off somewhere else by then. Should have been a bit quicker off the mark, but one can't be everywhere, can one?'

'That was you?'

'Of course it was. You as good as told me you had it when we had lunch.'

'I said nothing of the sort.'

'Body language, Tom. That's all I needed.'

'You bastard.'

'Possibly. But given that I've got the gun, I'd suggest keeping the insults to a minimum. Anyway, the case. How did you open it?'

'I guessed the right combination.'

'Which was?'

Shit. If only I hadn't shredded Dorothy's Post-It note. My mind was a perfect blank. I couldn't remember the damn thing at all. Maybe I could reconstruct it from scratch.

'Um… it was the first six digits of π plus that other one.'

'"That other one"?'

'Yes. The other one. You know. The other number. The one that Archie was known by. Pye was π and Archie was… the other one.'

'Come on, Tom,' said Fairbanks, frowning. 'This isn't very good, is it? "The other one" doesn't cut it, I'm afraid.'

I thought hard. Then I remembered. That was it! Dorothy's tattoo! Oiler! 'e. Archie was known as e.' I sat back in my seat, triumphant and smiling.

'π plus e?' said Fairbanks. 'That's mathematically illiterate. Don't believe you.'

'Burgess wasn't a mathematician,' I said.

'But he didn't set the combination, Tom. It was Vavasor's case.'

I hadn't thought of that. 'Maybe he isn't much of a mathematician either,' I said.

'Possibly,' said Fairbanks. 'Anyway, what are the first six digits?'

Shit. 'π or e?' I said.

'Both.'

This wasn't fair. I hadn't come all this way to indulge in some perverted maths test. It was worse than being back in school. But then I remembered Pye's message: 'How I wish I could fornicate my lovely vixen.' Yesssss!

'Three one four one five nine,' I said. GO ME!

Fairbanks raised an amused eyebrow. 'Well,' he said. 'You're full of surprises today, Tom. Tell me the first six digits of e and I'll believe you did solve this on your own.'

'I can't,' I said, eventually. I didn't know where to begin. If I could remember the actual combination, I could have subtracted π from it, but that had vanished into some dark hole in my brain where numbers went into hiding. 'No one knows e!' I said.

'A mathematician would,' said Fairbanks. 'A true Vavasorologist would know, too. It's two point seven one eight two eight.'

'Oh,' I said. It did sound vaguely familiar.

'Oh indeed, Tom. Who's helping you?'

'No one! Honestly—'

'Honestly? HONESTLY? Come on, Tom, I am very good at telling when people are lying and you currently have a big, red, flashing neon sign positioned above your head with the word LIAR on it.' He stroked his chin for a moment. 'It's odd,' he said. 'You're supposed to be a PR man, but you're extraordinarily inept at telling porkies.'

I shook my head. There wasn't anything I could say.

'So what are we going to do with you, Tom? If you're not going to tell me, I'm going to have to extract the information from you.'

'What? I mean, how?'

'I've been wondering about this. That's the thing about serial killing. It's an absolute bugger sticking to the script.'

'What do you mean?'

'What I mean is I'm going to have to devise some kind of mathematical way to kill you, Tom.'

'But—'

'It's all right, I'm not asking for suggestions. I was wondering about gagging you with duct tape folded into a Möbius strip.'

'Sorry?'

'A Möbius strip. That's where it's folded over once and connected to itself to form a surface with only one side. Trouble is, I realised it wouldn't stick properly.'

I stared at him.

'Then I thought about graph paper.'

'Graph paper?'

'Yes. Scrunch up a few dozen sheets and shove the lot down your throat, one by one.'

Jesus. The man was off his head.

'Hold on,' I said. 'I wouldn't be able to tell you anything then, would I?'

Fairbanks nodded. 'I came to that conclusion too. So I'll just have to shoot you. In a nice equilateral triangular pattern. Oh, come on, Tom. Keep up. An equilateral triangle is the one where all the sides and all the angles are equal.'

I knew that. Really I did. I was just feeling nervous.

Fairbanks picked up the gun and aimed it in turn at my upper left chest, my upper right chest and then down at my crotch.

'Right,' I said.

'Don't worry about the mess,' Fairbank added. 'This is a modern kitchen. All the surfaces are wipe-clean.'

'That's nice.'

'So, what's it to be, Tom? Are you going to cooperate?'

I thought long and hard. Something deep inside me still wanted some kind of closure. If I could somehow keep him talking, there was still the teeniest outside chance the cavalry might still turn up. It was a pretty long shot – something like twice the distance to Alpha Centuri and back, give or take a parsec or two – but it was better than sitting there waiting for a bullet. Three bullets.

The one thing I had on my side was that Fairbanks liked the sound of his own voice.

'I'll do a deal,' I said, trying to keep my voice steady. 'I'll tell you everything. But I want to know what it's all about first.'

'What's what all about?' said Fairbanks.

'All of this. All these deaths. All these secrets. Please. I want to know what's going on.'

Fairbanks considered this. 'This is better, Tom,' he said. 'I like a man who's prepared to do a deal. But can't you work it out yourself?'

Then again, the only thing that Fairbanks liked more than the sound of his own voice was establishing that he was in the presence of an inferior human being. I had to play along.

'OK,' I said. 'Your wife had an affair with Archie Vavasor. And another one with Pythagoras. Did anyone else know about them?'

'No.'

'But you wanted to keep a lid on it, right?'

'Of course.'

'But it can't have been just to avoid embarrassment, can it?' Then it hit me like a bolt of lightning. 'Oh God, I've got it,' I said. 'You wanted to keep it quiet because it linked you to the Vavasors. But why would that be a problem? Unless...' I scoured my brain for information. There was something there, just out of reach. The Belarusians. That was it. 'Unless it somehow connected you to the Belarusian mafia.'

Fairbanks didn't say anything.

'That rumour,' I said, 'that rumour that Pye was assassinated by the Belarusian mafia. Where did that come from?

'When the authorities were investigating the Vavasor deaths, they looked through the papers and found a number of significant references to the Belarusian mafia and deduced that Archie and Pye had got themselves mixed up with them. So for a time, they did indeed think that Pye had been killed by the mob. But the physical evidence ultimately pointed towards Archie.'

'Regardless of whether Pye was killed by the Belarusians,' I said,' the Vavasors were involved with them at the same time as they were carrying on with your wife. And you didn't want that link to come out.' My delight at working it all out was immediately tempered by the realisation that the fact that I'd worked it out had just signed my death warrant. There wasn't going to be any deal now.

'Bingo, Tom. Yes, it all goes back to shale gas. I'd set up a finance deal for a bunch of guys in the Pripyat basin and it turned out they were well connected in the local *cosa nostra*. Asked me how I felt about cleaning up some of their other operations.'

'You mean money laundering?'

'Shame it's got such a bad name, but yes, that was the long and short of it. There was a considerable fee involved, so it was very hard to say no. I needed to put together a complex investment strategy to hide everything so I called on Pye Vavasor to develop the algorithms.'

'Didn't he worry about the ethics of it?'

'Tom, he was a mathematician. All he cared about were his bloody equations. Mathematicians are pretty amoral people. Maybe that's why I like them. Didn't expect him to go and seduce my wife, though.'

'Are you sure you didn't have him killed?'

'Must admit I considered it. But Archie stepped in before I had a chance. Turned out she'd been at it with him, too, before Pye even got involved. In fact it was Archie who was originally working for me, not Pye. Unbeknown to me, Pye stepped in to share the workload when Archie was briefly indisposed and he decided he might as well share Cress as well. Archie found out, went ballistic and you know the rest.'

Jesus.

'All a bit of a balls-up,' said Fairbanks. 'I've resolved never to work with identical twins again.'

'And no one asked any questions about your wife?'

'Fortunately,' continued Fairbanks, 'Isaac Vavasor turned out to be very helpful. Wasn't sure at first how much he knew, but it soon became obvious that he had his own reasons for keeping the lid on the story. I joined a few of the Vavasorologist forums and watched with amusement as the conspiracy theories began to bloom. I even contributed a few of my own, anonymously of course. Dinsdale Mazloumian owes his entire career to me, you know.'

'You're kidding.'

'Am I? Think about it, Tom. What better way to hide the truth than to spin a web of conspiracies around it? The ultimate PR exercise, if you like.'

I chose to ignore the jibe at my former profession. 'And ten years on,' I said, 'George Burgess pops up.'

'Yes, Burgess. Turns out bloody Isaac's got sick of the conspiracy theories and he's commissioned the idiot to come up with the definitive story so he can be left in peace. God knows why he chose him.'

'I can answer that. Cressida's brother knew Burgess. Worked on his first book, in fact. Probably gave a copy to Archie.'

Fairbanks stared at me. 'Good heavens. Bloody Colin! Are you sure?'

I nodded.

'How extraordinary. I will enjoy letting her know that I know.' Fairbanks chuckled softly to himself. 'And him even more. Anyway, Isaac goes and gives Burgess access to the Vavasor papers, including the Marginalia that everyone's so excited about ever since Margot Evercreech got involved. And no, I didn't provide her with any crackpot theories – she was perfectly capable of making up several thousand of her own.'

'Do you think she knows anything?'

'I doubt it. The thing about the Vavasor papers is they're so impenetrable and ambiguous that no one outside the family has had enough time to make any sense of them. Old George is probably the only one.'

'So you thought there was a chance that, given time, he could have worked something out?'

'Yes. So I had to stop him or at least get the papers away from him before he managed to find out anything. Of course when I dropped in on his house that night, I couldn't find them because they were in the case that he was in the process of leaving behind on the train. He found me rummaging through his study, we struggled and I lashed out with the nearest thing that came to hand which happened to be a compass. Didn't really mean to kill the man, but it made me think.'

'Bloody hell.'

'On my way home,' continued Fairbanks, 'I began to wonder who else he might have blabbed to along the way and I realised they would have to be silenced too. It was just a matter of working out how to go about it. Then the somewhat unusual manner in which I'd accidentally dispatched Burgess gave me an idea: what better way to lay a false trail than to adopt the persona of a serial killer? Particularly when I had a cast iron alibi for the first one. Rather serendipitous, I felt.'

'But you weren't just pretending. You actually ended up being a serial killer.'

'Details.'

'But you've really killed people,' I said. 'With your bare hands. Hilary van Beek. Benjamin Unsworth. Mrs Standage.'

'Who's Benjamin Unsworth?'

'Hilary van Beek's intern. Went missing after she was killed. Hasn't been seen since.'

'Wasn't me. Not my style. Sounds more like the work of the Gretzkys.'

'The who?' I said, trying to sound as if I'd never heard the name before.

'Belarusians. They've never really trusted me and they wanted to cut me out. Heard some story they'd tried to get one of the Vavasors' old students to work for them instead – one of their fellow countrymen, Maxim something-or-other – but he wouldn't play ball. So they tried to get their mitts on the papers instead. Obviously thought the investment algorithms were in there somewhere. Still, they're not a problem any more. Blown to buggery in the middle of Somerset last night.'

'Good Lord.' Yes, very convincing, Tom.

Fairbanks frowned. 'I don't understand why you're so squeamish about a bit of killing, though, Tom. I've made investment decisions that have caused far more deaths than this lot and I haven't been clapped in irons for that.'

'Yes, but—'

'It's just these people are a bit closer to home. You're a bloody hypocrite, Tom. Listen. I invest in companies that sell cigarettes to teenagers, strew cluster bombs over the Middle East and dig mines that poison the water supplies to African villages, and my investors think the sun shines out of my fundament. Kill a handful of idiots in this country and I'm suddenly a despicable murderer. It's not as if many people are going to mourn the Burgesses and van Beeks of this world. I could kill every single person in Burgess's address book and the world would keep revolving.'

'What about me?' I said.

'What about you? Tom, you're a bloody PR executive. They're not going to be holding candlelit vigils for you, sunshine. There won't be any online petitions to name a constellation after you or whatever it is they do when some pop star dies. It'll be "Remember that bloke – what-was-his-name? – Winscombe?" "Who? Oh that twat." Think about it, Tom. I'm doing the world a service here.'

'What about Mrs Standage, then?'

'Collateral damage. Fog of war. It happens, Tom.'

'You bastard.'

'Is that the best you can do?'

'You fucking bastard.'

'Scarcely an improvement, Tom. But you can insult me all you like. You're still going to tell me who's helping you, aren't you, Tom?' He picked up the gun and carefully took aim at each of the three points of the triangle in turn again. 'Aren't you?'

Chapter 33

There was a long silence.

'Come on, Tom,' said Fairbanks. 'I'm waiting.'

'If you kill me, you'll never find out.'

'Not entirely true, Tom. It'll just take a bit longer, that's all.'

Bugger. The silence continued.

'OK,' said Fairbanks. 'I'm getting bored with this now. I'm going to count to ten and then it's all over. One. Two. Three.'

'Wait a moment—'

'Well?'

I couldn't think of anything to say.

'Four. Five. Six. Seven. Eight. Nine.'

'No, please! One more moment. Please!'

Then we were both distracted by the softest 'Pffft!' sound from the television screen as it went blank.

Fairbanks sighed and put down the gun. He picked up the phone and started bashing away at it. Nothing happened.

'Bloody thing's buggered,' he said. 'It's locked me out.'

At that point the window blind suddenly whizzed up before coming straight back down again.

My heart skipped a beat.

Fairbanks was still stabbing at the phone and getting angrier by the minute. The kitchen door flew open and closed again, then continued flapping backwards and forwards. Fairbanks stood up, picking up the gun. He continued pointing it at me as he headed for the door to try and close it again. But before he got there something new entered the room. It was one of those Roomba robot vacuum cleaners and it was heading purposefully towards Fairbanks. He realised just in time and stepped aside to let it pass, giving it a kick as he did so, sending it on a new diagonal trajectory.

'What in God's name—' began Fairbanks, spinning round. He put the gun down again and picked up the phone. I seized my moment and reached across the table. I wasn't quick enough, however, because Fairbanks saw what I was doing, dropped the phone and made a grab for the gun himself. But before he got hold of it, I managed to knock it out of his hand and it flew off the table onto the floor, where the door, still swinging backwards and forwards, caught it like a flipper in a pinball game and sent it off to the opposite side of the room, right in the path of the oncoming Roomba.

As the Roomba collided with it, the gun went off, sending a bullet straight towards a mixer on the work surface. The bullet ricocheted off the bowl and changed course for one of the coffee machines, which it duly smashed into several thousand pieces, most of which landed where Fairbanks and I were tussling on opposite sides of the kitchen table. The Roomba continued on its merry way, pushing the gun in front of it, while we both tried to brush fragments of glass and plastic off ourselves.

We both realised at the same moment that the Roomba was about to hit the wall and that there was every chance that the gun would go off again. It did. This time the bullet skittered across the room at floor level, narrowly missing both our legs. I was now nearer than Fairbanks to the Roomba, so I lurched after it, but Fairbanks saw what I was intending to do and leapt onto me before I could get there and we ended up sprawled in an ungainly heap. At this point, we both became aware of an unpleasant burning smell. The electric hob had been switched on and several pieces of broken coffee machine plastic were now beginning to melt all over it, releasing a pungent smoke as they did so.

Before either of us could do anything, the smoke detectors in the ceiling picked up on the burning plastic and decided to join in the fun, and in no time at all the room was being doused in a fine rain. Several worktop appliances had now also woken up and the air was filled with the sound of beaters twirling backwards and forwards and blenders whizzing round at high speed. Alongside these, a large toaster had come to life and it reacted badly to the unforeseen shower. In no time at all, sparks were flying and a small electrical fire was beginning to get underway.

'You little scumbag,' hissed Fairbanks, as I tried to wriggle free from him on the slippery floor. 'You had this planned all along, didn't you?' I kicked out, but he was too bulky for me to escape and he very quickly had me pinioned.

'It's over, Fairbanks,' I said, more out of hope than any sense of reality. 'Your little game's finished.' I don't know why I added that last bit. It just seemed right.

'I don't think so, Tom,' said Fairbanks, placing his hands around my neck. 'I rather think it's over for you.'

The sprinkler system had by now either run out of water or simply given up, but the fire in the toaster was still going strong and it had now spread, via a pair of carelessly-positioned oven gloves, to the cupboards above the work surface. The fan over the hob now came on, but it couldn't cope with the sheer density of smoke and began blowing it back into the room instead. Some of it wafted into Fairbanks's face and he developed a coughing fit, during which he relaxed his grip sufficiently for me to break free. I staggered to my feet and I'd made it part of the way towards the door when I noticed that Fairbanks had managed to intercept the Roomba and as a result was now back in possession of his gun. This was now pointing straight at me once more.

Fairbanks stood up, wiping his face with a silk handkerchief. Despite the chaos enveloping the room, he still commanded the scene, like Napoleon at the battle of Austerlitz. Something like that, anyway. Maintaining a grip on the gun in one hand, he managed to locate a fire extinguisher with the other. Very soon, the conflagration had been smothered in foam and a kind of normality had returned to the kitchen. Or at least the kind of normality where the atmosphere consists of fifty per cent acrid smoke, everything is covered in foam or water, and someone is waving a gun about in the middle of it all.

'Sit down,' said Fairbanks, putting down the fire extinguisher and motioning me back to the table.

I have to say I felt more than a little disappointed. I had this terrible feeling of having blown a brilliant opportunity. On the plus side, I was still alive, which was more than I'd anticipated being a few minutes previously. On the minus side, Fairbanks was still the only one out of the two of us who was armed. The situation, however, was still not entirely under Fairbanks's control. Behind him, one of the blenders was working itself up into an orgasmic ecstasy. Next to it, the beaters on the mixer were still spinning around with gay abandon. A microwave oven was also now trying to attract our attention by pinging away in an exceptionally annoying manner, and a speaker in the fridge door was blasting out German military band music. Meanwhile, the kitchen door was still banging backwards and forwards as if in a hurricane.

'All right, Tom, I'd – Jesus buggering Christ, I can't even hear myself think – ALL RIGHT, TOM, I'D APPRECIATE IT IF YOU COULD STOP THIS NOW.'

'I HAVE NO IDEA WHAT YOU'RE TALKING ABOUT.'

'YES YOU DO, TOM. SOMEONE IS HACKING MY BLOODY HOUSE. I WANT YOU TO MAKE THEM STOP.'

'I DON'T SEE WHAT I CAN DO—'

'I JUST WANT YOU TO – JESUS, I'VE HAD ENOUGH OF THIS!' Without taking his eye off me and still aiming the gun at my chest, Fairbanks began thrashing about with his free hand behind him, trying to find a way of stopping all the noise. The first appliance he managed to locate was the blender.

'Ooh, I wouldn't do that,' I muttered to myself as his fingers started to feel their way towards something that was definitely not the off switch.

As the fridge oom-paa-paa'd its way towards a climax, Fairbanks found what he thought he was looking for...

and the top of the blender flew open...

releasing the rotating blade...

which shot upwards out of the container...

before caroming off the underside of the work surface towards the mixer...

where, still rotating at high speed, it collided with the spinning beaters...

which sent it whizzing through the air like a weaponised Frisbee...

before falling back towards Fairbanks...

who turned round just in time to see it coming his way...

but not in time to stop it from scything a ghastly fissure that went halfway through his neck.

Fairbanks went down, hitting the floor with a dull thud. The gun clattered away from him as a crimson jet spurted from his body, daubing the cupboard doors with a fresh layer of paint. Shaking, I pulled myself to my feet and went over to where he lay writhing as his life flooded out onto the kitchen floor. His head was hanging off at a unnatural angle from the rest of his body. He tried to gurgle something at me before his eyes glazed over and he went silent. There was nothing I could do for him.

Everything in the kitchen slowly began to return to normal. The mixer stopped beating. The microwave stopped pinging. The fridge fell silent. The kitchen door came to rest in the open position, and as I turned round to face it, a slight figure walked through, holding my laptop in front of her.

'Tom?' said Dorothy in a quiet voice. 'Are you OK?'

'Yes,' I said. 'I think so.'

'Is he…?'

'Yes.'

'I didn't mean to—'

'I know.'

'I just meant to mix things up a bit. I really didn't mean to…' She was sobbing now.

I got up and went over to her. 'I know you didn't,' I said, taking hold of her shoulders. 'But he was trying to kill me, and you saved my life. Thank you.'

She shook her head and wiped her eyes. 'It's nothing. I owed you one. I would have got here earlier, but I had to download the hacking tools and it took me ages to find a decent torrent and then all the Wi-Fi hotspots along the way were protected and then when I got here I couldn't find a way into the network and in the end the only thing that didn't have a password was the washing machine and that was on a different subnet to almost everything else so I had to find a route out of there via the central heating boiler and—'

'Hey, it's OK. It's OK.' I stroked her hair and she looked up at me, her eyes glistening.

'I'm glad you're OK, Tom,' she said, putting her arms round me and pulling me close. 'I really am.'

'I'm glad I'm OK, too,' I said. I was shaking now. Christ, that had been horribly close.

There was a moment's silence while we held each other. Then Dorothy pulled away.

'So I take it you worked everything out?' she said.

'About Fairbanks doing the Belarusians' money laundering? Yep.'

'As soon as I found out who Cressida Fox was married to, it all fell into place.'

'I know.' For some reason, the fact I'd worked it out independently of Dorothy gave me immense satisfaction.

'Speaking of which, where is she?' she said.

'I don't know. Fairbanks said she'd gone out with friends.'

'You don't think—'

'What? Oh my God. You're not suggesting he's done her in too, are you?'

'Nothing would surprise me.'

'We could always wait until she comes back.'

Dorothy looked at me and frowned. 'That maybe one of the worst ideas you've ever come up with, Tom. Think about it. Even by your standards, it's awful. Imagine her walking in here, finding this scene and us in the middle of it all.'

I could see her point.

'Actually,' she continued, 'maybe we need to think about making a hasty exit. But first, there's one thing I need to check. Your laptop is showing a hell of a lot of traffic coming into this building.'

'What do you mean?'

'Looks like data. Financial data, most likely. I think whatever he was doing with the Gretzkys' cash was too sensitive to handle anywhere but here. I'd love to take a look at the machine that's sucking it all in.' She had put the laptop down on the kitchen table and was now clicking her way around the screen. 'Ah, hang on, I'm in,' she said. 'Whoa. That's a powerful box he's got there.'

'You're not proposing to hack your way around his computer network now, are you?' I said. 'We don't know how much time we've got until Cressida gets back.'

'I guess you're right.' She gave the laptop one last wistful look and then shut the lid. 'OK,' she said. 'Let's go.'

If the truth were told, I wasn't enjoying sharing a room with a corpse. But I still felt uneasy about just running off. 'Shouldn't we wait for the police or something?' I said.

'That could get very complicated, Tom. For one thing, if they find the hacking software on this laptop of yours, we could be in some very deep shit. Actually, you might want to think about wiping it completely.'

'The laptop?'

'Don't worry, I'll get it back up and running. More importantly, I can't afford to hang about any longer. I have some software to deliver.'

'Surely we've got some sort of duty to stay here?'

'Possibly, but I don't think you understand. If Ali and I don't have the software ready before the start of the week, we're in serious trouble.'

'But tomorrow's Sunday!'

'Doesn't matter. It's a 24/7 business and I can't afford to be delayed here any longer than necessary. Ali's already in meltdown. We need to get going right now. We can go to the police and explain it all in our own time once the heat is off.'

I couldn't fault Dorothy's logic. 'But won't we be on Fairbanks's CCTV records?' I glanced up at the tiny camera hidden in the corner of the room.

'He'd already switched off the recording in this room. I turned everything back on when I was outside so I could find where you were but I can't find any video records here.' She was back at the laptop, scrolling through a directory listing. 'Oh, hang on. There's you walking up the drive. Wait a moment, who's that?'

'It's the maid.'

'Did you give her your name?'

'No, I made one up. Jim Beam.'

'Oh great. Still, chances are as soon as she gets wind of all this, she'll be on the first plane back home. OK, I'll get rid of that video. And that one. One more, then we're done. Nothing left to connect us.'

'I still think we should call the police,' I said. 'From his phone at least. I'd hate his wife to come home to this.'

Dorothy looked at me and then gave a reluctant nod.

'OK, but be careful,' she said.

'I will.' I found the phone and called the police, adopting something close to a Yorkshire accent in an attempt to disguise my voice. Dorothy looked at me as I did this and shook her head from side to side with a sad smile on her face.

'Wonder what they're going to make of it,' I said when I'd finished giving them the address.

'Dunno,' said Dorothy. 'Although if you're looking for a mathematical aspect to it, this place is a pretty good example of chaos theory in action. Come on, let's go.'

Chapter 34

On the way back to London, we sat in an empty train carriage leaning against each other, not saying a lot at first. Then I remembered something I wanted to ask.

'What *did* you mean about letting you down again?' I said. 'Can you tell me now?'

Dorothy sighed. 'I suppose so. You remember the bunch we used to be in back in the sixth form? You, me, Gaz, Bilbo, Sheena and Tina, Ed, Zoë and the rest?'

'Yeah. I remember Sheena and Tina anyway.' They were hot, but well outside my price range.

'Shut up, Tom. You know what I mean. Now, do you remember I suddenly wasn't part of the bunch any more?'

Oh God, I did remember something now. What had happened?

'We were all going to the end of term dance, remember?' said Dorothy. 'And I sort of thought we were going to it together? You and me? Part of the group, but you know, together? I mean, we weren't going out or anything, but – well, you know.'

We were. But something happened, didn't it? Wasn't anything to do with me, though, surely?

'Week or so beforehand, we were going back to the sixth form common room after lunch. You guys were up ahead and I was with Sheena and Tina and Zoë and a couple of the other ones – I can't remember – and we were talking about the dance and wondering who we were going to end up with and, like a fool, I said you. And they all laughed at me. All of them. Zoë said, "You're a geek. No one's going to want to dance with you", and then Sheena said something horrible about you not liking Chinese girls anyway.

'I was mortified. I wanted the ground to open up there and then and swallow me whole. Then I saw you turn round and look at me. Like you'd heard every word. And I was willing you to wait back a moment and say something. But you didn't, Tom. You didn't say a bloody thing. You just smiled at Zoë – not at me, Tom, – at Zoë. And then you turned back to your friends, laughing. And when I didn't turn up to the dance, you went off with Zoë instead, as if it didn't even matter.'

Oh God, Zoë. What a nightmare. That didn't end well.

Did I really do that?

Was I that much of a shit?

'I don't know what to say,' I said after a while. 'I honestly don't remember doing that. I just thought one day you were coming to the dance and the next day you weren't. I thought – I think I thought – you'd gone off me or something. That you didn't like me after all.'

'Well, I didn't like you. Not after that, anyway.'

'Oh God. Look, I'm sorry. I didn't mean to hurt you. I don't think I did. And if I did, I'm different now. Aren't I?' I hoped I was.

'Yes, Tom,' said Dorothy. 'I actually think you are.'

We didn't say another word for the rest of the journey.

It was past ten o'clock when we got back to Dot Chan World Central. Only one of the occupants of the office seemed pleased to see us, and it wasn't the human one. As soon as we walked in the door, μ trotted over to see us and began rubbing herself against our ankles. I bent down and picked her up and was pleased to note that she appeared to have been fed and watered and generally looked after over the last couple of days. I was about to make a point of thanking Ali before I saw her face. To say it was like thunder would be to understate the full range of varied meteorological phenomena that could currently be observed in Ali's facial microclimate. The twelve numbers on the Beaufort Scale were insufficient to encompass the full scale of her fury.

'WHERE THE FUCK HAVE YOU BEEN, DOT?' she said, getting up from her workstation. 'We're going to have to re-run the unit tests on half the weaponry objects, one of the zombies starts wobbling round in circles if you approach it from the wrong side and sometimes ten thousand points get added to your score for no good reason. Also, one of the cut scenes has gone missing – no, I don't know where, Chennai haven't a clue – and we're going to have to code round it.' She paused and then adopted a more conciliatory tone. 'Good to see you're still alive and all that, by the way.'

'Cheers,' said Dorothy.

'You're welcome. And you're alive too?' said Ali to me with some surprise.

'Yeah.'

'He saved me,' said Dorothy.

'And then she saved me,' I said.

'Well, that's nice,' said Ali.

'And we solved the mystery,' I said. 'Didn't we?'

'Yeah,' said Dorothy.

'Well done Secret Seven,' said Ali. 'Now can we get to work, please?'

'Sure,' said Dorothy. 'One moment.' She turned to me and took hold of my arm. 'This way,' she said, leading me to a door at the far end. I'd assumed it led to a cupboard, but it turned out it was actually a small room with a mattress on the floor.

'You mean you live here as well as work?' I said. I hadn't had time to wonder what kind of place Dorothy might call home.

'Yeah. It's cheaper that way. Look, I'm going to have to get some work done. Catch up with you later, OK?'

The significance of what she was saying didn't register for several seconds, and then my internal organs performed a neat, synchronised somersault while my heart began filling the tiny enclosed space with a note-for-note rendition of the Anvil Chorus.

'Er, yeah, right. OK,' I said, trying to remain calm.

'You OK?'

'Yeah. Yeah. I'm fine. Just a bit tired, that's all.'

I wasn't lying. It had been the second traumatic day in succession and I was absolutely exhausted. As soon as Dorothy went back to work, I lay down on the mattress and I was asleep within thirty seconds of pulling the covers over me.

At around three in the morning, I was aware of Dorothy getting into bed beside me.

'Everything sorted?' I said.

But she didn't answer. She was already fast asleep.

A few hours later, I was woken by Dorothy shaking my shoulder.

'Huh?' I said.

'I've got it,' she said.

'Got what? What time is it?'

'Dunno. 'Bout seven, I think.'

'Jesus, Dorothy. It's Sunday.'

'Yes, but this is important. I've just realised something.'

'What?'

'I don't think the papers were blown up after all.'

'Sorry? Look, can't this wait? Especially as we seem to have found ourselves in bed together for the first time.'

'Oh yeah. Hi,' she said, leaning over to kiss me. Then she sat up again. 'No, this is really important. Look, you gave the case to this Sergei guy, right?'

'Yes.'

'But he – probably – used to work for the Vavasors.'

'Yes, but…' I wasn't getting any of this. My brain was still somewhere in Rufus Fairbanks's kitchen.

'Don't you see? Before he planted the bomb in the case, he must have removed the papers. He knew how important they were. They're still out there somewhere, Tom!'

'He probably just took them back to Isaac Vavasor.'

'Maybe. Or maybe he's on the way back to Minsk. Don't forget, there are almost certainly a few remnants of the Gretzky gang still around. If I was a fugitive Belarusian and I wanted to blend into the surroundings, I'd pick somewhere where they speak my native language.'

'OK, but… look, does all this matter? We found out why Archie killed Pye. We found out why everyone else died. We know everything now, Dorothy. It's all over. Isn't it?'

She shook her head. 'No, Tom. There's still something important in those papers. From what I saw – and I mean I didn't have a lot of time to look and they were full of weird shorthand and stuff and frankly they could have meant almost anything – they could revolutionise everything.'

'OK. But do we have to—'

Dorothy ignored me. 'The thing is,' she said, 'I mean, what if they really did manage to prove the Riemann hypothesis?'

'Huh?'

'Think about it, Tom.'

'I don't want to. It's seven o'clock on Sunday morning.'

'It's simple, Tom. Look, maybe you don't appreciate how important this is. I'll try and give you a quick overview.'

'God, you really are going to sit there and explain this to me, aren't you?' I said.

I sighed. This was all wrong. I was in bed with a woman I'd fancied for years, we had a whole Sunday stretching out in front of us and we were about to start talking about mathematics. I sat up and turned towards her.

'Look,' I said, softening my tone. 'Can't we save this for later?' She was about to say something, but I put my arm round her and gently pulled her towards me. She didn't resist.

Acknowledgements

Archie and Pye made their first appearance in my story 'Mathematical Puzzles and Diversions', which was performed by Sabina Cameron at Liars' League in London on September 9th, 2008 and subsequently appeared in my first short story collection, *Dot Dash* (Salt, 2011). The use of grandmothers as an investment vehicle was first mooted in my story 'Financial Engineering or Whatever Shall We Do With Grandma?', which appeared in my second collection, *Dip Flash* (Cultured Llama, 2018).

Many thanks to Donna Gagnon Pugh and Doug Pugh for posing the challenge that resulted in me inventing Archie and Pye, to Katy Darby for accepting the story for Liars' League, and to Richard Kerrigan of Bath Spa University for inadvertently providing me with the impetus to turn it into a novel. Especial thanks to my brilliant tutors Celia Brayfield and Maggie Gee for constantly nudging me in the right direction and also to my fellow students who provided some excellent critique. Thanks to my beta readers Liz Friend and Steve James for their valuable time and extremely helpful advice. Thanks as ever to my wonderful family Gail, Mark and Rachel for putting up with me while I wrote this thing, and especial thanks to Mark for the loan of his Euler tattoo. Thanks to the unbelievably awesome team that Farrago assembled to make this book the absolute best it can possibly be, and humungous thanks to Abbie and Pete at Farrago for having the confidence to take the project on. Finally, my eternal gratitude to the late Mike Rawlinson, the most inspirational maths teacher that ever walked the earth.

About the Author

Jonathan Pinnock is the author of the novel
Mrs Darcy Versus the Aliens (Proxima, 2011), the short
story collections *Dot Dash* (Salt, 2012) and
Dip Flash (Cultured Llama, 2018), the
bio-historico-musicological-memoir thing *Take It Cool*
(Two Ravens Press, 2014) and the poetry collection
Love and Loss and Other Important Stuff
(Silhouette Press, 2017). He was born in Bedford and
studied Mathematics at Clare College, Cambridge,
before going on to pursue a moderately successful
career in software development. He also has an
MA in Creative Writing from Bath Spa University.
He is married with two slightly grown-up
children and now lives in Somerset, where he
should have moved to a long time ago.

Preview

A QUESTION OF TRUST

Dorothy has gone missing, along with all of the company's equipment and the contents of its bank account, leaving Tom and Ali to eke out an awkward shared bedsit existence while they try to work out what she is up to. Meanwhile, Tom has other things on his mind, including how to unwind his father from a cryptocurrency scam and how to break into a hospital in order to interrogate an old acquaintance. And what is the significance of the messages he's been receiving from Rufus Fairbanks's LinkedIn account?

A Mathematical Mystery, Volume Two

COMING SOON

Note from the Publisher

To receive updates on new releases in the Mathematical Mystery series – plus special offers and news of other humorous fiction series to make you smile – sign up now to the Farrago mailing list at farragobooks.com/sign-up.